Rivo: Blade of the Shooting Star

Matthew Linton

Matthew Linton

This book is dedicated to my late parents, Wesley and Virginia. The lessons they taught me and the wisdom they shared still help to carry me through the storms of life.

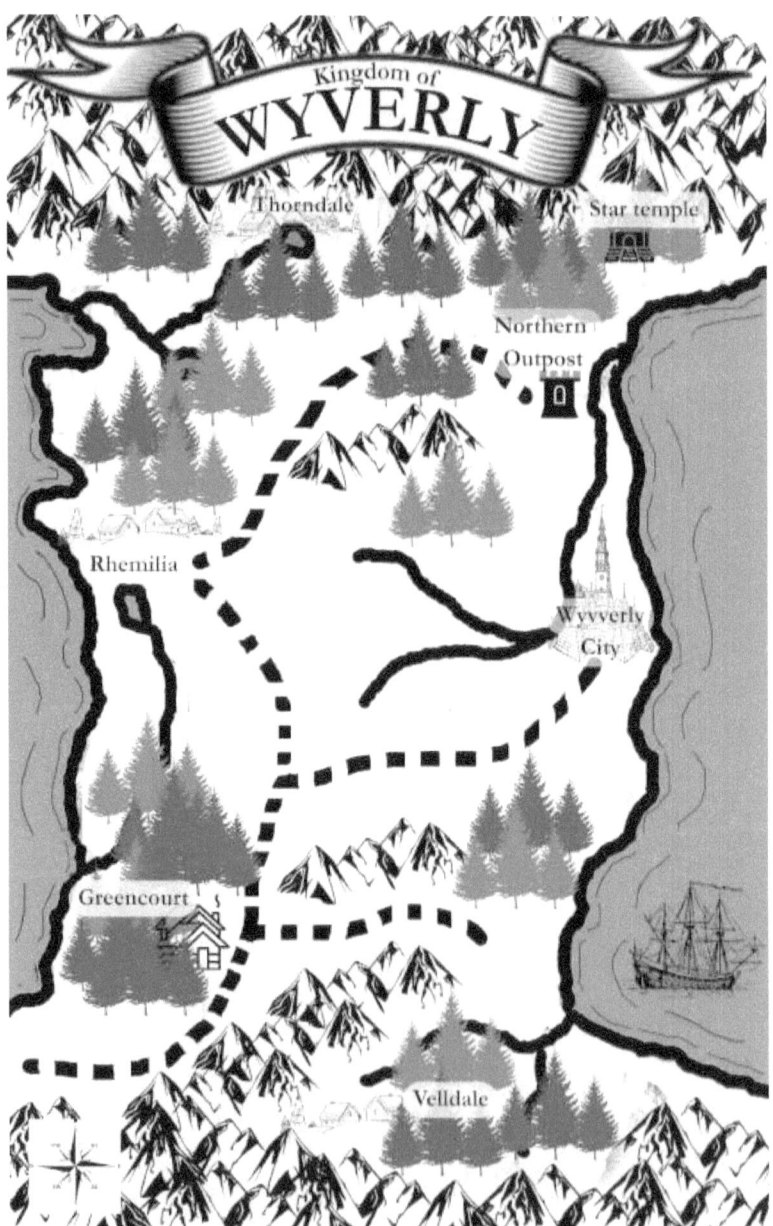

Contents

From the Captain's Memoirs

The old stories say that long ago, we worshiped the stars. The stories said we used to look to them, seeking their wisdom, power, and protection.

As time went on, we stopped looking to the stars. It wasn't long before it became little more than a superstition we held on to out of nostalgia.

Then, when frightened children would ask about the monsters from the stories, we would tell them the same things our elders told us when we were small.

We told them there was nothing to worry about.
We told them none of it was real.
We told them the stars had no power.
We told them monsters would never come to get us.
We told them we didn't need heroes to rise up and save us.

We were wrong.

R. Magnus Tremlee,
Captain, North Wyverly Battalion (Retired)

Chapter 1

From Finish to Start

"So then, the mighty Demon King Garel took the magical orb that he had stolen from the heavenly realm and placed it on his chest, right over his heart, rendering himself invincible. He left his demonic minions to terrorize the forests, hunting humans for food and sport. Garel then brought forth the four kings of the forest lands. He commanded them all to bow down before him and declare him ruler of their kingdoms, but the brave warrior kings refused. They banded together to fight him one last time.

As the brave kings battled the evil demon, they lured him to the Temple of the Stars, in the heart of the forest. Garel, drunk with pride, chased after them, not realizing that they had laid a trap.

For in that temple dwelt Wyverly, the Star Sage, the wisest and most powerful man the land had ever seen.

Upon entering the temple's sanctuary, the Demon King Garel and Wyverly did battle. It was then that Garel realized that the Star Sage had been granted the power of the Guardian's Glare, a gift from the stars to the one who was deemed worthy. He defeated the Demon King and then called up to the heavens to send one of its glowing minions.

The heavens answered, and a giant star was seen dashing through the nighttime sky.

Upon seeing the shooting star, Wyverly wished that Garel and his minions would be sealed away. So gone forever went the defeated Demon King and all his followers.

Peace was restored to the land, and the people forever celebrated Wyverly, the Star Sage."

Frank closed his copy of *Tales of the Star Sage* and looked at his young son, sitting up in his bed, the boy's eyes open wide with wonder.

"Well, what did you think, Rivo?" Frank asked.

"Wow, Father. That was great!" the boy said with a smile.

"I figured you'd like it, son," Frank replied as he rocked back and forth in his chair.

The boy's smile slowly faded as he started rubbing his chin.

"Something wrong, Rivo?" asked Frank.

"I was just thinking," the boy said, looking at the book on his father's lap. "Remember the nursery rhyme you and mother taught me?"

"Which one?"

"The one that goes, *nobody knows how the shooting star hears, but a shooting star's wish can last ten thousand years.*"

"What about it, Rivo?"

"Well, the story you just read says Garel was sealed away forever because of a wish. But the nursery rhyme says a wish can last for ten thousand years, not forever."

Frank chuckled at his son's clever connection. "That's because *forever* doesn't rhyme with *hears*, Rivo."

"But what if it's true?" the boy asked nervously as he fidgeted with the buttons on his shirt.

"Oh, honey, you don't need to worry about that. It's just an old fairytale," his mother, Gwen, reassured him as she walked in to close his bedroom window.

"But what if Garel wasn't sealed away forever, and tomorrow is the end of the ten thousand years? What will we do?" asked Rivo, as his voice quivered.

"Son," Frank said in a calming voice as he leaned toward the boy. "Don't you know anything about fairytales?" he asked. "When the monster comes, a hero *always* rises up to save the day."

The boy's eyes shot wide again as he gasped in excitement. "Do you think I could be that hero, father?" he asked eagerly.

"Rivo," Frank said as he leaned back. "I think you could be an amazing hero. You just need to be brave and to care about others more than yourself," Frank answered as he arose and tousled the boy's hair before turning to leave.

"And you need to get a good night's rest, like all of the other good little boys in Wyverly," Gwen added, as she tucked her young son in bed and kissed him goodnight.

As Rivo lay in bed, he looked out his bedroom window and saw a shooting star. "Mother, Father, look, a shooting star!" he exclaimed as he sat back up.

"Oh, really?" Frank asked as he turned around. "Did you make a wish? You know we all get one wish on a shooting star," he said with his hands on his hips.

"Yes, I did. I made a wish!" the boy exclaimed.

"Well, don't say what it is out loud, Rivo, or else it won't come true," said Gwen with her eyebrows raised.

Frank put his arm around his wife's shoulders as they watched their young son staring at the nighttime sky in wonder. "Oh, he doesn't need to tell us. I think we know exactly what our little hero wished for."

***

Rivo opened his eyes, as if waking from a deep sleep, his mind scrambling to piece together and recall what had just happened. He stood amid the wreckage of an ancient temple, unused for millennia, maybe longer.

Gray and brown rubble stretched around him, with broken stone and debris scattered about in jagged piles.

The battle, he recalled. *It started collapsing afterward. But why am I here? How am I still standing... still alive?* he wondered. He scanned the debris, catching faint shouts in the distance. *Cheers, maybe?* He thought. *We must have won. The war's over!* Excitement flickered through him, tangled with confusion.

Where is everyone? He looked around frantically. Large pieces of stone still falling all around him. He ducked and dodged to avoid being struck by the falling debris. *I've got to get out of here or else I won't make it,* he thought, panic taking over. As the large stones continued to fall, he flinched, swearing that one had struck him, though he didn't feel any impact.

This is not good. If I don't leave now, I'm dead.

The hollering and shouts outside continued, though too faint to make out. "Can anyone hear me?" Rivo yelled. "Cade? Pearce? Naomi? Anybody?" No response came.

Then, as he walked across the dirty stone floor, he saw it—the body of a boy, half-buried under the wreckage that once made up the structure of the ancient temple. He looked to be about seventeen, Rivo's age. He stepped closer.

A red handkerchief circled the boy's left arm, tied midway up the bicep. "A Wyverly soldier, like me," he remarked. "How'd he get down here?" The boy had light brown hair dusted with ash, black pants that ended below the calf, with buckled boots that rose just above the ankles, and a sleeveless blue vest with golden embroidery. "That's my vest," Rivo whispered in bewilderment.

He then saw a chain around the young soldier's neck; it was a star pendant, just like the one his father had given him before he passed away. He peered at the boy's face, caked in dust and blood, but unmistakable. "This boy... is me."

Fear gripped him as reality began to sink in. He knelt and reached out to touch the body, only for his hand to pass right through. Rivo gasped and shot back up. "Am I... dead?" he whispered.

He began studying himself, looking at his arms, legs, and torso. His body was translucent. "Is this what death is like?" He looked about his surroundings, desperate for some idea of what he could do, for some way to come back to life.

"Somebody, please help me!" he shouted. Still no response.

At that moment, the temple walls slowly blurred and faded. A gust of wind tugged at him, pulling his spirit upward like a loose fabric in the wind.

Seconds later, he was floating in a dark void. "What... what's happening? Is there anyone else here!?" he shouted desperately.

He began to hear a faint but familiar voice. He couldn't make out exactly what they were saying, but the voice was getting louder and louder, "It's the Captain! Thank the stars! It's Captain Tremlee! Captain, can you hear me? It's me, Rivo," He shouted, glad to feel as though he wasn't alone.

The jubilation didn't last long. He could hear Captain Tremlee's voice, but there was no reply. It was as if he were just listening in on a conversation like a fly on the wall. The void around him morphed into a familiar-looking room.

He scanned his new surroundings: a large room with wooden floors and walls. "I recognize this place," he said. It was daytime outside, and about two dozen kids his age stood in rows of six, facing a man at a small podium.

"I'm sure you all understand the severity of the circumstances that have brought you here today," said the speaker, a short, middle-aged, mustachioed man. His head was shaved bald, and he wore a standard military-issued uniform: a blue beret, a thin, long-sleeved blue shirt, accompanied by black cloth pants and boots.

"Oh, it is him, Captain Tremlee. I knew it!" Rivo said with excitement. "But why can't he hear me?" he asked as he began to scan his surroundings. "Wait... this place... it... It's the town hall in Greencourt. Why am I here? Why is the Captain here?"

Rivo studied the room as Captain Tremlee recited the soldier's creed aloud. Familiar faces filled the crowd, kids from his hometown of Greencourt, all about his age.

Then his focus shifted to a young man and woman, a couple of years older than himself, standing toward the center. "Pearce and Naomi?" he muttered, his eyes widening with a quizzical expression. "What in the world are they doing here?"

"So what am I watching? Why are we in a room with Captain Tremlee and everyone else?" asked Rivo, "he hasn't been in Greencourt since..." He froze, his gaze darting around the room again as the Captain droned on in the background about military formalities.

At the back of the room stood a familiar figure—himself. "That's me!" Spirit Rivo gasped. "I see now, we're in the past! This is recruiting day, a couple of months back." He marveled at the reality of seeing himself from this perspective.

"I'm sure most of you understand the threat we face," Captain Tremlee stated to the new recruits, "but you may not understand the full magnitude of this threat and how the entire kingdom of Wyverly is in danger." He paused so as to make sure the group had time to take in everything he was saying.

"Why am I in the past? Is somebody or something behind all of this?" he asked, staring at his past self, who stood listening attentively to the Captain's address.

"It started several months ago," Captain Tremlee continued. "First, there were reports of folks going missing, followed by the bodies of slain travelers and vagrants being discovered. It was clear that some sort of wild animal killed the poor souls." He again stood silent for a moment. "Then things got worse. Groups of traveling merchants, and in some instances, entire villages were attacked and wiped out."

"By the stars, Captain, I don't need anyone telling *me* about the Haundo," Spirit Rivo remarked.

The Captain once again took a moment and tightened his jaw. "Scouts were sent out to gather more intel. Several of them never returned, and those who did brought back horrifying news."

"Those monsters," said Spirit Rivo, his ghostly fists clenched, "They just kind of came around Wyverly out of the blue. The people were terrified, we'd never seen anything like this... like those terrifying creatures."

"They are called the Haundo," the Captain went on. "Have any of you encountered them as of yet?" Captain Tremlee asked, scanning the crowd, only to see that no hands were raised. "Consider yourselves fortunate," he added. He went on to describe the Haundo to the new recruits, though they all had heard the stories.

"When we first heard of these wolf-like monsters roaming the land, we thought it must have been some sort of bad joke taken too far, "Spirit Rivo reflected. "But the stories kept coming. Merchants started coming through town less and less often, bringing with them horrifying stories when they did."

"From all reports we've received, there appear to be two classes of Haundo," the Captain continued. "The smaller ones have brown fur and are about the same size as a fully grown man; the larger ones have white fur and stand over a head taller than the rest. We call them the Greater Haundo; they are pack leaders of a sort to the others. If you ever encounter a Greater Haundo, run."

"Sometimes, running isn't an option, Captain," Spirit Rivo scoffed.

"All the kingdom's military resources and personnel are going towards fighting this enemy," the Captain announced as he rubbed his chin." Our forces are dwindling; we need all of the help we can get."

"Things got bad," Spirit Rivo said somberly. "Real bad. The kingdom got so desperate that they started recruiting women and children. That's why Captain Tremlee came and set up the recruiting station. To get us all to sign up," he added with a cynical chuckle, "like we had a choice."

"Our goal is not to put you young kids on the front lines fighting the Haundo," announced the Captain. "Your responsibility is to go out to the other remote towns in the kingdom of Wyverly and recruit more soldiers." He continued, "Myself and these other officers here are needed elsewhere in this war. Our services are most useful in areas of combat and military strategy, which is why we are commissioning you to do the recruiting from this point on." His voice changed to a lower tone, "Your focus is first to recruit those with the most combat ability," he said, pausing as murmurs rippled through the recruits. "But you understand the desperate situation we currently face. If there aren't enough, any able-bodied person will do."

"I was terrified," said Spirit Rivo, "I think we all were, but I guess, for some reason, I just knew we'd pull through."

As he was reflecting, an officer was going around the room tying red handkerchiefs around their left biceps, signifying that they were now part of the Wyverly kingdom's military. "Red for the blood that's been shed under the stars that guide us," announced the Captain, quoting an old song of Wyverly's founding. As everyone else gathered their gear, the real Rivo also opted to grab a blue headband from the supply chest.

"I thought it would make me look tough," Spirit Rivo recalled with a chuckle.

"Well, my stars, an elite guard vest," remarked a middle-aged officer to Rivo as he made his way around the room. "I haven't seen someone wear one of these vests in ages," he muttered as he studied the vest's golden embroidery.

"It was my Father's from when he was a soldier," Rivo replied as he proudly patted his chest.

"Good," the officer said with a nod as he kept walking, "they don't make them like that anymore."

Pearce walked up beside Rivo after the officer passed by. "You know, wearing that vest might be like putting a target on your back, Rivo," he whispered. "The other soldiers might see this as you trying to show off."

Pearce was about the same height as Rivo, but with broad shoulders and a muscular build. He had short, dark brown hair that he always kept well-combed, parted down toward the side. He often kept a short stubble to look a little older than he really was.

"You think so?" Rivo asked as he looked back down at his vest. "Well, it belonged to my father. I'm gonna wear it proudly," he said as he raised his chin. "If they don't like it, that'll be their problem."

"No, Rivo, it'll be *your* problem," Naomi said as she walked up and put her arm around the waist of her childhood sweetheart, and now husband, Pearce. "Look, I loved Uncle Frank, too. He was like a father to all three of us, but there are other ways to pay tribute to him."

"I'll be fine," Rivo replied dryly.

"Yeah, you will, Rivo," Naomi said with a snarky tone, "because I made sure they had the three of us placed together. That way, I don't have to worry about you getting yourself killed doing something stupid like jumping headfirst into a fight with a Greater Haundo."

Naomi wore her light brown hair straight down, just above her shoulders, with a pink hairband over the top of her head, keeping her hair pulled back and exposing her forehead. She was pale-skinned and petite. She had blue eyes like Rivo, and people often thought they were siblings.

"My loving and overbearing cousin, Naomi," Spirit Rivo sighed. "All of two years older than me, yet she's always treating me like a child."

He watched on as everyone gathered their gear and made their way out." In spite of everything going on, I was proud at that moment, officially a soldier," said Spirit Rivo with a slight smirk. "So," he continued, "what now? Who or whatever is behind this didn't bring me back just for me to watch myself get recruited, did they?"

At that time, another gust of wind came through, seemingly lifting him up. The room slowly warped and faded away as Rivo braced himself, unsure of where his spirit was being sent next.

Chapter 2

We Could Use Another Clown

The two young girls were dashing through the streets of Wyverly. In and out of alleyways they went, evading any potential captors. They had never been caught, and they weren't about to let their luck run out today.

Shouts echoed through the market: "Thieves!" "Sneaks!" "Tramps!" yelled the merchants as they realized some of their goods were missing. They had just pulled off another heist, and by the time anyone noticed, it was too late. Fourteen-year-old Vickie and her eleven-year-old sister, Renee, had just finished another successful free shopping trip at the market.

Witnesses were at a loss to describe to the authorities what exactly they had seen. They all seemed to remember the gorgeous fourteen-year-old flirting with the boys running the stands. Still, nobody could quite pin a good description of the mysterious cloaked figure who moved about the market like a wraith, nabbing whatever goodies she could get her hands on. All they knew was that when the pretty girl walked by, their merchandise vanished.

"This is almost getting too easy, Renee," Vickie said, chuckling as she finished the last bite of a stolen apple and then tossed it to the ground.

"I'm good with easy, Vick," remarked Renee, eyeing their haul. "This'll last us a while."

"Well, I don't know about you, but I'm up for a challenge," Vickie said as she tugged on the sleeve of Renee's cloak, pointing in the direction of a group of wagons outside of a circus tent. "Whatcha think?"

"Oh, Vick. I don't know," Renee groaned. "That seems a bit too risky."

"Yeah, but I bet it's a gold mine. Let's at least scope it out."

Renee reluctantly trailed her older sister, gripping her cloak. "Vick, last time we pushed our luck, we almost got caught," she whispered as they surveyed the circus wagons, peering around while trying to remain discreet.

The two could clearly see there was plenty to be had. From clothing to weapons, drinks, and food, there was more than they could ever hope for lining those wagons.

"Stars be damned, Renee, can you believe this!?" exclaimed Vickie, her eyes gleaming with mischief.

"Woah, Vick. It's like a small town on wheels!" Renee gushed, clutching her cloak.

"Yeah, and it's my town!" barked an angry voice from behind, heavy footsteps crunching closer.

The girls spun around, gasping. There stood a massive, muscle-bound man with his head clean-shaven.

They stared wide-eyed at the giant of a man, their mouths agape. "I'm sorry, sir. We were just looking," Vickie stammered.

"Yeah, I bet. You two little thieves were eyeing the wagons for somethin' to steal, weren't ya?"

"No, sir. We were just looking around. We'd never seen anything like this," Renee squeaked.

"*Just lookin' around,* my foot!" grunted the man.

"We're sorry, sir. Honest!" Vickie pleaded. She and Renee began shaking in fear. Caught at last, they were completely at this giant's mercy.

The man threw his head back and laughed out loud. "You should see the look on your faces! As if I could ever hurt two sweet-looking girls like you!" He gave a dopey-looking, crooked smile. "The name's Judd. Nice to meet ya!"

The two sisters were taken aback by the man's sudden change in demeanor, but relieved nonetheless. "I'm Vickie, and this is my sister Renee," Vickie said as the two both sighed in relief.

"Pleasure to meet you, Vickie and Renee," Judd said with a nod. "Hey, Sundry! I found 'em!" he shouted.

Out came Mr. Sundry, the ringmaster. He was a short and pudgy man with a comically long mustache that curled at the ends. "Ah, yes, our little guests. So glad you decided to make an appearance," he said with a wide grin.

Vickie and Renee stood frozen in place, unsure of how they should proceed.

"So, young ladies, where are your parents?"

Neither spoke up.

"I'm pretty sure they're orphans," Judd chimed in.

"Ah, I see," Mr. Sundry said with a nod. "Well, that's too bad." He gave a thoughtful pause, "ya know, we have lots of orphans working the circus, don't we, Mr. Judd?"

"Yes, Mr. Sundry. I should know. I'm one of 'em."

"Of course," Mr. Sundry remarked. "And you know who else is? Me."

The sisters both looked puzzled, at a loss for words.

"The only problem is, we don't tolerate thieves," Mr. Sundry said as he paced back and forth, twirling his mustache. Vickie and Renee exchanged nervous glances. "Our performers earn an honest living. I pay them fairly, so they don't need to steal things." He stopped and leaned in closer, eyes gleaming, "What do you say, ladies? You work for me, and instead of stealing food and clothing, you'll be stealing the hearts and minds of the people. No more sleeping out in the cold, wondering where your next meal will come from. No more living in loneliness and fear."

Mr. Sundry took a step back as Judd lumbered forward, extending his massive hands, "Take my hands, ladies. You're coming with us. Now, let's all go see the world together," he said with his dopey, crooked grin.

Vickie caught Renee's eye, her heart pounding with hope. They looked at each other and both nodded as one. The two sisters turned to the towering strongman and each clasped one of his hands.

"A wise choice, ladies," said Mr. Sundry, his gentle grin widening his mustache and showing his pearly white teeth. "I promise you won't regret it."

***

As the breeze subsided, Spirit Rivo found himself in the nearby town of Rhemilia, about half a day's hike from Greencourt. A quaint and charming town, much larger than Greencourt, but still small compared to the Capital. He remembered how, when he was small, he and his family would go there a few times a year, whenever there was a fair or a circus in town. Coincidentally, the circus was in town that day as well.

"Ah, I'm not going to be caught off guard this time," Spirit Rivo said in a wry smirk. "This was a couple weeks after recruiting day, right after we finished our basic training. Our first recruiting trip," he added, as he noticed himself, Naomi, and Pearce getting off a wagon by the town entrance. It was shortly after daybreak. There was another wagon with a small group of people unloading by a circus tent about twenty paces away from the three. "Ah, yes. Vickie, Judd, and Renee, my recruits," he remarked.

The three performers all looked to have tanned skin from spending so much of their time in the sun. "There's good ole Judd, carrying that big barrel of something on his shoulder," he said, pointing at a large, muscle-bound man with a clean-shaven head unloading the wagon." People think he looks scary, but he's just a teddy bear."

"And there leaning on the wagon, is Vickie, she's a little full of herself, but she's a good person," he said, as he looked at a beautiful young woman about twenty years of age. She had a haughty look in her eyes, deliberately examining her fingernails.

Vickie was a striking beauty from head to toe. She was wearing a long violet dress that complemented her figure well. A perfectly proportioned figure at that, with curves in all the right places, long, wavy, jet-black hair, pouty lips, and mesmerizing eyes that were complemented by her violet eye shadow. It was obvious by her appearance that she put a lot of time and effort into her looks. It was also clear that she had no issue attracting the attention of any man she was around.

"And last but not least, Vickie's younger sister, Renee. She can be a little standoffish at times, but she's really sweet," Spirit Rivo remarked, now looking in the direction of a thin, petite young woman wearing her jet-black hair in a long pixie cut, with bangs that would cover her eyes when she didn't brush them to the side.

She wore little to no makeup; her face was cute, yet it lacked distinct features. She was standing with her arms crossed, shaking her finger at the wagon, as if she was counting something, going through a mental checklist. Renee was more slender and not as curvy or well-proportioned as her sister. From her practical haircut to her low-profile, slide-on canvas shoes, it was clear by the way she dressed and carried herself that comfort and simplicity were her primary concerns.

Spirit Rivo then turned his focus to himself, the real Rivo, who was talking with Pearce and Naomi.

Rivo took a moment to admire Rhemilia and reminisce. The small rolling hills in the distance, the noisy market streets, and the series of small cottages that served as the family homes of the locals. *It still has all the charm it did when I last came*, he thought. *However, it does seem smaller than I remember.*

Rivo hadn't been to Rhemilia since his parents died. He had been living with Naomi ever since, and she would never let him leave Greencourt.

It's understandable that Naomi, or anyone else for that matter, who at the tender age of twelve had to take on the role of guardian for her younger cousin, might be overprotective. She had to grow up quickly, after all. But Rivo often felt this might stem from her once witnessing a coyote almost attack him when he was two years old. He was too young to remember, but Naomi recalls it vividly. She said it was about to snatch him up when his Mother, Gwen, jumped in and chased it away.

Once he finished his reverie, he spotted the young circus workers. "Those look like good candidates, don't ya think, Pearce?" he asked.

"Yes, I noticed. The big guy, especially," said Pearce, pointing towards Judd. "You two wait here, I'll go have a talk with them."

"Try to relax and be approachable, please," Naomi told him, as she knew he had a tendency to be blunt and intimidating to strangers.

As Pearce headed in the direction of the circus wagon, Naomi turned to Rivo. "Could you at least go and see about a room at the inn for us?" she asked in a nagging tone. "And by the stars, Rivo, straighten up that vest, we're trying to give a good first impression."

"I'll head there in a minute, I want to see how he does first," Rivo replied, not even turning to look at Naomi as he spoke, his eyes fixed on Pearce.

"Well, at least stop leaning against the wagon, you look like a slacker," Naomi said sharply as she adjusted his vest for him.

Pearce spoke with the three performers for what seemed like less than a minute and turned to head back to Rivo and Naomi. His face didn't seem to express any emotion, though it seldom did, so it was hard to say how the conversation went by that alone.

He shrugged as he walked past Rivo and Naomi. "They aren't interested," he mumbled, starting to unload bags from the wagon without even making eye contact with them.

Naomi drew a deep breath and sighed in frustration. "Well, what happened exactly?"

"I told you, they said they're not interested."

"Pearce, honey, this is our job; we need to recruit. What exactly did they say?" asked Naomi with her hands on her hips, her irritation starting to show. "You weren't talking with them for long at all."

"They said *we're not interested* as soon as I told them we were part of the Wyverly military," replied Pearce, seeming unfazed by Naomi's attitude.

"Well, I guess they're just not Wyverly material, then; it's settled," Naomi concluded as she waved her hands dismissively. "Rivo, go get a room while we finish unloading."

"Can I talk to them?" asked Rivo.

"Fine by me," replied Pearce, still going through the wagon.

"No," replied Naomi, now transferring her frustration towards Rivo. "I didn't want you signing up for the service in the first place, but we weren't exactly given a choice. Kids like you belong in school, not here. You need to focus on doing what you're told. You need to focus on thinking about what you're going to do with your life when this mess is all over."

Rivo shook his head and huffed at her last comment. "Well, like you said, we didn't really have a choice. So let's all chip in," he replied, knowing she wouldn't like his response.

"You can *chip in* by seeing about our room, you don't need to do the adult stuff, we'll take care of that," she barked.

"I'm gonna have to learn this stuff one way or another. I'll go introduce myself," Rivo said as he began to walk towards the circus performers.

"Ouch!" he hollered. Naomi pinched him hard on his arm as he was walking away.

"That's what she'd do to me anytime I made her mad, she'd pinch me. She's been doing that ever since I was a toddler," Spirit Rivo said as Naomi began scolding the real Rivo in the background. "As much as I hated it, I'd give anything to have her pinch me like that one more time," he added with a sigh.

"Just let him go, Naomi," said Pearce, now looking directly at them. "What harm could it do?"

"Fine!" Naomi grunted as she grabbed Rivo's bag out of the wagon and dropped it on the ground. "We'll be at the inn, get your bag, and meet us there when you're done making a fool of yourself."

Rivo approached the circus wagon, a little nervous, but still with an upbeat spirit. "Hey, I'm Rivo, of Greencourt," he started. "We—"

"We know," said Renee bluntly, not even taking her eyes off the wagon.

"Oh," he replied, a bit taken aback. "How did you—"

"The other one told us already. And those are your cousins and comrades, *Piss and Moaning*," Vickie interjected dryly, still more focused on her nails than she was Rivo.

"Umm... that's Pearce and Naomi," remarked Rivo, oblivious to her joke.

Vickie gave an exhaustive groan and rolled her eyes in disbelief. "Whatever, child. We already told the other one, we aren't interested in fighting your war." *He's clueless*, she thought, smirking.

"Wait, what was that?" Spirit Rivo remarked in bewilderment. "I just heard Vickie call me clueless. I don't remember her saying that."

"Well, it's not exactly *our* war. Do you know what's going on?" Rivo argued. "The Haundo-"

"We know all about the wolf people," replied Judd, in a deep, throaty voice. "We don't want to get involved; we have a good gig here."

"Look, I didn't want to get involved either. Sometimes war comes to you. You think I want to be here doing this?"

"Oh, so you're here talking to us against your will? Trying to get us to join you against our will?" Vickie said obnoxiously. "That's not exactly a good sales tactic, child."

Rivo clenched his fists, her condescension stinging like one of Naomi's pinches. *Man, this lady's annoying,* he thought, just *like Naomi.*

"You mean the kingdom drafted you? You're just a kid, and they're making you fight?" asked Renee, now looking at Rivo and genuinely bothered by this revelation.

"Well, I'm about the same age as you. You're at work too, aren't you?" Rivo asked sarcastically, his irritation with Vickie starting to show.

"Yes, but we're performers in a circus," Renee replied, her voice softening. "You're fighting for your life."

"Ah, well, not our monkey, not our circus," Vickie added, laughing at her own joke.

Rivo bit his lip and closed his eyes. *She's so disrespectful*! he thought.

"We're not looking to join you all, but you're still welcome to come watch our performance tonight, I promise you'll enjoy it!" exclaimed Renee, trying to both smooth over tension and bring in an audience.

"Yeah, sure, maybe we can recruit him to join our circus; we could use another clown," Vickie scoffed.

I can't take this much longer, Rivo told himself. *I want to wring her neck, but I'm not gonna let her know she's getting under my skin.* "You know what? Sure, we'd love to come. We'll see you there!" he said with a wide smile.

"Perfect!" Renee replied. "By the way, my name's Renee, that's my big sister Vickie, and the big guy is Judd, he's kind of like our adoptive older brother and bodyguard."

"Nice to meet you all, we'll see you this evening," replied Rivo as he headed off.

"He seemed like a nice boy, Vick," said Renee. "Did you have to be so rude?"

"He's a fool, Renee. He's gonna get himself killed, and he'll bring you down with him."

"I liked him," said Judd.

"Of course you did," Vickie sneered as she walked away.

"I'm as uncomfortable now watching that as I was back then going through it," Spirit Rivo said, a pang of longing in his voice. "But I'm glad I did."

Chapter 3

I Need a Distraction

Rivo trudged toward the inn, dreading Naomi's inevitable lecture. After her nagging and Vickie's jabs, his nerves were frayed. *I need a distraction*, he thought. Then he spotted a group of children kicking a ball in a field past the inn. "Perfect," he muttered, a grin creeping in. "Hey, you kids need another player?" he called, jogging over.

"Rushball. I loved that game as a child," Spirit Rivo murmured, watching from the sidelines. "Two teams facing each other, seeing which side could kick the ball in the other teams goal. Hadn't played much since Mother and Father died, though."

The children cheered, squabbling over which team got the older boy. As the game kicked off, Rivo's skill outshone them all. He juggled the ball with his feet, dodging their clumsy tackles, but held back—no goals, just fun. A wide smile lit his face.

Regardless, Rivo's team won. "So how about best two out of three?" he said with no hint of being winded.

"Yes, definitely!" answered Gordon, one of his teammates. He was a tall, lanky boy with dirty blond hair.

"Oh no, you don't!" a female voice shouted from across the field. They all turned to see Renee stroll up, a coy smile on her face. "Rivo of Greencourt, isn't it? What? Are you trying to recruit these young kids now? I don't think so."

"What are you talking about? I'm just having a little fun, they said I could join them."

"Well, that's just as bad, a young man like yourself running circles around these little kids? That doesn't sound fair to me," she said, still wearing that wry smile as she slowly walked toward the group. "I was watching you this whole time. Ya know, you should be ashamed of yourself."

"Oh really?" Rivo's eyebrows raised. "Are you gonna even the odds?" he replied with a playful grin.

"I think I will. C'mon, kids, let's put this overgrown child in his place," she said, staring down Rivo with her dark brown eyes; he couldn't tell at the time if her glare was that of playfulness or derision.

As the next game went on, the teams were now much more evenly matched. Renee was fast and knew how to play the game. She was good, but not as good as Rivo. As he dribbled past all the other kids, the only one standing in his way was Renee.

No worries, I can handle this, he thought as he prepared to dribble past her. That was, until she stepped on his foot and kicked the ball out from under him. She passed the ball to a nearby boy, who kicked it between two rust buckets used as goal markers. Game over.

"That's cheating, ya know!" Rivo hollered, chuckling.

"I don't see any referees, do you?" Renee replied, laughing as she ran past him to celebrate with her teammates.

"Oh, whatever, we have one more game," Rivo said as he gathered his team. He gazed across the rolling fields and saw Rhemilia Lake in the distance, its waters reflecting the sunlight. He remembered swimming there a few times as a child. "On second thought, who's up for a swim? I know I'm hot!"

The kids all cheered in favor of a swim in the lake.

"So the lake it is, c'mon Renee!"

"That's enough, Rivo!" a sharp voice cut through the air and stopped the children dead in their tracks. Naomi stood by the inn, scowling with her hands on her hips.

"Oh, hey Naomi. Sorry, I guess I lost track of time." Rivo remarked, rubbing the back of his neck.

"Yeah, I bet," she replied, "say goodbye to your friends and let's go to our room."

Gordon and the other youngsters ran to give their new playmate a hug and say their goodbyes. Renee stood behind the crowd with her arms crossed, a gentle smile on her face. "Goodbye, Rivo of Greencourt," she said mockingly as Naomi escorted him away, giving him another pinch on his arm.

"Ya know, they invited us to see their performance tonight. I'd like to go, I think we should," said Rivo as they were walking to the inn.

"Why?" Naomi scoffed. "Sounds like a waste of time."

The Rhemilia Inn was a simple, two-story brick building with about twelve rooms on each floor. For a town the size of Rhemilia, it would suffice. The two entered their lodging together, where a small plate of food was set out on one of the beds in the cozy room. The cramped space, with a window overlooking the field where he and the children had been playing, held just two beds, a small area for luggage, and little else.

"Why couldn't I just get my own room?" He mumbled under his breath. Though Rivo wasn't normally one to complain, he wasn't looking forward to sharing such tight quarters with those two.

"I made a plate for you. Pearce and I ate already while you were goofing off," Naomi said as she pulled a coin purse out of her bag. "Go ahead and eat. Pearce is waiting for me by the shops down the road. I'm gonna go see him now and get some supplies. Please just stay here until we get back."

As Naomi left, Rivo quickly scarfed down his food, then decided to use the free time to grab his parents' old copy of *Tales of the Star Sage*. It was an ancient collection of texts that everyone in Wyverly was required to have some familiarity with. There wasn't any clear consensus on who wrote it all. The book contained various tales from Star Sage's various adventures, though most thought they were heavily embellished, if they were true at all. The book was mostly considered a collection of fairy tales, along with some sayings that were used as nursery rhymes.

Rivo thumbed to a section about the Guardian's Glare, a mysterious ability the Star Sage had acquired and used to defeat Garel before sealing him away. Little was said about this power, except that it was believed to grant the one who possessed it a brief burst of supernatural strength and that the power could be activated if the one who bore it believed their loved ones to be in danger.

"Well, I guess they needed some way to explain how that old man could beat a demon king," Rivo said sarcastically, as he flipped to another section of the book.

He came across another section with some of the nursery rhymes he had learned at the schoolhouse. *Nobody knows how the shooting star hears, but a shooting star's wish can last ten thousand years.*

He kept flipping pages and came to another section, this time about the death of the Star Sage. There, it talked about how shortly after he defeated Garel, Wyverly the Star Sage had lain on his deathbed and called his children to his side. A shooting star had just crossed the sky, and he had made a final wish. Wyverly made known his wish to his children, but commanded them to tell no one, so to this day, Wyverly's final wish remains a mystery. "I thought if you told someone what your wish was, it didn't come true," Rivo remarked, as he shrugged and then tossed the book back into his pack.

He lay down in his bed and closed his eyes. *How do they expect us to get recruits at a time like this,* Rivo wondered, *especially in a place like Rhemilia. Who would wanna leave here and fight monsters in a war? It's not like we have someone like Captain Tremlee here to compel anyone to join. And those circus people? Talk about a dead end."*

"I didn't know it then," Spirit Rivo remarked, as he hovered above." But this was a big day. It was the day everything changed for us all."

*　　　***

Pearce and Naomi came back to the room later that afternoon. "Well, we have a little bit of good news, I suppose," Naomi said as she put down a bag of supplies they purchased, along with a small brown envelope.

"Really, what's that?" asked Rivo, sitting up in his bed.

"We met the circus promoter, Mr. Sundry," Pearce said as he set down a bag of his own. "We struck a deal of sorts with him. He said if we sponsored his show and helped him with the clean up afterward, he'd introduce us to the crowd and encourage them to enlist."

"He only asked for a few silver pieces, so we figured it was worth it. If we just get one or two recruits, I'd say it was a job well done," Naomi chimed in with a hint of optimism that Rivo hadn't seen in a while. "Besides, he gave us three tickets," she held up the brown envelope. "So, Rivo, it looks like we get to go after all."

"Let's get settled for a bit, then we'll head out for the show," said an exhausted Pearce with a sigh as he sat down on the bed.

A strong breeze carried Spirit Rivo away again. This time, he found himself in a large tent, big enough to fit over half the townsfolk. It must have been early evening that same day. "I figured this was coming," Spirit Rivo said somberly, "here we are... at the circus..."

Chapter 4

Stealing the Show

Spirit Rivo found himself near center stage in the large, sprawling circus tent. It was early evening, hours after the rushball game had ended. The tent's canvas walls were vibrating from the noise of the excited crowd. It was completely packed with the townsfolk of Rhemilia, no doubt all desperate for a distraction from the events surrounding their kingdom. Though night cloaked the sky, glass bulbs blazed overhead, their cables leading to a crank outside. Workers spun the crank in shifts. When the bulbs dimmed, they'd crank again. "I'd heard of those before," remarked Spirit Rivo as he watched on, "but actually seeing it for the first time? Surreal." It was the same for most folks in places like Rhemilia and Greencourt. In years past, gas lamps were used, but these new lights were much brighter.

Judd and Renee were part of the sideshow before the main event started. Rivo sat in the audience along with Naomi and Pearce, a couple of rows back from the front.

Judd demonstrated some feats of strength, bending metal bars with his bare hands, lifting giant logs over his head, and even wrestling a bear.

Spirit Rivo looked on, watching Judd's act, just as impressed now as he was back then. "That guy," he chuckled. "He never ceases to amaze me."

Next up was Renee, who had a magician act; she was billed as "the invisible girl". She performed some illusions and card tricks, always involving members from the crowd to keep the audience engaged. Many of whom were plants working in cahoots with the performers, though Rivo had no clue about that part.

She was now about to start her final act: "Well, we just need another volunteer from the audience, who else wants to join me?" she asked, pretending to scan the audience full of eager volunteers. The plant, who was to assist in her final act, a man in a yellow shirt, one of Mr. Sundry's employees, stood up, ready to be called. "Yes, you, sir, in the yellow sh-"

"Rivo, stop! What are you doing!?" shouted Pearce.

"You idiot! Don't make a spectacle of yourself!" yelled Naomi.

It was too late to stop him. "I'll do it!" Rivo volunteered himself as he jumped the rope separating the audience from the performers. He stood near the center stage, just a few yards from Renee. She took a step back, stunned. Rivo had just ruined her act.

Vickie, watching from backstage, put her head in her hands. *What an unbelievable moron*, she thought.

"There it is again," Spirit Rivo said in shock. "Am I... hearing Vickie's thoughts?"

"Oookay, well, uhh... it looks like we have our volunteer, the boy in blue! What's your name, kid?" Renee asked, feigning ignorance for the crowd's sake.

"My name's Rivo of Greencourt. I'm a member of the Wyverly militia," he said, puffing out his chest. "We came here to find some recruits," he added, making sure to promote the cause. This didn't impress Pearce and Naomi, though. Pearce stood with a stone-cold expression, staring Rivo down for drawing attention to himself like this. Meanwhile, Naomi was beyond embarrassed; she had her hands covering her face, wishing she were somewhere else.

As the crowd applauded Rivo, as much for his bravery running on stage as for his military service, Renee approached him. "Rivo of Greencourt," she whispered mockingly, "you dope. We had a plant in the audience that I was supposed to work with." She pointed to a dumbfounded and frustrated-looking man in a yellow shirt standing in the front row, the same one she was about to call in before Rivo ran in.

He stood frozen with embarrassment. *Oh no, I really messed up! No chance of winning them over now,* he thought to himself.

"Don't worry, we have backup plans for when guys like you show up," she reassured him. "Alright, we're gonna change things up a bit," she announced to the crowd. "Let's get a few more volunteers from the audience, you, sir, in the yellow shirt," she pointed at her audience plant, having to come up with a different trick than she had planned. "And how about you and you, come on down to the stage," she said, randomly picking a couple of volunteers. "Watch this," Renee whispered to Rivo with a wink as she walked past him.

"Okay, volunteers, I want you all to think of a number, any number between 1 and 10," she heard playful jeers from her fellow performers, accusing her of trying to take the easy way out. "Oh, is that too easy? How about between 1 and 100? Still not good enough? Fine, let's do between 1 and 1,000!" she announced to the massive cheers and applause of the audience.

She used Judd as her assistant; his job was to hold a bucket and follow her as she performed. She asked each volunteer to state their name, then had Judd give them each a sheet of paper, an envelope, and a small lead stick to write with. "First, I'm going to walk behind the volunteers, turn my back to them, and blindfold myself for good measure."

She walked up to Rivo, "I'll need this," she said as she took his headband off and used it as her blindfold. Renee walked about ten paces behind the volunteers, turned her back, and then blindfolded herself.

"Now that we know that I can't see what they're writing, I'd like our volunteers to think of a number and write it down on their sheets of paper. I would like them to show their number to the audience long enough for everyone to take a good, long look, but please, nobody say the number aloud," she announced. The volunteers all displayed their numbers as told.

"Once they're done and everyone sees their number, I will need the volunteers to place their sheet in their envelope and write their name on that envelope. Once this is done, Judd will take them and place them in the bucket, which he will then bring to me."

Once everyone had handed in their envelopes, Renee employed a classic magician's sleight of hand. First, she called out the plant's number, a number she already knew, then made the audience think she was opening his envelope to confirm her guess was correct, when in fact she was opening the next volunteer's. From this, she was able to read the next volunteer's number, with the audience thinking she was doing nothing more than revealing the number she had already predicted. She did this for all the other volunteers, allowing her to call out their numbers accurately.

The audience could not have been more impressed; their awestruck applause filled the air. Renee took a bow and sent the volunteers back to their seats, giving Rivo a sideways glance as they walked past each other in opposite directions.

"That was incredible! How did you do that?" asked Rivo.

Renee turned toward him as she kept walking. "If I told you, it would ruin the magic," she replied with a smirk.

She then did her final trick. Judd handed her a long black sheet, which she used to cover her whole body. He then counted to three and pulled the blanket off, revealing that Renee was nowhere to be seen. "The invisible girl!" Mr. Sundry announced to the amazed audience.

"Well, I guess I'm not getting my headband back," muttered a wide-eyed Rivo.

He walked back to his seat, next to Naomi. "By the stars, what were you thinking!?" she said through her clenched teeth as Rivo sat down.

"Well, I thought maybe getting out there would put us in their good graces, "he replied defensively.

"Are you crazy?! You looked like a joke down there. We'll be lucky if anyone wants to join up after your antics!"

"We don't need any more of those little tricks, Rivo. This is business; we aren't here to be a part of the show. At least, not like that, "Pearce interjected as he shook his head.

The next set was the rope dancers. There were four of them, each tied to a rope suspended from a large beam on the ceiling. Vickie was one of them, introduced as "the mysterious beauty," and the only one Rivo recognized. All the dancers were impressive, but Vickie was on a whole other level. Her unmatched beauty aside, she would swing, spin, and cradle with the rope as if it were an extension of her own body. The crowd watched in stunned silence. It was a type of elegance and skill like they'd never seen before.

The dancers' performance came to a close. The silence of the audience broke into thunderous applause, mixed with catcalls from some of the less restrained men in the crowd. There was no doubt about it, for those few minutes, the love and admiration of the people of Rhemilia belonged to Vickie.

"I remember that," said Spirit Rivo. "Looking back, I can sure see how all the guys fall head over heels for Vickie; she's something else."

As the performers left the stage, Spirit Rivo's breathing started to become erratic, and his nerves began to fray, but it wasn't because of Vickie. It was because he knew what was coming next. "Do I have to watch this? "Why can't I look away?" he groaned as his ghostly eyes welled with tears. "I don't want to see this again, please!"

The stage was set for the main act, and the performers brought out all the performance animals: lions, bears, monkeys, and even an elephant. The audience was cheering so loud that nobody could even hear themselves talk. This was what the crowd was waiting for all evening. The roars of animals rang through the massive tent. The lights began to dim, and the crowd was still cheering, thinking it was part of the show, but it wasn't.

The performers looked confused, shrugging their shoulders at each other as if they didn't understand what was going on. The animals looked nervous and started to move around frantically; their handlers tried to get them under control. It was then that the audience began to realize something was wrong. The lights dimming wasn't part of the show, the workers weren't turning the crank, and the animal roars that were heard weren't from the circus animals. The crowd then fell silent and could hear the roars mixed with the screams of the workers outside—screams of terror.

"This was hard enough the first time," Spirit Rivo moaned. "I can't even close my eyes or look away. Why?"

It wasn't the roars of the circus animals they were hearing at all. They grew louder, unnatural, and guttural. The Haundo had arrived, and Rhemilia was under attack.

Chapter 5

The Need for Creed

Assess, but don't hesitate.
Act, but not rashly.
Attack if you must,
defend at all costs.
The people of Wyverly,
They are the heart of the kingdom.
Without them, we have nothing worth fighting for.

-The Soldier's Creed.

"Assess, but don't hesitate. Act, but not rashly..." The voice of Rivo's father, Frank, echoed in his mind. This was the soldier's creed; Rivo had to memorize it, every word. Frank, a former soldier himself, took pride in the role, and he ensured his son knew the noble creed, with every word etched into his heart and mind. Now, as screams filled the circus tent, those words anchored Rivo against the rising panic.

They had to repeat it every day in basic training as well. With only two weeks among the recruits, Captain Tremlee, like Frank, emphasized why they fought: to protect Wyverly's heart. It wasn't just about how to fight, but what they were fighting for.

Assess, but don't hesitate. Act, but not rashly. Attack if you must, defend at all costs. The people of Wyverly, they are the heart of the kingdom. Over and over again, these words kept replaying in Rivo's mind. They were on repeat, haunting him as he, Pearce, and Naomi scanned over the frenzied crowd, trying to gain some semblance of where exactly the threat was coming from and how bad it really was.

Rivo's heart raced as he fought off his own panic. *No way, I'm gonna have to fight through this fear,* Rivo thought, his heart racing and his fists clenched. *I've got to push through. This is it; this is real. For me, the war starts today.*

"If it wasn't for Father's words, I don't know if I could have made it through," said Spirit Rivo, his voice quivering.

Pearce's eyes met his, stone-cold, and Naomi's were sharp—they all knew.

"Two entrances," Pearce said. "I'll take the right. You two cover the left. Move."

Their gear sat back at the inn; only the small daggers in their belts remained, but they needed more. They bolted towards the left entrance. Rivo snatched a broken stool leg, while Naomi grabbed a brick she found lying on the ground. They weaved their way amidst the panicked crowd, trampling over each other in a state of chaos, all trying to get as far away from the entrances as they could for fear of the Haundo barging in. The people needed a leader, but without anyone to provide them with a clear understanding of what was happening outside, there was no way to know how or if a safe escape was possible.

As Rivo approached the entrance, he saw one for the first time. Creeping through the entrance, a ferocious, brown-furred creature came crawling in on all fours, to the screams of the nearby onlookers. It stood up on its hind legs, snarling as it scanned its surroundings. *A Haundo,* Rivo thought as he found himself frozen in fear.

The Haundo stood still for a brief moment, then quickly bolted toward the audience members and snatched up an elderly woman who was cowering nearby.

The beast handled the woman like a rag doll and turned to flee the tent with its prey, but just as the Haundo turned, Rivo threw his chair leg at the beast, striking it across the head. The creature began to turn back to see what had struck it. Without hesitation, Rivo lunged forward with his knife, stabbing the Haundo in its left arm, the arm holding the woman. It dropped her and shifted its focus to Rivo, who stood ready to attack again.

With so much going on, it didn't register that the lights in the tent blazed bright again. The crank was located near the other entrance that Pearce went to. He had made it safely to the outside and had gotten somebody to turn the lights back on for his comrades.

As Pearce and some armed townspeople fought off the Haundo at their entrance, the panicked crowd began to flee to the town hall, a brick building nearest to the tent entrance across from the inn.

Back inside the tent, Rivo and Naomi weren't quite as lucky. After he had attacked the Haundo, it quickly retaliated and struck Rivo across the side of his face with the back of its fist. Rivo got jarred by the blow, but was so full of adrenaline that he didn't feel it at the time. He retaliated in kind, slicing the beast across its face, following it up with a punch across its mouth.

As Rivo faced off with this beast, Naomi threw a brick, striking the creature square in the nose, a brief yelp escaping its mouth. It was hurt, the Haundo was stunned by the blow and was struggling to come back to its senses.

It's hesitating! Rivo thought. He charged at the beast, stabbing it in the side of the neck. It collapsed to the ground, blood spilling out of the wound as it fell down, dead.

Rivo stood panting, his knife dripping with blood. He looked down at the creature to make sure it was dead, but this proved to be a mistake. As he looked upon the dying Haundo, another one charged Rivo, head-butting him in the chest so hard it put him on his back. The creature then jumped on top of a stunned Rivo. Naomi slashed the beast across the side of its face, but was then herself tackled by one of its comrades.

Rivo and the Haundo were struggling with each other, trading blows. He was blindly taking stabs with his knife, periodically stabbing the creature in its side. The beast would return with strikes to his ribs. The Haundo was clawing and biting him on his forearm, drawing blood. He could tell the thing was hurting and not at full strength. When the hound again bit his arm, he returned the favor, biting the beast as hard as he could in its furry arm. Rivo was fighting for his life.

Just then, the Haundo was cracked across the skull so hard, it fell off dead to Rivo's side. As he tried to get a hold of his senses, he looked to see who had hit the beast with such force. It was Judd, holding a blood-spattered wooden post.

"Judd?" Rivo said as he grunted, holding his arm.

"Get out of here, Rivo, you're hurt," he said as he extended his hand to get Rivo back to his feet.

"Naomi! Is she okay!" Rivo hollered, desperately looking around as he came to his senses.

"Over here," Naomi called back, her voice exhausted but steady. She was scraped up, but otherwise fine. "I'm glad we got some help," she said as Vickie and Renee helped her to her feet.

"Where did you all come from?" asked Rivo.

"You're welcome, Rivo," Vickie replied dryly as she brushed some dirt off Naomi's back.

"We were in the staging area in the back when we heard what was going on," Renee remarked as she held Naomi's arm. "Vickie and I went to find some daggers and hatchets to fight with while Judd charged on ahead. We saw him running towards you already, so we went to help Naomi."

"And as you can see, they both have deadly accurate aim," added Judd.

As Rivo began to get his bearings straight, he could see at the opposite entrance the last of the surviving audience members leaving, one of the townspeople, holding a bloody sword in one hand, guiding them out. The man then turned to Rivo and the gang, frantically beckoning them to come towards him.

Throughout the tent, Rivo saw dead and critically injured Haundo, along with a few dead audience members. The handlers had released their animals on the beasts. At some point during the skirmish, the elephant rampaged out of the tent, trampling on several Haundo before finally being overcome. There was still a lion on the inside, two Haundo were on all fours, staring down the lion, but were wise enough to keep their distance.

A roar shook the air, low and guttural, just outside. "Who killed my hounds!?" A voice growled deep, commanding, and fueled with fury.

Vickie's eyes shot wide. "Mother of the stars, what was that?"

Rivo and Naomi looked at each other, both their mouths agape. "Oh no," Naomi's voice quivered. "Those things can talk?"

"What things?" asked Judd. "Who is that out there?"

"It's a Greater Haundo," Rivo gasped, swallowing a lump in his throat, the pit of his stomach in knots.

"What does that mean?" asked Renee, her eyes darting from the direction of the voice to the group inside.

"It means," Naomi's voice cracked. "We've got to get out. Fast!"

It was too late; the tent wall shuddered. A massive shadow loomed beyond the fabric. Dark claws slashed through, ripping the canvas wide. A hulking, werewolf-like beast stepped in, its gray fur glinting in the flickering light. The Greater Haundo stood, glaring at them with its golden eyes. "So," it growled with a voice that shook the tent, "Who dies first?"

Chapter 6

A Different Type of Magic Trick

The massive gray beast stood on its hind legs; it was at least seven feet tall. It was holding a large club, covered in blood—no doubt the blood of some unfortunate Rhemilian citizens who met a horrific end.

"That was the most terrified I'd ever been," Spirit Rivo said. "By the stars, I wish I didn't have to watch this again."

Without wasting any time, the large hound charged at the stunned group. Rivo lunged toward the beast without hesitation. "You've got to be joking!" the beast said as he swatted Rivo aside like a fly. He hit the ground but jumped right back up to his feet, ready to attack. He felt a surge of power run through him. It wasn't adrenaline, it was something completely different.

With everyone else keeping their focus on the giant Haundo, they didn't notice Rivo's eyes had turned a bright amber for a brief moment.

"That's it!" exclaimed Spirit Rivo. "It has to be."

"Looks like I finally found one of you humans with some fight!" the Greater Haundo said as he inhaled deeply. "Black fang!" it yelled as it opened its mouth wide, and a wave of black energy shot out like a hundred arrowheads, striking Rivo.

Rivo screamed in agony as he collapsed like a marionette with its strings severed. He lay on the ground, groaning and writhing in pain. It felt as if he had sharp fangs digging into every pressure point in his body all at once. Every time he tried even to flex a muscle, the pain got worse, shooting through his body like a hundred wolf bites.

"I'll never forget that pain," said Spirit Rivo. "It was unlike anything I'd ever felt before, real yet unreal."

"Rivo!" Renee screamed, frozen yet scrambling for a plan. She ran over to aid him, but there was little she could do.

Naomi jumped towards the Greater Haundo to attempt a lethal stab to its neck. The beast reacted in time to strike her in the torso with its forearm, knocking the wind out of her and causing her to fold over.

The monster continued charging towards the rest of the group, only to be met head-on by Judd. The big man threw the wooden post he was holding directly at the creature, striking it right in the chest. The Greater Haundo let out a brief gasp but didn't slow down. The two met, and Judd lifted the beast up and body slammed it into the ground with so much momentum that Judd fell down on top of the giant hound.

The large beast dropped its club but didn't show signs of pain, immediately clinching Judd, biting him on his shoulder hard. He let out a shout, but then proceeded to continually bash the beast on its side with his rock-hard fists. Judd relentlessly pounded on the beast, who still had its teeth sunk in his shoulder. Renee had no choice but to leave Rivo's side to try and aid their friend. She and Vickie rushed to help, but were knocked to the ground by a sweeping strike from the Greater Haundo, who was still wrestling with the strongman.

The beating that the beast was receiving began to take its toll. He released Judd and began to back away, only to receive a vicious right hand across his mouth from the bald strongman. The giant Haundo let out a brief, deep yelp, then stared back at Judd with a sinister, bloody sneer.

The Greater Haundo, with blood dripping from its fangs, continued to stare down Judd. Both Judd and the beast were breathing heavily—they were hurt.

"This is a waste of time," the large beast growled. "We came here to feed, not to fight these human freaks. Let's regroup and gather up the humans we've already slain," the Greater Haundo shouted, as he barked at the other two Haundo who were still in a standoff with the lion.

After the large creature gave its orders, the other two Haundo ran past it out of the tent on all fours. The Greater Haundo backed up, still standing on his hind legs and still staring down Judd, who was holding his right shoulder, dripping with blood. The strongman staggered, but glared back at the beast; he was not intimidated. The massive hound scoffed and then turned his back to the group as he left the shredded tent.

"We gotta go, now," Renee said, hauling herself up. She turned to Rivo, who was still on the ground, his breathing labored. "Rivo, are you okay?"

"Ugh," Rivo breathed in short, sharp gasps. "I... I think the pain's fading a little. What..." he paused to gasp for more air. "What was that?" he asked as he slowly sat up, the pain still surging, but not as intense.

"Blackmagic—it had to be," Vickie replied, steady despite the chaos. "We've heard about it in our travels. It should pass soon."

He began checking his arms and legs for fresh wounds; aside from the streaks of blood on his forearm from the other Haundo's bite, there looked to be none. "It... it felt so real, but I swear that I felt his bite."

"That's how black magic works," replied Renee as she started to help him up. "You weren't being attacked, but your mind thought you were."

"We can talk about that later," said Vickie as she inspected Judd's injured shoulder. "Let's get out of here. We have to get Judd to a medic."

"Naomi!" A familiar male voice shouted from the far entrance. It was Pearce; he was breathing heavily and holding a bloody sword that he must have gotten from a fallen local. He appeared to be a bit scraped up, but not nearly as bad as Rivo or Judd, especially.

"Pearce! Thank the stars!" shouted a relieved Naomi as she ran towards him and embraced while the rest followed.

"Everyone's holed up in the town hall and the inn," Pearce told them as they all ran out of the tent. They could hear the barks and growls of the Haundo echoing in the distance through the cool night air.

They ran as fast as they could to the town hall building nearby. Renee was helping Rivo along, the lingering pain of the dark magic making it difficult for him to keep up with the rest.

As he and Renee trailed behind the rest, he noticed drops of blood from Judd splattering the ground. "He's bleeding pretty bad. Is there a medic in there?" Rivo asked.

"I don't think so," replied Pearce. "I heard most of the wounded went to the inn. I believe there's some medics treating people inside."

"We'll have to take him there; we need to stop the bleeding," said Vickie. She had been holding Judd around his side, helping him along as best she could.

"Understood, replied Pearce. "Naomi, you and Rivo stay here at the town hall. I'll take them to the inn."

"I'll go," said Rivo. "You stay here, you need to be with Naomi," he added, now able to move a little more freely. The pain from the Greater Haundo's magic at that point reduced to a pins-and-needles sensation.

"That pain started to fade," Spirit Rivo remarked. "But then the very real pain from the bites and pounding I took from that other Haundo bastard started to set in."

"Rivo!" Naomi hissed through her clenched teeth. "We can't separate!"

"I'm not leaving these three out in the open in this condition. I'll be fine," he said, wincing as he and the three performers made their way to the inn just a couple of buildings down on the other side of the road.

"Here it is. We made it," Rivo rasped, still catching his breath and grimacing from the pain of his injuries, which felt as if it was spreading across his entire upper body. "We're safe. For now…"

Chapter 7

Calling the Bluff

"Vickie! Judd! Renee! Thank the stars you're all okay!" a concerned Mr. Sundry exclaimed as he saw the group enter the lobby of the inn. The clerk and another inn worker then barricaded the door with some heavy crates after the four were let in.

"Yes, barely," Vickie panted, "but Judd's hurt, he needs a doctor."

"Rivo too, he's hurt," added Renee.

As soon as they had entered the inn, Rivo sat on the ground next to the door, his legs splayed out and his back against the wall. His eyes stared blankly, mind reeling. He had a dazed look on his face, still trying to process everything that had just happened.

"The Haundo, the lifeless bodies of the townsfolk, blood everywhere," Spirit Rivo lamented. "It was a lot to take in."

Each breath sharpened the throbbing in his skull and ribs. "I think... I might've overdone it a bit," he gasped, pausing to gulp air.

"That's putting it lightly!" Renee exclaimed as she wiped down his scrapes with a clean rag and a bucket of cold water. She then dipped the rag back into the bucket to get it soaked, then placed it against the side of his swollen and bleeding face.

I feel like I just got kicked by a horse, Rivo thought.

"You look like you just got kicked by a horse," Renee remarked as she inspected the bruising on his face. Rivo couldn't help but chuckle at her comment.

"Renee. What was that Vickie was saying about the black magic that thing used on me?" he asked, catching his breath.

"Black magic attacks the mind somehow," she answered as she wrapped a cloth around the bite marks on his forearm. "At least that's what I've always heard. I don't know a whole lot about it, just bits here and there. Some people say that the same attack won't work on the same person twice."

"Really?" His brow furrowed. "Is it something you build an immunity to?"

"That's just what I've heard. I wouldn't try to push it again if I were you."

The town doctor, along with a nurse and a handful of others with some medical know-how, were doing the best they could to care for the wounded. They started treating Judd, who was sitting in a bed. The nurse poured some alcohol on his wound, which was thankfully not as bad as was feared. The blood started to clot quickly. The doctor bandaged him up, urging him to rest for a while. There had to have been over a hundred people packed in that inn, many of the wounded lying on a bed.

"Any idea how many people were killed?" asked an exhausted Rivo.

"No telling right now," said a somber Mr. Sundry as he looked out the lobby window. "I know I lost a few fine performers, and probably all my animals by now... damn those monsters."

"I think they were after the adults more than the kids. More meat, I guess," said Gordon, one of the boys Rivo and Renee had played rushball with earlier that same day. "I ran here because my parents weren't at the house. I just hope—" the boy began to sob. Renee got up and hugged the young lad, providing what comfort she could. There were no doubt several children in the same situation. One could only hope they were safe and sound, somewhere in the town.

A young man about Rivo's age approached him. "I saw you fightin' those things," he said excitedly. "Stars be damned, that was impressive."

Rivo looked up at the young man. He recognized him as one of the workers at the inn. "Oh, uh, thanks," Rivo replied faintly.

"The name's Murphy," he said, as he brandished a shiny sword. "And next time, I'm gonna fight those things off just like you did."

"Murphy," Spirit Rivo sighed. "Too brave for his own good... Though I guess I'm not one to talk."

Their conversation was cut short by the barks and howls of the approaching Haundo.

"Humans! Humans!" boomed a loud growling voice from outside.

Oh, no. That's got to be that damned Greater Haundo again, Rivo thought.

"C'mon, answer me!" it shouted again. "One of you can talk, can't you? I am Drokner of the Haundo. Now show yourselves, you cowards!"

The night air fell silent, only to be interrupted by a loud voice from a cracked window at the town hall. "What do you want with these people?" Pearce hollered. "These are civilians, this isn't some military outpost. They have no quarrel with you."

"We came to feed. We need more man flesh," Drokner shouted back. "Give us ten more humans to feed on and we'll leave the rest of you be."

"No way, you've terrorized this town enough," Pearce answered.

"Then we'll tear this whole town apart and kill every last one of you!" growled an angry Drokner.

"Let's not be rash," Pearce replied. "I'm sure we can work something out. There's got to be some livestock or something that you can take instead."

I know Pearce, Rivo thought. *He'd never bargain. He must be trying to think of some way to stall them so he can come up with some sort of plan.*

"He's bluffing," said Rivo to the others as Pearce and the beast continued to argue.

"Who's bluffing?" Murphy asked as he peeked out the window.

"That monster, Drokner. We may have lost people, but so did they. I don't think they have the numbers and strength. Not if we fight."

Rivo glanced out the window, seeing shooting stars streaking across the sky. "Anybody care to make a wish? We could use one right now."

"A star isn't going to help us out of this one, child," Vickie interjected as she walked into the lobby. "Let's get real, just what exactly can we do?"

"Can one of you hand me that green bag in the corner? It has my gear," he said as he motioned towards the far corner of the room.

"What on earth are you planning, Rivo?" asked Renee.

"We have to take action now. This is our best shot; they won't be expecting it. Please, can someone just hand that to me?" Rivo asked, again motioning toward the bag.

Judd picked up the bag and brought it to Rivo, dropping it at his feet. "You can't do this alone," he said.

"I know," Rivo replied as he began to go through his bag. He started putting on his brown leather gauntlets around his forearms, wincing as he tied one over his injured forearm. His arm throbbed, but the thought of losing Rhemilia would hurt worse. *This will help guard against the Haundo's teeth,* he thought. He then grabbed his weapons of choice, two short swords.

"You can't be serious! Rivo, you're in no condition," Renee pleaded.

"We don't have a choice; this is our last stand. Let's make it count," he responded, somehow managing to get back on his feet. "I need everyone who's able to chip in, grab whatever you can find, shovels, chair legs, wine bottles. Let's give them everything we've got. I'm gonna go after them. Anyone who can join me, please feel free. The rest of you, get on the rooftop and start pelting these things with any and everything you can get your hands on."

"I told you I liked him," Judd said to Vickie with a crooked smile.

Vickie eyed Judd's wounded shoulder and sighed, "That boy's reckless and stupid, but he's right. We don't have much of a choice."

"I'm in," Murphy added, swaying his sword in front of him.

Judd, Vickie, Renee, and others all grabbed anything that could serve as a weapon. Murphy removed the barricade from the front door. Rivo closed his eyes and drew a deep breath. *Pearce, Naomi. I'm banking on you guys having the same thing in mind. Let's make this work.*

"Okay, everybody," Rivo instructed the crowd. "We charge out in three," he paused to take another deep breath, "One... two... three!"

Rivo and the group charged out of the inn, shouting at the beasts. He cut through two Haundo before they knew what hit them. Vickie, Renee, Judd, and Murphy right there with him, slashing and pounding at the beasts in their path.

It was at that time that Rivo realized his gamble had paid off. Pearce, Naomi, and a slew of armed townsfolk came running head-on towards the beasts. Those with weapons cut, stabbed, and bashed the beasts, while others pelted them with bricks, glass bottles, wooden chairs, and anything else at their disposal.

An enraged Drokner had no intention of going out quietly. He let out a roar and began pounding, clawing, and biting any who came near him, delivering fatal blows to several who were unfortunate enough to be in his path.

While Drokner was occupied fighting off the brave crowd of people, Judd, holding a melon-sized rock, bashed him across the face so hard it practically took him off his feet. Drokner had an unbelievably high pain threshold and showed little sign of pain. He bashed Judd across the left side of his face with an equal degree of force, causing the strongman to wobble backward, but somehow he stayed standing.

The giant Haundo was about to lunge at Judd, but was interrupted by Rivo leaping at him with a sword in each hand. Drokner took a back-handed swing at the young warrior that barely missed, due to Rivo changing course at the last second to avoid the potentially deadly blow. The parry may have avoided the beast's attack, but he lost his balance in the process, falling on his back. Drokner took advantage of the situation and stomped on Rivo's forearm with his massive foot, pinning him to the ground. The beast loomed over his young opponent, as if to relish the moment before he finished the boy off. Rivo did not hesitate and used the sword in his free hand to slice the great beast's leg, midway up the calf. The cut went so deep it practically sliced through the monster's calf muscle.

Drokner howled in pain. "Retreat!" it hollered, barking sharply at the surviving Haundo, whose numbers had significantly dwindled. The beasts were sent fleeing back to the nearby forest, Drokner on all fours, limping badly as he fled.

The battle was over, and the people had won. Cheers rose as Rivo struggled to stand, arm throbbing. He started to slowly sit up when he felt an arm wrap around his, elbow to elbow. It was Renee.

"Rivo, are you okay? Can you hear me?" she asked.

"Yeah, yeah, I think so. It's just my arm," he said, wincing in pain.

He felt a large hand grab him by the back collar. "Up you go," said Judd as he effortlessly lifted Rivo to his feet. He looked back at the strongman, who had his signature crooked smile, but Rivo could tell he was hurting. *That blow to the side of the face Judd had suffered from Drokner had done some damage,* he thought.

"Rivo of Greencourt, you reckless fool," said Vickie with a relieved smile on her face. "You were amazing." She walked up to him, gave him a hug around his neck, and kissed him on his cheek. "You may be an idiot, but you're a heroic one."

Spirit Rivo chuckled. "I guess she just got caught up in the moment."

"Rivo!" A voice yelled. It was Naomi. She ran up and embraced him. "I'm glad you're alright!"

Pearce wasn't far behind. He gave Rivo a side hug and rubbed his head. "That was great, Rivo! I'm glad we were thinking the same thing. Perfect timing, they never saw it coming!"

"I'm glad too," said a relieved Rivo. "I'm just thankful you all are okay. I wonder if those things will come back."

"No telling," replied Pearce as he turned his gaze in the direction of the forests on the outskirts of town that Drokner and the remaining Haundo fled to. "But we can't take our chances. We aren't out of the woods yet."

"What do you mean?" asked Renee.

"We may have won this time. But there's a good chance they'll be back, maybe in even greater numbers. We have to go take them out now while they're weakened," Pearce explained.

"You can't be serious! Right now?" exclaimed Vickie.

"Yes," Pearce replied. "Like I said, now is the best time." He turned to Rivo. "Rivo, can you still fight?"

"No way! He's hurt," Renee said adamantly.

Pearce rubbed his forehead in frustration. "I understand. But if he can still fight, we want him to come with us. We work best as a team."

"He. Is. Hurt!" Vickie said slowly and emphatically, as if speaking to an unruly child.

"We. Know!" Snapped Naomi in kind, mimicking Vickie's tone as she took a step toward her. "*He*. Is on our squad. *You*. Are not. We asked you and you told us to get lost, remember?"

Vickie glared at Naomi, then went to check on Judd.

"That's enough," said Pearce, pinching the bridge of his nose. "Rivo, can you still fight or not?"

"Uhh, yeah. Yeah, I can still fight," replied Rivo as he flexed his hand to see if he could still hold his sword.

"Rivo," Renee pleaded as she sighed and dropped her shoulders.

"Perfect. Naomi, let's go get our gear and get ready. Rivo, just sit tight 'til we get back. Anyone else who wants to join is welcome," Pearce announced. "We'll make sure we tell the townspeople to stay armed and ready. There's no telling what the Haundo's plan might be."

"I'll go," hollered Judd.

"Excellent, we'll be back shortly," replied Pearce as he and Naomi walked back to the inn.

"Judd, no. Please," begged Vickie.

"I've got a score to settle with Drokner," Judd told her.

"I'm going too," volunteered Renee as she looked at Rivo and shook her head.

"Stars be damned, have you all lost your minds?" Vickie pleaded, throwing her palms in the air.

"Somebody has to make sure Rivo of Greencourt doesn't get himself killed," replied Renee.

"I can't believe this," Vickie sighed. "Fine, I guess that means I'm going too." *I knew this kid was gonna get us all killed,* she thought.

"Was that Vickie again?" Spirit Rivo asked. "Thanks for the vote of confidence, Vickie."

Pearce and Naomi returned, gauntlets on, dual swords in hand, matching Rivo's.

"Well, looks like we got ourselves a decent-sized team," remarked Pearce as he joined his new squad. "Judd, Vickie, Renee, go ahead and get yourselves armed and get to it. We have some Haundo to hunt down."

"I'm going too," added Murphy as he approached the group.

"Who are you?" Pearce asked as he eyed the young man.

"Well, I'm—" Murphy started.

"Not leaving me here!" A young woman hollered, running up and wrapping her arm around his. "Murphy, I was scared to death when I saw you charge in there like that. Please, can you just sit this one out?" she pleaded.

"Myra?" Murphy replied. "Well, uhh—"

"Just stay here, kid," Pearce interrupted. He looked at Rivo and shook his head. "What in the star's name did you do to get that kid thinking he could fight with us?" he whispered.

The squad of six got armed and ready as best they could and set off into the wilderness to hunt down Drokner and the rest of the Haundo.

Chapter 8

Watch Out!

Rivo could hear nothing but the sound of his own heavy breathing. "It's best to wait a good forty-five minutes before tracking if you want to find the animal you've wounded. Look for blood spatters and trails. Don't forget to find their tracks in the ground and always look for things like rubs and scat," said Frank to a young Rivo, no more than eight years old at the time. They had just wounded a wild boar and were now tracking the animal.

"What do we do when we find it, Father?" asked young Rivo.

His father was about to answer, but noticed the wounded boar in a clearing nearby. It was limping badly, with an arrow sticking in its hind leg.

"We found it, Rivo," he whispered. "Son, it's hurt, so it can't move fast enough to charge you. Can you handle this? Keep calm, stay focused, and don't make any noise. I'll be close by."

Rivo nodded his head and cautiously approached the boar, spear in hand. As he got close enough to touch it, he froze. The boar realized he was there, swung around, and knocked the boy to the ground.

As the wild animal prepared to attack him, the boar was stuck in the back of its neck with a spear. It fell dead to the ground. Frank walked over the beast's dead body and held his hand out to help his son up.

"Are you okay, Rivo?" he asked. The boy rose to his feet and nodded. "Listen, Rivo. You can't freeze like that out here; you do, you're in trouble. You must strike when the time is right. Don't let your head get in the way. It could be a matter of life or death."

"But how do I know when the time is right?" the boy replied, his lower lip quivering.

Frank put his hands on the boy's shoulders and looked him in the eye, "You'll know, Rivo."

***

"Rivo, Rivo!" Naomi said in a sharp whisper, "c'mon, stay focused."

Rivo and the gang found themselves in the dark forests outside of Rhemilia. It was about midnight. The air was cool but not unbearable. The only light they had was the dim blue light of the moon.

Keep calm, move slowly, and most importantly, don't make any noise. The voice of his father played through his head as the squad carefully made their way through deep, dark woods.

Judd was large and clumsy; his steps were too heavy, and the sounds of twigs snapping under his feet could be heard every few paces. Pearce kept motioning for him to keep quiet. Poor Judd tried his best, but tracking wasn't his strong suit.

"Oh, Judd," Spirit Rivo remarked. "That man couldn't be quiet if he was standing still."

As they kept making their way through the forest, Rivo trailed his hand over branches, feeling for blood. A low limb gleamed, wet with fresh blood. The Haundo weren't far away.

Rivo motioned to Pearce, signaling that the enemy must be nearby. The group quietly gathered close together; one wrong move, and the hunter could become the hunted.

Just then, Rivo thought he spotted something in the distance from the corner of his eye, watching them. Just as quickly as he turned his head to look, it vanished. *Was that... a child?* Rivo turned back towards the rest of the group and again noticed movement in the corner of his eye. He turned quickly and saw it clearly, if just for a split second. No doubt about it, it was a young boy, a few years younger than Rivo. He had disheveled hair and wore tattered clothes.

"Psst! Pearce!" Rivo whispered.

"What is it? Did you find something?" Pearce whispered back.

"Somebody else is here. It looked like a child, a little younger than me. I saw him, just for a second."

"What!? No way. Out here? Are you sure?"

"Yes, positive. He was dirty looking, with messed-up hair and clothes."

"Feral people. It has to be," Pearce remarked.

"Feral people? You mean the Forest Folk? I'd never seen one before."

"Yeah, sounds like it. They're thieves and scavengers, every one of 'em. We're not gonna worry about that now. They won't bother us. Let's keep moving."

As they advanced at a yet slower pace, the sound of a twig snapping was heard in the distance, not even a hundred feet away. Rivo and the others crept forward, pausing frequently to search for any other signs of Haundo. It was then that Naomi spotted something; it looked like a large wolf den, dug into the side of a slope by a stream. The opening was larger than that of a standard wolf den; it was large enough for a full-grown man to fit through easily.

As they approached the den, they saw several dead bodies of the townspeople from the recent attack. Rivo, filled with rage and disgust, had to fight to stop himself from gagging himself at the sight.

"Even seeing this again turns my stomach," Spirit Rivo said.

Rivo took a moment to collect himself. "What should we do now? Did anyone see how many had fled the town?" he whispered.

"Hard to say, maybe six or so, plus the leader. Who knows if there wasn't more that stayed behind?" Pearce replied.

"There's one right there," Naomi whispered, pointing to the right of the entrance to the den. A Haundo was sitting on its hind legs, watching guard. Thankfully, it hadn't spotted the group that was standing at about four o'clock in relation to the den entrance, about fifty feet away.

"Ladies, is your aim as good with those bows and arrows as it is with the throwing knives?" Pearce asked Vickie and Renee, who both grabbed some as they left town.

Vickie and Renee both nodded with confidence.

"Good. Vickie, you and Judd stay here. Naomi, you and I are going to get into position directly in front of the entrance, keeping the same distance as we are now. Rivo, you and Renee go take position at about eight o'clock. Vickie, give us some time to get in position, I'd say count to about two hundred," said Pearce.

"Then what?" replied Vickie.

"Then I want you to shoot, get a kill shot if at all possible. This, I'm sure, will startle the others. When that happens, I want you and Renee to pick off as many as you can. The rest of us will jump into action, and we're going to charge in as fast as we can. Once we get close, I need you two to switch to your short-range weapons and back us up," said Pearce. "Judd, if you spot that big one, you know what to do, right?"

"Right," answered Judd.

The group stealthily moved into position so as not to make a sound. So slowly that Rivo was worried that Pearce telling Vickie to count to two hundred wasn't enough time. Thankfully, it would seem Vickie was thinking the same thing. It took what seemed like ages for everyone to get into position, but they all finally got there.

Rivo was holding his two short swords, his right arm throbbing from when Drokner had stomped on it earlier, but he still felt he had a good grip. Renee stood ready with her arrow pointing at the den's mouth. He noticed more shooting stars streaking across the sky. The *stars must really want someone to make a wish*, he thought.

It was then that the battle began. Vickie's arrow zipped through the air at a ferocious speed, striking the Haundo that was standing guard straight through the side of the head. Two other Haundo leapt out of the den and were both picked off, one by Renee, the other by Vickie.

Rivo's heart began to race, fear and anxiety setting in. This was it, either they would kill all the Haundo, or the Haundo would kill all of them. *Don't freeze, you can't freeze, not now.*

Rivo and the others sprang into action. Pearce and Naomi ran straight for the mouth of the den and were met by two other Haundo. Judd charged in as well, tackling another one that had been standing guard somewhere past the entrance. As Rivo sprinted to help, he was tackled by another, who, it turned out, was only a few feet from where Rivo and Renee had been positioned; they had somehow missed the creature that had likely fallen asleep.

As Rivo was wrestling with the creature on the ground, he was able to block the beast's bite with his leather gauntlet on his already hurting right arm. Thankfully, the monster wasn't able to bite through the gauntlets, so Rivo was able to use the sword in his left arm to slice the right side of the beast, allowing him to push the creature off of him, and Renee finished it off with an arrow to the side of its neck.

"Thanks, Renee," Rivo said as he lifted himself up. "I don't know how I missed that—"

"Watch out!" shrieked Renee.

Rivo felt a large hand grab him by the back of the neck and throw him like a ragdoll into a nearby tree, his torso smacking against the large trunk with ferocious force. He had the wind knocked out of him, and a sharp pain reverberated through his ribs.

There stood an infuriated Drokner, looking to see who it was that attacked his den. "You again!" he growled as he advanced toward Rivo. "I should have eaten you alive when I had the chance."

He stood over Rivo, ready to pounce, when an arrow was shot into his side. Drokner let out a howl and then turned to look at Renee, who was nocking another arrow.

Without saying a word, Drokner sprinted towards her, she dropped her bow and arrow and opted to grab her knife, unsure how much damage it could do to a beast of that size. Just then, Drokner's onslaught was stopped by Judd, who tackled him from the side.

Yet again, Drokner and Judd found themselves battling on the ground. Drokner sank his teeth into Judd's shoulder, reopening the wound and causing the strongman to holler out in pain. The large beast pushed the hurting Judd off of him and smashed him across the side of the face. Renee tried to aid her ailing comrade and stabbed the monster in his shoulder, which did little more than anger the beast. Drokner swatted her to the ground with a back-handed swing and then picked up a large stone nearby to finish off Judd once and for all.

"What a nightmare," Spirit Rivo said, his ghostly eyes glaring at Drokner. "I thought it was over for us."

Chapter 9

The Glare

.

"Rivo, I want you to understand what I'm about to do and why," Frank told his young son as he knelt in front of him. "You say you want to be a warrior, you want to protect the people you love and the land you call home, right?"

"Yes, Father, that's what I want. More than anything," young Rivo answered. Pearce was standing just past him, wooden staff in hand, ready to spar.

"What is about to happen is going to hurt. I'm not doing this in anger; you didn't do anything wrong, I'm not upset with you, and you're not in trouble. This is about knowing what it takes to fight. A warrior needs to know what it's like to get hurt and keep on fighting, do you understand?"

"Yes, Father, I can handle it," the boy replied, determined with his eyebrows furrowed.

"Very well." Frank straightened up and nodded to Pearce, who spun around and swung his staff, striking young Rivo with a forceful blow to the gut. The boy fell to the ground, gasping for air.

"Get up, Rivo! You have to get up! This is a matter of life and death!" Frank urged him.

"I can't... I can't breathe... Father," the boy groaned.

"Rivo! You must get up! They're here, Rivo! They're going to kill me! They're going to kill your mother! They're going to kill Naomi! Rivo, you must get up!"

The boy worked up the strength to stand, his legs quivering. He felt as if he was going to vomit.

"That's it, Rivo! Now fight! Fight!"

Rivo took a sloppy swing with his staff and hit nothing but air. He collapsed back down to one knee.

"That's not good enough!" yelled Frank. "Focus! Fight! Get up, Rivo! This is a matter of life and death! They're going to kill everyone! Get! Up!"

Rivo stood up, his eyes burning a bright amber color. He could feel power surging through him. Pearce's eyes shot wide, and his mouth gaped open; he was the only one to see it. Rivo let out a shout and lunged at Pearce, taking one directed swing, then another. Pearce stumbled, struggling to keep up with the sudden onslaught. Rivo then did a backhanded swing with his staff that might have nearly separated Pearce's head from his body had Frank not stepped in to block the attack.

"Perfect, Rivo! That's it! Just perfect!" Frank hugged his young son to reassure him. Rivo was leaning against his Father, breathing heavily, the amber light having faded from his eyes. He was staring blankly into the distance. "Rivo, I am so proud of you," he gently patted the boy on the back. "It's okay, son, I'm here. It's over, everyone is safe."

Rivo slowly collected himself and looked up to meet his Father's eyes. Frank put his hand to his son's cheek. "You did good, son. Real good," he said, as he smiled proudly at the boy. "You got up and kept fighting to protect those you love. That, Rivo, is a warrior's heart."

Meanwhile, Pearce stood in stunned silence, unsure if what he had just seen in Rivo's eyes was real or if it was all in his head.

***

The Greater Haundo loomed over the injured strongman, ready to bash his skull in and finish him off once and for all. As Rivo lay on the ground, gasping for air, the words of his Father echoed in his mind, *"Get up, Rivo! This is a matter of life and death! They're going to kill everyone! Get! Up!"*

Drokner's growl echoed through the forest. He raised his arm, rock in hand, poised to crush Judd, but his attack was cut short as he buckled to one knee, howling in agony. He had just been stabbed in the same place on his leg where he had been cut earlier. With the beast now unable to stand, Rivo lifted himself up. Vickie and Renee watched, in shock, as they saw Rivo's eyes, furious and burning bright amber again. His sword cut through the air in a vicious backhanded strike, but this time, Frank wasn't there to stop him. Rivo's blade went deep into the back of the Greater Haundo's neck.

Drokner fell to the ground. Dead.

"That was it again!" Spirit Rivo exclaimed. "That's got to be it. The Guardian's Glare..."

Vickie and Renee both looked at each other, mouths gaping, then at Rivo. *Stars be damned,* Vickie thought as she and Renee both stood in disbelief at what they had just witnessed. *What kind of kid is this?*

"I can still hear Vickie's thoughts," Spirit Rivo remarked in bewilderment. "And, it seems, *only* her thoughts..."

Chapter 10

A Boy in the Woods

As Drokner lay dead on the leaf-covered forest floor, Rivo fell to one knee, then collapsed on his side, doubled over in pain.

"Rivo! Judd!" hollered Renee as she ran to check on them.

"I'll be okay," said Judd as he slowly got to his feet, bracing himself against a tree trunk.

"Rivo! Are you okay?" Renee asked frantically as she knelt beside him.

"Rivo! Rivo! We're coming!" yelled Naomi as she and Pearce ran to his aid, having finished off the Haundo they were battling.

"It—it hurts when I breathe," Rivo groaned, his eyes clenched. Leaves, damp with the morning dew, stuck to his skin. His breathing was sharp and labored, the cold forest air stinging his lungs.

"It's okay. We're here with you. The Haundo are dead. We're safe now," Pearce said calmly with his arm around Naomi's shoulders.

"Judd. Is Judd okay?"

"Yeah, Rivo, thanks to you," Judd replied as Vickie checked his injuries.

"That's good," whispered Rivo as he drew some shallow breaths. "I'm glad."

"Rivo, honey, can you move at all?" Naomi asked softly as she knelt by his side. "We need to get you back to town and have a doctor take a look at you. Maybe we can carry you there."

"Okay," rasped Rivo, trying to lift himself but collapsing back down after bracing his injured right arm on the ground to sit up. The damage caused by Drokner's stomp earlier was really starting to set in.

"Rivo, don't! We'll help you," said Renee. She and Vickie got on either side of Rivo, placing his arms over their shoulders and slowly lifting him to his feet.

"Let me help," said Naomi as she placed her hands on the sides of his face.

"Not now, Naomi, there may still be some Haundo around. I think we should scout the area while they head back," said Pearce. "You were great, all of you. We couldn't have done this without you. And Rivo," Pearce added as he walked up to him and placed his hand on the back of Rivo's neck, "that was incredible, really incredible."

"We're so proud of you, Rivo, really. We love you," said Naomi as she kissed him on the forehead.

"You two don't wander off too far," hollered Judd as they began to slowly make their way toward town.

"We won't," replied Pearce as he studied his surroundings. "This shouldn't take long. One way or the other, we'll plan on being back by sunrise." He paused to gaze up at the tree tops. "And that feral brat better hope we don't catch him if he's still out here."

"Judd," Naomi called out as they parted ways. "Please keep an eye on him."

"Yes, I will. It's the least I could do," he replied.

As the group dispersed, the young feral boy Rivo had spotted earlier stood perched atop a high tree branch, watching them. "Beastkiller... " the boy whispered.

"I see you there, little rascal," Spirit Rivo remarked as he watched on.

The four slowly made their way back, with Rivo helped along by Vickie and Renee. Judd followed, lugging all their weapons along with him.

As they walked back to Rhemilia, Renee looked to Rivo with a relieved smile. "Rivo of Greencourt," she said with playful mockery. "So reckless. I don't know what we're gonna do about you."

Vickie glanced at Renee over Rivo's drooping head. *Renee*, she thought to herself, in thoughts that were once again being heard by only Spirit Rivo, *usually the quiet and cynical type. You're seldom this talkative and friendly outside of your performances, especially around boys.*

"I guess I just have that effect on people, Vickie," remarked Spirit Rivo as he hovered beside them. "Everyone except you, it seems."

They came back to town to the cheers of the townspeople. The group's return could mean only one thing: the Haundo were gone. "Everybody, we're alright!" hollered Judd with a wide grin. "The Haundo are defeated and Drokner is dead!" They marched down the main street, the people pressing against them as they made their way through the town. "And it was all thanks to this boy. Rivo, the hero of Rhemilia!"

Rivo couldn't help but blush at the praise and attention the people gave him, in spite of his injuries. Vickie and Renee both shook their heads in amusement when they noticed his red cheeks. "Let's get you to the inn so they can take a look at you, hero," Renee said sarcastically.

As he was getting treated by the medics, Vickie noticed how comfortable her typically stand-offish sister seemed around the boy. As he was lying, propped up in bed, the two were teasing each other about their rushball game earlier. Renee couldn't contain her giggling when Rivo brought up a rematch. Vickie smiled at Renee as she watched.

I don't remember the last time I saw you laugh like this, Renee. There is something special about this kid, isn't there? You just can't help but like him, but Renee, please be careful with this boy. Breaking hearts is what they do.

"Breaking hearts?" Spirit Rivo said, bewildered. "What's she talking about?"

Interlude

The Festival of Celestial Lights

Part 1 of 2

It was just a few weeks after young Rivo's sixth birthday. He was awoken by the sounds of his mother in the kitchen, humming a song and preparing a special meal for a special occasion. The sound of her voice and the aroma of the food wove throughout their small cabin, creating an atmosphere that felt almost magical to young Rivo.

Today was the day of the annual Festival of Celestial Lights; Wyverly's most beloved holiday. The largest festival was held in the Wyverly capital, which was located on the other side of the kingdom from Greencourt. Rhemilia, however, held its own festival. It wasn't quite as large and as grand as the one in the capital, but it was still spectacular in its own right. Gwen would always volunteer to bring food for the community meal everyone would eat after the closing ceremony.

As the years went by, Rivo would look back and realize that it wasn't any sort of magic that made the atmosphere in that cabin so special; it was his mother's love.

As young Rivo approached his mother, Gwen, she was busy preparing the food she would bring to Rhemilia for the festival. She was startled to see her young son had woken so early.

"Rivo," she gasped. "You're up early."

"So today is the day of the Festival," young Rivo remarked with excitement. "When are we going to Rhemilia?"

"The sun hasn't even risen yet, Rivo," She told him as she set her attention back on the meal she was preparing. "You know this year's festival is more special for us than most, don't you?"

"Why's that, Mother?"

"Your father has been invited to perform the closing ceremony. Why don't you go check on him, Rivo? He's out in the woods, practicing. Let him know that we'll be ready to head out soon."

Young Rivo left the family's cabin to find his father. The sun was just beginning to show through the horizon. He greeted people in town who were already set to leave for Rhemilia, no doubt not wanting to miss a moment of the fun to be had.

The boy walked through the woods to the clearing that his father would often use for training with Pearce and Naomi. Sure enough, as young Rivo approached, he could hear the grunts and heavy breathing of his father practicing his sword play.

He peeked through the bushes and saw his father, Frank, handling his sword and maneuvering with mastery. Each swing of the sword, each step taken, served a purpose. Rivo watched in awe, believing that there wasn't anything his father couldn't do.

As he stood in amazement watching his father practice his swordplay, he accidentally stepped on a twig and snapped it. His father jerked his head over in the boy's direction.

"Rivo!" Frank hollered with a smile. "I should have figured you'd try sneaking up on me. What are you doing out here?"

"Mother told me to come get you. She said it's almost time to leave."

"Already?" Frank said, wiping his sweaty face with a rag. "Well, I guess we'd better head back."

As the two started back to the cabin. Rivo turned to his father. "Father," he asked eagerly. "The way you were moving with that sword. Is that what you train Pearce and Naomi to do? Could you teach me that stuff, too?"

Frank stopped walking and knelt down to be eye level with his son. "You know what, Rivo? I think you're ready to start training with Pearce and Naomi. You can start training with us at the next session. How does that sound?"

The boy nodded with excitement.

"Just remember, Rivo," his father explained. "These things take time to master. You won't excel overnight. Always keep that in mind, son."

Frank and Rivo helped Gwen load up the food on their wagon and headed off to Rhemilia, along with most of the town of Greencourt.

As they entered the large-by-Greencourt-standards town, they got off their wagon and walked through the bustling streets of Rhemilia. The sound of music, the joyful laughter, and friendly chatter rang throughout, as the savory smell of freshly baked breads and various spiced meats from all across the land roasting filled Rivo's senses. He loved this time of year more than any other. The people always seemed so merry, and the food was delicious.

As they proceeded through the town, there were various arts and crafts tables and Rivo's favorite, carnival games. The games consisted of activities like ring toss, bobbing for apples, and throwing darts, among many others. This was one of the few times when Frank and Gwen would pull out a few extra coins to let Rivo have fun and win prizes, usually wooden swords and candy.

The day flew by in what felt like a matter of minutes. Evening was approaching and Frank changed out his tunic for his golden embroidered blue vest that he received when he was in the Wyverly Guard. It was said that only well-reputed soldiers were given those vests. It was the same one that Frank left to Rivo when he passed.

Chapter 11

New Recruits

A few days had passed since Drokner and the Haundo were defeated. Rivo had some heavy bruising on his sides and arms from the battles. Judd's wounds were healing well. The rest of the group had some scrapes and bruises, but were about as good as new.

Despite the townspeople of Rhemilia begging for the group to stay, it was time to move on. They were on a recruiting mission and weren't supposed to hang around for long.

"I know, considering all that happened with the Haundo's attack, that this might be of little encouragement," Pearce told Naomi and Rivo as they were packing their bags in their room, "but this was a successful recruiting trip."

They had about a dozen townspeople agree to sign up, including Murphy and his girlfriend, Myra. Captain Tremlee and the others at Greencourt had moved on some time ago to assist more elsewhere. The closest outpost was located a few weeks' travel east along the route they were taking. The recruits would go through training. Those who were deemed fit would be sent to battle, and the rest would be used for recruiting and other supporting roles. Though there was no promise of an easy trek, reports of Haundo sightings along with rumors of aggressive Forest Folk had begun to spread.

Spirit Rivo found himself whisked away to another room at the inn. There, he saw Vickie and Renee getting ready for the day. Vickie just finished doing her hair and was now putting on her makeup in front of the mirror. She could see Renee sitting on the bed behind her, huddled with her knees drawn to her chest and her arms wrapped around her legs, something she often did when her thoughts weighed heavy.

"Something on your mind, sis?" Vickie asked as she was applying her mascara.

"Vick, what...what do you think about Rivo?" Renee asked with hesitation in her voice.

Spirit Rivo watched intently. "Wait, what are they talking about me for? I don't get it."

"Rivo?" Vickie was silent for a moment, a thoughtful expression on her face. "Well, he's not the brightest star in the sky, but he's brave, he's got a big heart. We're lucky he's on our side." A mischievous smile then crept across her face as she saw in the mirror that Renee's body language hadn't changed. "And," she added, giving a dramatic pause. "He's got a certain charm about him. Oh, and let's not forget how handsome he is. You know, now that I think of it, maybe he and I could—" she stopped to see Renee's reflection in the mirror, glaring at her.

Vickie let out an obnoxious cackle. "Oh, Renee, what's with that look?" she said in a pouty tone. "You don't need to worry, little sis, I'm not going to let you blame this on me. Besides," she added as she finished putting on her makeup. "If I were you, I'd be more concerned with what to do about that mother hen who's always hanging around him."

"*Mother hen?*" asked Spirit Rivo quizzically.

Renee hopped off the bed abruptly. "I don't know what you're talking about!" she snapped as she stormed out of the room and slammed the door.

"Huh?" Spirit Rivo continued watching the bizarre squabble. "What in the world was that about? Girls are strange."

They left the inn shortly after dawn and met with their recruits at the town square, the scent of freshly cut wood the townspeople were using to rebuild filling the air. The town was generous enough to give them another wagon along with enough food and supplies to last a while.

"Perfect, looks like everyone's here. Let's say our goodbyes and get moving," Pearce announced to his new group as he and Naomi started loading up.

"I'd like to say bye to Vickie, Judd, and Renee if that's alright," said Rivo, as everyone else was huddling near the wagons. "Also, I'd like to check on Gordon and make sure he's doing okay." He was worried about his former rushball teammate. The last time he saw the boy, he was crying at the inn the night of the battle.

"That's fine, just make it quick," answered Naomi.

Thankfully, it was quick. Gordon came running up to Rivo, giving him a big hug. "Thanks, Rivo, for everything. You guys are the best!"

"Gordon, I was just gonna go look for you. I was worried about your parents."

Gordon pointed to his mother and father off in the distance. "There they are! As alive as ever!" The two were both carrying an armful of supplies, no doubt to get started on rebuilding the town infrastructure.

"Oh, thank the stars! I'm glad to see you're all back together," Rivo bent over to talk to the boy, face-to-face. "Listen, Gordon, you treat them good and do as they ask. They won't be around forever, ya know. Got it?"

The boy looked back, almost intimidated. "Yes, sir," he said sheepishly as Rivo smiled and turned around. Gordon made one last plea, "Please, all of you, come back and see us again sometime. After you kill the rest of them monsters."

He looked back to face Gordon and winked, "You bet, kid. I'll come back, I promise."

He was now off to look for Vickie and the others. He figured he'd never see them again, so he wanted to make sure he thanked them for their help and said his goodbyes. Just then, the three performers approached the group, each carrying their backpacks. Judd was with them, carrying the bulk of their belongings. He had his signature crooked smile.

"Oh, hey guys! I was just going to look for you. I wanted to make sure I told you three goodbye," Rivo shouted.

"Really? What for? We're going with you," said Vickie as she walked past Rivo to the wagon so she could load up her bag.

"Oh, wow, that's great! What about Mr. Sundry and the circus?" asked Rivo.

"It'll be a while before they can get back on the road," Vickie replied. "It sounds like most of them are going to stick around here for a bit. Besides, when we told Mr. Sundry how you saved Judd's life, he understood how we wanted to return the favor." She smirked and shot a sideways glance toward Renee. "Oh, and I think Renee wanted to come along as well, right, Renee?"

Renee sneered at her sister, then turned toward Rivo. "We just thought with everything going on, there wouldn't be much need for a circus for a while. Besides, you saved Judd's life, so it seemed like the right thing to do."

"Oh, please!" Vickie said provocatively. "Like you didn't want to join them from the get-go."

Renee closed her eyes and clenched her teeth. "Cut it out, Vick!" she growled.

Rivo's eyes darted back and forth between the two of them, unsure of what he should say. "Well, uh, either way. We're glad you all are coming along."

Judd walked back from loading their belongings. "I owe you my life, Rivo. This is the least I can do," he interjected as he put his hand on Rivo's shoulder to direct him away from Vickie and Renee.

"Judd, you don't owe me anything," replied Rivo. "But I'm definitely glad you're on our squad."

"Rivo. You three, if you're coming with us, let's go," Pearce hollered from the front of the pack.

They loaded the last bags on the wagons, keeping only a small backpack, and prepared to head out.

"There isn't enough room on the wagons for the supplies and us," remarked Rivo. "I'll walk. Why don't you ladies hop on? Me and Judd,

I think we'll just go ahead on foot. We'll see you all when we make our first stop."

"I'll let Renee make that call," Vickie sighed. "Well, Renee?"

"I think I'd prefer to go on foot too," answered Renee as she walked up to Rivo. "Come on, Rivo, let's go."

Of course. Stars be damned, how did I know? "I guess I'm walking too," she announced loudly.

Spirit Rivo smirked as he watched himself and the three performers gather together. "For as shrewd and tough as Vickie puts on, she doesn't like being separated from her sister."

So, off the now-larger group of nearly twenty went. Pearce and Naomi at the front, with Rivo, Vickie, Judd, and Renee holding up the rear.

Chapter 12

Scrap!

"It's believed that a long time ago, all humans dwelt in the forest, but at some point several thousand years ago, they split and went their separate ways," Rivo's mother, Gwen, had once told him when he was a boy. "Some left the forest to explore and build the civilization we now know, while the rest chose to stay behind in the forest."

The Forest Folk were considered more of a nuisance than anything else. They weren't known for violence and typically avoided contact with civilians. They were thieves who would steal from travelers as they slept or took their eyes off their belongings. These feral humans were also scavengers who would scour battlefields, searching for any and everything they could take for themselves. They could use a few words, but typically communicated with hoots, whistles, and growls.

"It's been said that if they ever came across wounded humans, they would render aid if at all possible," she once told him. "There've been tales of soldiers left for dead on the battlefield, who would return home alive after being tended to by these strange humans. They say the Forest Folk are a very superstitious people, and see that leaving behind the wounded to die is bad luck."

***

The group was a few days along in their trek to the outpost. Things had been going well, and they were able to keep a steady pace. They had two wagons full of supplies, each led by horses. A couple of older gentlemen from Rhemilia were kind enough to volunteer their services in manning the wagons. These wagons typically led the way, followed by Rivo and all the other recruits walking on foot, each carrying a backpack with some personal belongings. Pearce, Naomi, and Judd would typically be at the front of the pack, with Rivo, Vickie, and Renee at the back.

The bulk of the journey between Rhemilia and the outpost was along commonly traveled trade routes spanning the northern region of Wyverly. There wasn't much to see, as there were typically woods on either side most of the time. There was, however, little interaction with traders, since many lived in fear of the Haundo, and there was always the nuisance of the Forest Folk.

It was approaching sundown, and Pearce had the wagons pull over so they could set up camp and rest until morning. The group ate their supper and got settled, each in their own sleep sack, around the campfire under the open sky.

Sometime in the middle of the night, a rustle jolted Rivo awake. Shadows shifted near the wagons. Someone was rifling through their supplies. "Hey!" he shouted, waking the rest of the group. "We're being robbed!"

He went to grab his backpack with his weapons inside, only to notice it was missing. The others all jumped up and noticed their gear was gone as well. The creature that was in their wagons had been startled and ran into the forest.

"By the stars! It's got to be the forest people!" shouted Pearce. "Some-one guard the wagons; the rest, you go after the one that just ran away!"

As they all got up to run after the thief, they realized it was too late—they were surrounded. There had to have been over fifty of them, dirty-looking figures with matted hair and tattered clothes, holding weapons—their weapons. It was the Forest Folk, feral humans who lived in the mountains and forests of Wyverly.

Growing up, Rivo had never encountered any but had heard many stories. Pearce and the others were fairly certain that the child Rivo had seen in the forest outside of Rhemilia was one of them.

"Everybody, just stay calm," Pearce said in resignation. "They won't hurt us if we don't make them feel threatened."

As everyone in the group stood still, the Forest Folk made their way around them, looking for any additional valuables. All that could be heard was the crackling of the fire, the rustling of the Forest Folk, along with their hisses and incoherent babble.

Rivo whispered to Pearce, who was standing just a few feet away, "I always heard they avoided people. What is this?"

"They must be hungry and desperate, Rivo. With all the Haundo around, there haven't been as many merchants and travelers to steal from." Pearce whispered back.

Just then, one of the Forest Folk growled at them, as if to tell them to stop talking. They kept going around, picking up random items, a cloak left on the ground here, a blanket there. Then, one of them, a gaunt-looking man who appeared to be in his thirties, went to grab the cloak that Renee was still wearing.

"Hey, stop that! She's wearing it!" shouted Rivo.

The man snarled and growled at Rivo, as if to warn him to back off.

"It's okay, Rivo, it's just a cloak," Renee replied calmly.

"Growl at me all you want. You're not taking someone's clothes off their back!" Rivo hollered as he charged the man and pushed him to the ground.

"Rivo, don't!" Shouted Pearce.

As Rivo stood his ground, holding his fists up to fight, he was pushed down from behind by another Forest Folk, a larger, middle-aged man with long, tattered red hair and a red beard. The man had one of Rivo's swords and was pointing it directly at Rivo's face as he went to get up.

The red-haired feral man gave a low growl to Rivo, as if to dare him to try something. Just then, a loud voice rang out.

"Beastkiller? Beastkiller!" The voice shouted from a distance.

Out ran a young boy who appeared to be a few years younger than Rivo. He had sandy blond hair that covered half of his face. From the glimpse he caught back in the woods at Rhemilia, Rivo could tell it was the same boy. The boy leaped and placed himself between Rivo and the red-haired forest man.

"Beastkiller!" The boy again shouted. He was wearing a large, filthy cloth bag like a backpack, with a long piece of bamboo strapped to his back, each end sealed by a leather patch.

The red-haired man slowly lowered his sword. The boy then took his bamboo shaft off his back and opened one of the ends. From the bamboo, he pulled out several large pieces of parchment paper. After sorting through them, the boy pulled out one sheet and showed it first to the red-haired man, then to the rest of his fellow Forest Folk, before finally showing it to Rivo and the others. On the paper was a drawing in some sort of black ink or dye, which showed the image of a man with a sword that appeared to be stabbing an image of a large Haundo.

The boy kept pointing to Rivo, then to the man slaying the Haundo in the drawing. "Beastkiller!" he kept saying excitedly.

"What's going on?" asked Rivo.

"You, you Beastkiller," the boy told Rivo, pointing to the figure in his drawing.

"That was you, wasn't it? You were there," Rivo said in disbelief. "You were watching us. I knew it!"

"Aye!" the boy exclaimed, his eyes wide.

The red-haired man drew a deep breath and sighed. "Beastkiller, eh?" he remarked. He then turned toward his fellow Forest Folk and hollered, "Zon!"

Out from the crowd came a well-built young man with long, thick red hair. He had a rope tied around his forehead, like a headband. He was stocky and built like a warhorse.

That older man must be the leader, and this has got to be his son, thought Rivo.

"Aye!" the young man hollered back. He appeared to be about the same age as Rivo, maybe a little older.

The leader then spread his arms toward all of his followers, "Zon. Beastkiller. Scrap!" he shouted, as the Forest Folk cheered.

All, that is, except Zon. He gave Rivo a steely-eyed glare.

The young boy backed away, his mouth agape as he watched how Rivo would react.

Pearce walked up to Rivo, "I think they're wanting you to fight their best warrior, Rivo," he whispered.

"Yeah, I gathered that, Pearce," he replied.

The forest people formed a circle around the two as they continued their cheers. Naomi walked between the two. "Do we really need to do this right now?" she asked Pearce, her arms raised to her sides, expecting Pearce to somehow resolve the matter.

She was barely able to finish her sentence when the Forest Folk began to cheer, and she was pushed back by the crowd.

"What's the point of this exactly?" she hollered over the crowd noise.

The red-haired leader evidently decided it was worth clarifying what was at stake, "Want this?" he questioned as he waved one of Rivo's swords in front of him. "Win scrap!"

Pearce leaned toward Rivo. "Sounds like they're saying if you can beat that freak, they'll let us have our stu—"

"Yes, Pearce. I gathered that," Rivo interrupted.

"You've got to be kidding me!" Naomi hollered as she rolled her eyes. "Rivo, you don't have to do this. It's not worth getting killed over this."

Pearce went over to her and wrapped his arm around her in an effort to both comfort her and direct her away from the crowd that was becoming increasingly hostile.

"Naomi," he whispered. "I don't think anyone's gonna die. They want to see what he's made of. I don't like this either, but I have the feeling that if he doesn't accept this challenge, things will get worse. I think Rivo can take care of himself."

"Fine!" she shouted as she shoved him away. "But I'm not watching this. I can't believe men like this kind of stuff!"

"Judd, please do something," Renee pleaded.

"I'm not gonna let them kill him, Renee," he said passively, not taking his eyes off the combatants. "But right now, I think it's best to let Rivo deal with this." Judging from the smile on his face, Judd appeared eager to watch the two face off.

"They'll be fine, Renee," Vickie remarked dismissively. "Let's just hope he doesn't get his face messed up."

"Oh, Vick," Renee groaned as she placed a hand on her forehead. "What's wrong with you?"

Myra went up to Renee and put her arm around her, and pulled her in close to console her.

Too bad they aren't placing bets, Vickie thought. *I'd put fifty gold pieces on that muscle-bound stud knocking Rivo's teeth out inside of ten seconds.*

"Vickie, are you serious?" Spirit Rivo snapped.

Zon never took his gaze off Rivo the entire time, "Beastkiller," he said with a taunting tone as he beckoned Rivo to make a move. "Scrap!"

Chapter 13

The Spit Shake

"Rivo, you stay back. Let me take care of this," Frank told his young son as he approached a small group of ruffians who had just come to town. There were complaints of them stirring up trouble and threatening some of the townsfolk.

"Alright, gentlemen. I think you've all had enough for today," Frank said to the two scraggly-looking travelers who were causing a scene outside of the small tavern by the town entrance.

"Mind your own business!" shouted Mel, the shorter of the two. "We're just here to have a good time. Is that so wrong?" he asked sarcastically.

"There's nothing wrong with having a good time, gentlemen," replied Frank, with his arms crossed. "But you boys have been getting a little too loud and have been harassing some of the townsfolk. We can't abide that, fellas."

"We couldn't give a damn what you'll *abide*," replied Jarvis, the taller of the two. "Nobody tells us what to do. Now get lost before you regret it."

"Gentlemen," Frank said sternly, "It's time you leave this town."

He stared the two men down with a steely glare and uncrossed his arms.

"Oh, really?" Mel replied with a smirk. "Are you gonna be the one to see us out of town?"

Just then, Frank noticed Jarvis reaching for something in his pocket. He quickly grabbed the man's arm and used his free hand to strike the thug across his jaw, then hooked the back of Jarvis's feet with his leg and sent him to the ground.

"Why you!" Mel shouted as he went to take a swing at Frank, who blocked the punch with one hand while striking the man's collarbone with the other. Mel doubled over, holding his arm. Frank brought his elbow down on the back of his attacker's neck, sending him to the ground like a sack of potatoes.

"Father, watch out!" shouted Rivo as Brody, a massive, muscle-bound man, charged out of the tavern, hollering and tackled Frank to the ground.

Brody lay on top of Frank and began pummeling his ribs. Frank grabbed each side of the collar on the big man's vest in a cross-grip and cinched his neck until he had a firm chokehold on him.

"Father!" exclaimed Rivo as he watched on, horrified.

"Look away, Rivo!" his father grunted, as the big man continued to pound his sides.

Brody's punches started getting slower and weaker until they eventually stopped. The big man's body then went limp. Frank rolled him off and onto the ground next to him.

The townspeople all watched in amazement as Frank slowly got to his feet.

"Father, are you okay?!" Rivo asked frantically.

"Yeah, son. I'll be fine," he said as he winced and held his side where Brody had been pummeling him.

Rivo looked down at the big man lying limp on the ground. "Is he...?"

"No, he'll be fine, son," Frank said, still favoring his side. "But he'll wake up with one heck of a headache."

Jarvis sat up, his eyes wide as he saw his two friends lying face down in the dirt. He then looked to Frank and held his arms out in submission as he backed away.

"You see, it didn't need to come to this, now did it?" Frank asked the startled man, who was too afraid to get back on his feet.

"Please, sir," Jarvis stammered. "I don't want any more trouble."

"Good," Frank replied. "Now help me get your oversized friend up so you boys can get on the road."

As Brody and Mel were just starting to gather their senses, Frank and Jarvis helped the big oaf sit up.

"You gonna be okay there, big fella?" Frank asked as he slapped him on the back.

"Y—yes, sir," the muscleman stuttered as he slowly realized what had just happened.

"Good, now let's get you and your friends on your wagon so you three can go on to your next stop," Frank said as he grabbed his sack nearby. "Tell you what, here's some bread and cheese for the road. I don't want you gentlemen thinking the good people of Greencourt aren't hospitable after all," he added with a wink as he handed the men his small sack of food.

Jarvis looked at him with a mixture of fear and confusion. "Oh, uh, thank you, sir," he said as the three got on their wagon and left town.

The townsfolk all laughed and applauded as they patted Frank on the back and thanked him for his heroics.

"Father, that was amazing!" exclaimed Rivo. "What was that?" he asked as Frank put his hand on the boy's shoulder and started walking back home.

"A chokehold," Frank replied, still wincing and favoring his side from Brody's blows.

"A chokehold?"

"It cuts the blood supply off to the brain," Frank explained. "After a while, they pass out."

"That sounds scary."

"It can be."

"Will you show me how to do that?"

Frank stopped walking and knelt down, eye-level with his young son. "I can show you, Rivo, but you must understand when to use force and when to show restraint," he said in a soft tone. "That technique could kill someone if taken too far. I wasn't trying to end that man's life; I was only trying to restrain him. Do you understand, Rivo?"

"Yes, Father," the boy answered as he nodded.

***

Rivo could see his breath in the nighttime chill of the forest. He wasn't sure what the rules of engagement were exactly, but he knew he had to do something. He charged at the young feral man, attempting to do a double leg takedown, but the attack was easily parried, and Zon knocked him to the ground with a forearm strike to the side of the head.

Zon laughed at Rivo as he fell, "Ha, Beastkiller," he scoffed as he spat on the ground in front of his opponent.

"If I'm guilty of anything, it's pride," Spirit Rivo said as he watched Zon's disrespectful gesture once more. "I never liked to admit anyone was better than me, especially in combat. And I couldn't stand the thought of someone mocking me to my face like that."

He shook off the blow, hopped back up on his feet, and charged Zon again. The forest boy scoffed at him and drew back his right arm to strike his opponent once again. But this time, Rivo was prepared. He redirected at the last second and did an open palm strike to the warrior's collar bone, left exposed when he drew back his arm.

Zon howled as much out of pain as surprise.

Rivo quickly delivered a spinning elbow right to the forest fighter's mouth. He covered his mouth with his hand, only to look and see that his lip was bleeding. As Rivo was about to continue his offensive, Zon grabbed him by the waist and slammed him to the ground. He immediately jumped on him and punched him right in the mouth, returning the favor for the surprise elbow Rivo had just given him a moment ago.

He picked Rivo up off the ground like he was handling a sack of dirt and was going to slam him down again. As Zon had him slung over his shoulder for another vicious body slam, he didn't notice Rivo grabbing the collar of his vest. He continued his throw, but Rivo anticipated it and rolled into the maneuver, following the momentum instead of trying to resist. This caused him to land right at Zon's feet, with the forest fighter's vest firmly in his grasp. The angle of Rivo's fall, along with pulling Zon down by his collar, caused the brute to lose his balance and fall over.

Both fighters were now on the ground. Zon's eyes widened, and his jaw clenched as he was getting visibly furious with Rivo's antics and wasn't giving due attention to the fact that the collar of his vest was still firmly in his opponent's grasp. He lunged to get on top of Rivo in order to pummel him into submission. But Zon soon realized he fell into his trap yet again. Rivo crossed his free arm over and grabbed the collar on the other side of Zon's vest. He cinched his grips together and put the brute in a tight chokehold.

Zon was thrashing and fighting to break loose, but it was too late.

"Scrap! Scrap!" the fighter gurgled as he began to lose consciousness, his voice muffled by the firm chokehold.

"Aye! Aye!" the red-haired leader shouted as he tried to break the scrap up.

Rivo released his opponent as he realized what it meant. The fight was over, Rivo had won.

Zon was sitting on the ground, rubbing his neck. He looked dazed and was shaking his head, as if trying to wake himself up.

Rivo was lying on the ground, rubbing his face, just glad that it was over and that nobody got seriously hurt. Pearce and Judd both came up to lift him to his feet. Murphy ran up from behind and patted him on his back.

Pearce was beaming as he dusted the dirt off Rivo's back, "Hahaaa! Good job, Rivo, it's over!"

"Damn the stars, Rivo, you did it again!" exclaimed Murphy as he tousled Rivo's hair.

"I knew you could do it, Rivo!" said Judd as he inspected the blood on Rivo's lip. The strongman turned to Zon, "Hey, you! Next time, you scrap with me!"

Zon gave Judd a wide-eyed look as he was being attended to by his father. He didn't realize just how big Judd was until that moment.

The Forest Folk started to back off from the group. The red-haired man had a look of resignation on his face. He looked Rivo in the eye, then looked at the young boy. The man sighed in resignation. "Aye," he hollered. He motioned with a head nod to the rest of his Forest Folk. As he did, the tattered-looking group took all the bags they had stolen and set them down in front of Rivo and the others.

Naomi couldn't help but feel some pity for these people; it was obvious they were in need of food. "Are you hungry? Do you need food?" she asked the red-haired leader.

"We can share," added Pearce.

The man stood silent for a moment, his pride conflicting with his desire to help his people. "Aye. Food," he replied.

Slowly, Pearce, Rivo, Naomi, and the others began to set up some food for the forest people to take. They were hesitant at first, but began to cautiously take the food set before them and eat. Renee took her cloak off and gave it to the man who had tried to take it from her earlier.

"The Haundo, have you seen them?" Pearce asked the red-haired man, supposing him to be the leader. "Aye. Haundo. Kill. Kill us. Kill many." He replied as he motioned for Pearce to look upon his group.

"I'm sorry," Pearce replied. He pointed to himself and said, "Pearce." The red-haired man then pointed to his own chest. "Zim."

The Forest Folk began to show the group other pieces of parchment with drawings on them. It showed images of what appeared to be Haundo attacking and killing people. Zim began to choke back tears as the drawings were passed around.

"I'm sorry that this happened. We're here to fight them. We're here to kill the Haundo," Rivo told Zim.

"Aye," Zim replied, eyes watering, grateful to meet new allies.

The boy went up to Rivo and tugged on his shirt to get his attention, a look of admiration on his face. He was excited to show Rivo some more drawings he had made, including one of him killing Drokner.

"Wow, these are great!" he told the boy. "I'm Rivo," he said, pointing to his own chest.

"Bon," the boy replied with a smile as he patted his own chest. "Papa." He said as he pointed to Zim. He then pointed to Zon, who was sitting against a tree with his head down, "Bub-Bub."

"Ahh, so that's your dad and your big brother. Too bad, I would have loved to have taken you with us. I've always wanted a little brother," Rivo replied.

A huge smile spread across the boy's face as he held up one hand, "Rivo," he said, and he then held up his other hand, "Bon." The boy then clasped both of his hands together.

Rivo's face lit up with pride. He responded in kind, holding up one hand, "Bon," then holding up the other, "Rivo," and clasping them together. He knew this was the boy's offer of friendship. The boy gave a soft, joyful chuckle. He gave Rivo the drawing he had made of him battling Drokner. In return, Rivo took the red handkerchief off his arm and gave it to Bon. The boy took the handkerchief and wrapped it around his bicep, so he now looked a little more like Rivo.

Zon finally worked up the nerve to go speak to Rivo. He bowed his head to the young soldier, "Beastkiller," he sighed, his way of acknowledging that he had lost.

Rivo bowed in return; he didn't want Zon to think he held anything against him. "You're a good fighter, Zon. Keep it up, keep fighting for the ones you love."

The Forest Folk had finished eating the food that the group had shared with them. Zim and the others all gave a standing bow to the group, as if to thank them for their kindness.

The group all returned with a bow of their own and started to load up their wagons for the journey ahead. As they walked away, Rivo turned around to see Bon clasping his hands, reminding Rivo of their friendship. Rivo returned the gesture, much to the young boy's delight.

"Zim, Zon, and Bon," Spirit Rivo sighed as he hovered over the group. "It was good seeing you all again."

As they continued in their trek, Rivo remembered that Renee had given her cloak away. "Renee, was that your only cloak that you gave that man?"

"It's fine, Rivo," she quietly replied. "They needed it more than me. I'm sure I can buy one in the next town."

"I tell you what," Rivo said as he dug through his backpack, "take this one." He handed her a wrinkled gray cloak that he pulled out. "It belonged to my mother."

"You're mother? Rivo, I can't accept this," Renee replied as she tried to hand it back,

"I insist," he said adamantly as he pulled his arms back. "She would've wanted you to have it."

"Rivo," she pleaded. "I really don't feel comfortable taking this from you."

"Well, I'm not gonna take no for an answer," he said incessantly as he crossed his arms and wore a haughty yet playful expression on his face.

"Fine," she sighed wearily. "But I'm giving it back as soon as I can get a new one."

"Deal," he said as he stopped walking and extended his hand out to shake hers.

"What are you doing?" she asked with a quick giggle, staring cautiously at his hand.

"Shake my hand, Renee." He wiggled his hand in front of her. "My father told me that's how adults make deals."

"I don't think I've ever shaken someone's hand my entire life, Rivo."

"Well, that changes today," he said emphatically.

Renee realized that he was going to once again refuse to accept no for an answer. "Deal!" she said as she spat in her hand and grabbed Rivo's in a firm handshake, much to his horror.

"Renee!" he gasped loudly as he pulled his hand out of her strong grip and wiped the spittle off on his pants.

"Well, that's what I see the boys do," she replied as she couldn't help but laugh at his reaction. "You are different, Rivo of Greencourt," she added as she shook her head and started walking ahead.

"You're one to talk, Renee of spitting circus folk," he replied spitefully, looking at his hand in disgust as he caught up with her.

"Renee," Spirit Rivo said as he grimaced. "I almost forgot about that."

Chapter 14

The Agony of the Feet

It was over a week into their travels, and the group decided to stop for the day, much earlier than usual. Typically, other than brief stops, they would keep going until it got dark. Today, however, they pulled over with a few hours of daylight still remaining. It was a particularly hot day, and everyone needed a break; the heat had drained them. They had picked an area with a large clearing off the side of the path, an area otherwise surrounded by woods. Pearce was adamant that nobody go off on their own, fearing a run-in with a less hospitable Forest Folk tribe, or worse—the Haundo.

"I still remember that," said Spirit Rivo. "That must have been the hottest day of our travels."

Renee had been walking at the back of the pack with Rivo and Vickie the entire time. She had noticed Pearce, Naomi, and Judd looked like they could use a hand sorting supplies and preparing a meal. Murphy and

Myra, along with Vickie and the rest of the new recruits, all just wandered off, leaving the others to do most of the work, which had become an unfortunate habit of theirs.

As Renee went to give them a hand, Rivo had gone off to gather firewood. Once she finished helping the other three, she wandered a little way through the forest and decided to sit on a large, low-hanging tree branch and just wait for Rivo and Vickie.

As Rivo walked through the woods, he heard some rushing water and noticed there was a lake at the bottom of a small waterfall. Vickie and the others were all in the water to get some relief from the scorching heat.

"Everyone is doing their part to chip in, I see," he scoffed as he approached the group. "Mind if I join you all for a quick dip before getting back to it?"

Vickie noticed that Renee was no longer with him. "Rivo, where's Renee?" she asked.

"She was by the wagon last I saw," he answered. "Now step aside so I can jump in."

"Oh no, you don't!" she barked. "Not without Renee. Go get her; she needs to cool off, too."

"Fine," Rivo sighed as he turned back. "At least she did her part to help out," he said over his shoulder as Vickie pelted him in the back with a small stone.

While Renee was still resting under the shade of a tree near the wagons, Rivo showed up.

"Renee," he said with authority, "you're coming with me!"

"Rivo? What in the world?" She chuckled uncomfortably.

"Swimming. I came looking for you, c'mon, Renee," he said as he extended his hand out for her to grab.

Renee looked around with uncertainty. "Rivo? Do you mean it? You want to go swimming with me?" she asked sheepishly. "I don't really have the right kind of clothes for that."

"It's fine, Renee. Wet clothes won't kill you," he replied.

She hesitated for a moment. "Oh, okay. Sure. let's go!" Renee normally wasn't one to be impulsive like that, but this time she made an exception.

She clasped Rivo's hand as they dashed toward the lake, its roar growing from the waterfall crashing into the depths below.

"Ready to jump? Here it comes!" shouted Rivo.

Renee's heart was racing; she braced herself as they approached a small cliff over the water, still holding Rivo's hand. Following his lead, she and Rivo leaped together into the cold lake below.

As they surfaced, Renee's excited smile quickly vanished. She looked around the lake only to see Vickie and all the recruits that had wandered off earlier swimming and goofing off in the water. What Renee thought would be a special moment between her and Rivo was nothing more than a lake party with the recruits.

"Man, wasn't that fun!?" Rivo asked.

"Umm, yeah sure," she replied flatly, trying to hide her disappointment. "Actually, the water is a little too cold for me. I think I'll get out and dry off."

"Oh, okay... are you alright?" he asked, sensing the shift in her demeanor.

"I'm fine," she said bluntly, taking off her shoes. "I hate wet shoes," she mumbled under her breath. She then hopped on a boulder that was at the edge of the lake and sat huddled, hugging her legs with her back to Rivo and the gang.

Vickie, who had been playing around in the lake with the rest of the group, saw Renee sitting huddled on the boulder. *Oh no, huddle means trouble, what in stars' light did he do?* she thought. She knew she was upset about something, and it had to be over Rivo. She swam over to Renee to check on her.

As she passed by Rivo, she furrowed her brow at him. "You idiot! What did you do this time?" Vickie said sharply.

"What are you talking about?" he sputtered. The only thing that came to mind was that Renee might have felt left out. *I guess I should have thought to ask her from the start. It's not my fault; anyone else could have gotten her.*

Vickie pulled up on the giant rock next to Renee. "Renee, what did that moron do? Do I need to straighten him out for you?" she growled.

"It's fine, Vick... I just want to go hide under a rock somewhere or something. I think I just need to get away and be alone," she said, her eyes tearing up.

"You thought it was just gonna be the two of you, didn't you?"

"I don't want to talk about it right now, Vick," she murmured, looking away.

"Hey Rivo! Get over here, you dope! Now!" Vickie shouted to Rivo, who was wading in the water a little ways out.

"Vickie, stop it. He didn't do anything wrong. It's my fault for being so stupid and thinking anybody would ever do something just for me," she hissed, embarrassed and frustrated with herself.

"I'm sorry, sis. I saw that the two of you were together by the wagon earlier, so I figured I'd slip away for a bit. I didn't realize the dope wandered off by himself until I saw him here," Vickie whispered.

"And then you told him to come get your little sister, right?" Renee asked bitterly.

"Oh, Renee," Vickie giggled. "Dropping a hint doesn't always work with boys. Especially this one," she said, nodding toward Rivo.

"What are they talking about?" asked Spirit Rivo. "I can take a hint, Vickie. I'm not as dumb as you think... What was the hint?"

"I don't know. I still just want to get away from everybody." Renee moaned, her lip slightly quivering.

"I think I can make that happen. Watch this," Vickie whispered with a wink.

"Oh, Vick, please don't embarrass me," she pleaded.

"Stars be damned, Rivo. Hurry up!" Vickie shouted as Rivo made his way towards them.

"I'm here, okay, Vickie!" Rivo snapped at her as he came to them in the water next to where they were sitting. "Look, Renee. I'm sorry I left you at the wagons and for not inviting you. I was just hot and tired and wasn't thinking."

"It's okay, Rivo, I'm not upset with you," Renee said quietly as she turned her head to the side, hoping he wouldn't see her welling-up eyes.

She was then startled by Vickie, who grabbed Renee's bare feet and placed them in her lap, and started massaging them.

"Get over yourself, Rivo, that's not why she's upset!" barked Vickie.

"Well then, what is it? What did I do? Why are you being so mean?" he implored.

"We're ladies, dummy. We don't have those massive man-feet like you guys have," she said spitefully. "She's been walking non-stop for days.

Her feet hurt. We didn't have to come along, ya know. The least you could do is offer a lady a foot rub if she's been on her feet all day."

Rivo remembered seeing his father give his mother foot rubs every now and then after she had been out and about all day back when he was a boy. He remembered how it always seemed to help her relax. *Makes sense, I guess,* he thought.

"Okay, I'm sorry, Renee. I guess I didn't think about that. Are you feeling better now?" he asked.

"Yes, I'm fine," she replied uncomfortably.

"Well, I can't sit and do this all day," said Vickie. "Come take my place so I can head back. Are you watching me? Like *thiiiis*," she explained, in a condescending tone as she showed him how she was rubbing Renee's feet, as if she was instructing a child.

Renee shot her sister a wide-eyed glare to let her know she was embarrassed. Vickie returned with another wink, then hopped off the rock so Rivo could take her place.

"Okay, everybody," Vickie announced to the group, "let's head back. We've had enough fun today." She then turned to Renee and Rivo." And we'll see you two later," she said playfully.

"Vickie's one strange lady," remarked Spirit Rivo. "She never made any sense to me."

Renee could only close her eyes and shake her head. "What in the world is she thinking?" She mumbled under her breath. One thing was for sure, though: she was definitely glad that she had washed her feet that morning.

Rivo began gently massaging Renee's feet. She could feel her cheeks flush, but her nerves subsided a little as the rest of the group left. "I'm sorry Vickie spoke to you like that. I don't know why she thinks it's okay to treat people that way," Renee said with a sigh.

"I don't know either," Rivo replied sharply. "She just doesn't like me. Even though I've been nothing but nice to her." He drew a breath and sighed. "I swear, she's just like Naomi. Always talking to me like I'm a little kid."

"She really does like you, Rivo. I know it might not seem like it."

"It doesn't. But it's fine," he said as he closed his eyes and tried to calm himself down. "She's not exactly my type either."

Renee couldn't help but let the corner of her mouth curl up at his last remark. "Well, I'm sorry you feel you have to do this, but thank you. It feels nice."

"Oh, it's fine, Renee. My dad used to do this with my mom all the time."

There was a minute of silence between them. Renee ran her fingers through her damp hair. She looked at Rivo, his soaked hair glistened in the sunlight, his wet and well-toned arms and chest looked like they were carved from marble.

Rivo noticed Renee looking at him. "It's my hair, isn't it?" He directed his eyes up towards the wet mess of hair on his head, going in every direction.

"Huh?" Renee muttered, looking away in embarrassment.

"It's okay. It always looks wild when I swim."

"Oh, it's fine," she chuckled uncomfortably.

Rivo raised his jaw and looked proudly to the sky. "*His wet hair lay plopped upon his head like a dead octopus, but in a good way,*" he said in mock eloquence.

"Rivo, you are a strange one," she giggled, shaking her head.

After the laughter faded, Renee looked toward the waterfall, hoping the sight and sound would calm her. She drew a deep breath, unsure if she wanted to broach the next topic. "Rivo?" she asked pensively.

"What is it?" Rivo asked, meeting her gaze as he continued massaging her feet.

"You mentioned your parents," she said as she took a moment to collect her thoughts. "How old were you when you lost them?"

He looked thoughtfully up towards the sky. The sun was beginning to set. "Father died when I was ten; he got sick. Mother got sick and passed a few months later. She went downhill fast." He slowly shook his head. "They're flying among the stars now," he said gently.

"Oh," she replied, still unsure if she should have brought it up. "I'm sorry."

"It's okay," he said as he looked down toward the water. "I'm thankful to have Pearce and Naomi. They promised my mother on her deathbed that they would watch out for me. They drive me crazy sometimes,

Naomi especially, but I know it's because they care. She had to take me in when she was so young."

Renee noticed his eyes had started welling up; she swallowed, then looked away toward her wet shoes lying next to her. "What were they like, your parents?" she asked, trying to keep from tearing up herself.

"Oh man," Rivo chuckled, trying to find words that would do them justice. "They were something else. Father was a former soldier and a true outdoorsman. And with the right tools, he could fix anything. I remember thinking there wasn't anything that man couldn't do. He taught me everything I know," he said as he looked back up to the sunset, casting a pink and orange glow through the clouds. "And Mother, she was the best. Beautiful, caring, and man, could she cook. And her voice, her singing. It was like an angel. I still remember how she would just fill the house with her songs and sing me lullabies when I was small. It was the best. I really did have it good." Rivo was having to take deep breaths, fighting hard not to let any tears flow.

"A warrior dad and a homemaker mom. Sounds like something from a storybook," she teased.

Rivo laughed softly. "Mother was no one to mess with either."

"Oh, really?" She pulled her feet from his lap and sat cross-legged, facing him. "Do tell," she said, intrigued.

"Well," he said as he smiled proudly. "I was just a toddler when it happened, so I don't remember. But Naomi told me I almost got eaten by a coyote once."

Renee gasped. "My stars, Rivo, that's terrifying!" she said as she covered her mouth with her hand.

"I guess it's good I don't remember then," he laughed.

"Don't leave me hanging," she said as she motioned for him to continue. "What happened?"

"Well, Naomi says Mother came out of nowhere and knocked that coyote senseless with her bare hands!" he said as he shook his head, chuckling. "That thing must have run away with its tail between its legs. I'm guessing he told all his friends about the crazy lady that beat him up, because I haven't seen a coyote since!"

"Oh, Rivo!" Renee said as they both tried to control their laughter. "That's too much!"

Spirit Rivo watched on, laughing with them. "Renee... I forgot how much fun you were to hang out with."

Renee rubbed the tears of laughter from her eyes. "Well, Rivo," she said with a smile, "thank you for sharing that with me. It's obvious they really loved you." She drew a deep breath and sighed sharply. "And I'm sorry if I pried too much."

"Oh no, it's fine," he said as he waved her off. "I don't get to talk about them too often. It always depresses Naomi when I mention them. She was crazy about my folks."

Renee put her shoes back on, and they both turned to face the sunset.

"So what about you, Renee?" asked Rivo. "What was your family like?"

Renee's heart sank as her smile faded and her eyes drifted. For someone who was so good at weighing all possible outcomes, she failed to consider Rivo asking about her own family.

"Well," she hesitated, "my mother was gorgeous. She wouldn't leave the house unless she was all dolled up. All the men would fall at her feet; she was a natural beauty, and she knew it. As you might guess, Vickie takes after her." She fell quiet for a moment. "And Daddy, he was a lumberjack. He would be gone from home for weeks at a time." She abruptly cut herself off.

"Okay. So how old were you when they passed?"

"Daddy died in a work accident when I was seven. We lost Mom not long after. The two of us were out on our own. We did what we could to survive, stole food, scrubbed floors, and took whatever odd jobs we could. We met Mr. Sundry and Judd when the circus came to town. They asked us to work for them, and we accepted. I guess they just saw something in us. Mr. Sundry made us performers. Vickie was taught dancing, and I learned card tricks and illusions. Judd, over time, kinda just became like a protective older brother. That's about all there is to it."

"By the stars, you all sure went through a lot. I had no idea. So tell me what about—"

"It's going to get dark soon. I think we should go back," she interrupted as she stood up.

Rivo felt a pang of embarrassment as he got up as well. "Oh, right. Let's head out." *Should I not have brought that up?* He wondered as he buttoned his vest up.

"Poor Renee," said Spirit Rivo. "She had it rough."

They got ready and started walking back. Renee walked with her head down and her arms crossed. Upset with herself for pushing Rivo to share so much while she held back. As they were making their way toward the others, they were met by Vickie, who was waiting for them.

"So, did you all have a nice swim?" she asked with that same wry smirk.

"Vick, what are you doing here?" asked Renee.

Vickie turned to Rivo. "Rivo, would you mind grabbing my shoes? I left them out there to dry?" she asked, pointing to a large fallen tree branch with her shoes hanging in them.

Rivo gave a quick nod and went to retrieve the shoes. Once he was out of earshot, Vickie turned to Renee. "I have my reasons, Renee," she whispered. "Let's just say I don't want certain people getting the wrong impression by you two going off on your own. I figured it might look better if the three of us came back together."

Renee gave a slight nod. It made sense. The last thing she wanted was to have people gossiping about her. For all Vickie's hang-ups, she knew how to look out for her sister.

"Here you go," said Rivo as he handed Vickie her shoes.

The three got back to camp to notice the campsite was empty, with the exception of Pearce, Naomi, and Judd. And they didn't look happy.

"There's some food in the pot over there; it might be cold by now," Pearce said flatly. "We ate while you were having your little lake party."

"Where is everybody?" asked Rivo, "What happened to Murphy, Myra, and the rest?"

"I sent them ahead while you were goofing off," Pearce grunted. "They weren't really helping anyways."

"According to our map, there's a village called Thorndale up that way. It isn't too far off the path," Naomi chimed in. "We told them to try to pick up some more recruits there. Wyverly needs all the help we can get them."

"Nothing was stopping you two from joining us, ya know," muttered Vickie.

"Yeah, there was, Vickie," snapped Naomi. "Somebody had to stay and set up camp."

Vickie shrugged as she, Rivo, and Renee grabbed some food. The three sat down on a log nearby, Rivo in the middle with Vickie and Renee on either side.

As they passed the food around the campfire, Naomi leaned over to whisper something to Pearce, "Ya know, Pearce, there's something that's been bugging me ever since we were in Rhemilia."

"What's that?" he whispered back.

"It's Vickie. We tried to recruit her, and she said *no*. The next thing I know, she starts spending time with Rivo, and all of a sudden, she decides to sign up. Does that seem odd to you?"

"I guess I hadn't thought of that. You think she's interested in him?"

"There's definitely something going on. I've never cared for her, ya know. Her type has always gotten under my skin. And here she is, always hanging around Rivo."

"Could be harmless," Pearce interjected.

"Maybe. But look at her," Naomi replied. "She can have any guy she wants. So what exactly about him requires so much of her attention?" Pearce reacted with a shrug. "I've dealt with those types before," she added. "They take naïve and innocent types like him, chew them up and spit them out."

"So what do you want to do about it?" he asked.

"Tomorrow," she told him, "I think I'm going to walk at the back of the group, with Rivo."

"Ahhh, so that's what caused the whole big mess the next day..." said Spirit Rivo.

Chapter 15

Mother Hen is Watching

There was a certain double-edged sword to being the prettiest girl in the room. Without a doubt, there were benefits. Vickie had no shortage of praise from men, not to mention free drinks, meals, candies, flowers, and other gifts. She enjoyed all of those things. "So why not?" She would say to herself. But the drawbacks would always rear their ugly heads, from the lustful gazes and unwanted advances of ill-intentioned men, to the jealous glares and contempt of other women. Vickie had seen it all. So she was no stranger to the likes of Naomi, and she wasn't one to be easily outwitted.

***

It was daybreak now. The group just finished loading up, put on their backpacks, and started on their way. They all stood ready in what had become their usual formation: Pearce at the front along with Judd, and Renee stood at the back, waiting for Rivo and Vickie.

"Good morning, Renee," said Naomi with a fake smile as she approached the back of the group.

"Oh, hey Naomi. What can I do for you?"

"Oh, nothing, just in the mood for a change of scenery. I'll be traveling back here with you all today."

"Okay, great," Renee responded as she cast her eyes down. For some reason, this bothered her, but she wasn't sure why.

"Well, look who it is! Mixing things up today, are we?" Rivo asked with a big smile as he approached Naomi and Renee, oblivious to her motives.

"You could say that," Naomi replied. "Where's Vickie?"

"Right here," hollered Vickie as she met up with them.

"Perfect," said Naomi, still wearing a disingenuous smile.

Well, it would appear that despite my best efforts, the mother hen has taken notice and decided to make her first move, thought Vickie.

"Vickie, you and Naomi were so alike. Much more than you realized," Spirit Rivo remarked.

As they started their hike for the day, Renee was on one side of Rivo, and Vickie was on the other. He and Renee practically forgot that Naomi was behind them. She would offer them little more than a close-mouthed smile and an eyebrow raise whenever one of them looked back to check on her.

Vickie looked over at Renee and noticed that she was admiring Rivo's profile. There were times when he would catch her looking, and she would give a sheepish smile as she blushed and looked down. Rivo would smile back, thinking nothing of it.

Be careful, little sis, thought Vickie. *Mother hen is watching*.

"What in the stars' light does that mean? And why does Vickie keep calling her that?" asked Spirit Rivo.

Vickie had never really bothered to study Rivo's physique before, but couldn't help herself this time when she caught Renee staring. His skin, with little beads of sweat forming, appeared to glow with the backdrop of the sunrise. He was thin, but his body was fit and well-toned, and his high cheekbones and square jaw gave him the look of a storybook hero.

Stars be damned, sis, you're right... He is cute, she thought.

"Wait a second, what?" Spirit Rivo said quizzically. "Did Vickie...have a thing for me?"

I don't have a thing for him, Vickie thought, *but I can see why a girl might find the dope endearing*.

Naomi caught Vickie checking out Rivo, and she decided it was time to make her move.

"Hey Vickie," she called out from behind. "Would you mind keeping me company back here for a bit?"

"Here it comes," Vickie muttered under her breath.

"Oh, well, the four of us can just all walk together, Naomi," Rivo interjected. "There's no need for you to be back there by yourself. I would have offered before, but I just figured you wanted some alone time."

"It's fine, Rivo. We're just gonna talk girl stuff. Nothing you need to worry about," she replied.

Rivo was still looking back at her, with a puzzled look on his face. Renee gently grabbed his elbow, "Just let them walk together for a bit, Rivo. Come on, let's keep walking."

Naomi lagged behind enough to ensure the rest of the group was out of earshot. "So Vickie, why don't you tell me all about yourself? I feel like we need to get to know each other a bit more, ya know, since we'll be traveling together for a while."

Vickie didn't care for Naomi or her condescending and disingenuous tone. Especially in light of the prejudice she knew Naomi viewed her with. This was nothing new to her.

"I prefer for people not to know all about me, Naomi," she said flatly. "There's not really any benefit. I'm not looking to make new friends."

"Really? Well, it sure seems like you've hit it off with Rivo," Naomi said with an edge in her voice.

"What makes you think *that*?" Vickie asked, her eyes narrowed as she glared straight ahead.

"Do I have to spell it out for you?" Naomi pressed. "It seems like you're around him an awful lot. Now what does a woman like you have in common with a kid like Rivo?"

"I don't know what you're talking about," Vickie sneered.

"You don't?" Naomi asked as she widened her eyes, feigning shock. "Well, it seems like every time I see Rivo, there you are, too. Can't blame a girl for wondering what exactly you two are up to. You seem tight-lipped with me, but it sure seems like you enjoy his company."

"Maybe it's because he doesn't waste my time with stupid, insincere questions about things he knows nothing about," Vickie snapped as she picked up her pace to distance herself from her interrogator.

"Where do you think you're going?" Naomi barked.

"I'm going back to be with the rest of the group. Our conversation is over," snapped Vickie.

"I think you're fine right where you are. You don't have to talk to me if you don't want to. But I think you and Rivo need to take a little break from each other. Oh, and do me a favor and don't mention our talk to Rivo."

"Whatever you say, Naomi," Vickie sighed.

The two never spoke a word until their next stop.

"Those two are so alike, it's not funny. It's a miracle they didn't lock horns more often," said Spirit Rivo.

Chapter 16

The Wrong Sister

Her name was Leena. "The prettiest twelve-year-old in all of Green-court," many would call her, and she believed it. Even at such a young age, she knew how to break a young boy's heart. She wouldn't hesitate to use her beauty to get what she wanted, especially from the boys. Whether it was gifts, sweets, jewelry, or even getting them to do the chores assigned to her at the schoolhouse, Leena always got what she wanted. That was, of course, until she ran into a no-nonsense, overprotective fifteen-year-old girl named Naomi.

Leena, like a lot of the young girls in Greencourt, had her eyes set on one particular young boy named Rivo. Even back then, Rivo was a handsome young lad. The only obstacle was Naomi, who was known to intimidate the girls if she didn't like how they looked at or talked to her young cousin.

The problem with Leena was, she thought she was untouchable. It's not so much that she liked Rivo as much as she liked the idea of getting something that nobody else could have. Winning his heart would make all the other girls jealous, and this would cause her social standing to rise even higher than it already was. Then, she had already determined, when the excitement ran its course and she was bored with young Rivo, she'd just ditch him and move on to her next conquest.

Leena's grand scheme was cut short before it had even started. One day, as she was walking home from school with some of her girlfriends, Naomi happened to be waiting, leaning against a tree along the path and holding a small sack in her hand. The other girls saw her and backed up, except Leena, who was trying to put on a good show.

"Hey Leena," said Naomi, with a smirk on her face. "I heard you've been planning on courting Rivo. Word spreads fast in this small town, ya know." She went on, "May I ask, what does a manipulative, mean-spirited little brat like you want with my little cousin?"

"I don't know what you mean by that," Leena replied smugly. "I just think he's handsome and I'd like to get to know him better, maybe make a new friend. That's all."

"*A new friend*," Naomi scoffed. "I think you have enough friends. Are you sure you aren't just planning on using him to get more popularity in the school and then dumping him once you get bored?"

Leena stood shocked. Somebody close to her must have ratted her out. "I...I never—" she stammered as she tried to think of a way out of this.

"Come here!" snapped Naomi as she grabbed the young girl by the hair and pinned her against the tree, holding the small cloth sack she had in her hand up to Leena's face. "You see this? Brownberries, it's used as a dye for all kinds of things." She squeezed the sack, and dark brown liquid began to leak out. "Once it gets on a piece of fabric, it never comes out. You stay away from Rivo, you hear me? Or I swear I'll stain the back of every dress you own and make it look like you soiled yourself every day at school. Got it?!"

"Y—yes. I'll stay away. I promise," squeaked a terrified Leena as she started to tear up.

"Good," Naomi said as she left the shaken girl's hair loose and walked away. Her objective was complete, and Rivo was spared from Leena's scheme.

***

Pearce decided it was time to call it a day, another early one. They were making good progress, and there was no reason to rush. They found another good clearing in the middle of the woods with another decent sized lake.

"No wandering off and swimming this time, at least not until everybody does their chores, got it?" Pearce told the group. "Judd, you and I will head to Thorndale and see how the recruits fared."

Most days, Renee would pull Rivo away from the group to gather firewood while Vickie followed. Today was to be no different. "Let's go, Rivo," she said as she grabbed his elbow and directed him away.

Vickie began to follow, but was interrupted. "I think Vickie needs to stay here with me and help cut all these carrots and onions," Naomi said sternly. "You all can go get the firewood without her."

"Lovely," sighed Vickie as Rivo shrugged and walked off with Renee.

Naomi waited until everyone was out of earshot. "Ya know, Vickie. Pearce and I, we're all Rivo's got," she said as she began chopping away.

"Ya don't say..." Vickie mumbled.

"Well, the thing about Rivo is, he's got a really good heart. But he's also naïve and a little too trusting."

"Uhhuh," Vickie slowly moaned.

Naomi's jaw clenched and she started chopping the vegetables loudly, "He's impulsive and at times, stupid. If I'm not around to watch him, he might do impulsive and stupid things."

Vickie let out a loud, sarcastic chuckle, "That part, I believe, he is an idiot."

"I know you don't like me, Vickie. And I know you don't want to talk to me about this. But you are gonna listen to me," Naomi said firmly.

"What do you want from me, child?"

"Don't call me *child!*"

"Then speak plainly."

"Fine. I don't want you hanging around Rivo. A worldly woman like you has no business with a boy like Rivo!" Snapped Naomi.

"What do you mean, *a worldly woman* like me?"

"You know what I mean," Naomi scowled. "I've been protecting Rivo from girls like you his whole life. The type of person who uses people for their own gain and then disposes of them. Is that what you were planning with Rivo? Getting him to fall for you, then breaking his heart just because you're bored? Or is it that you want to corrupt him, make him cynical and jaded like you, so you can prove to yourself that you're right about the world? That people innocent and kind like Rivo don't really exist?"

"You don't know anything about me. I'm not that kind of person at all!" Vickie hollered back as she slammed her knife against the cutting board. "You don't know what you're talking about."

"Tell me what you want from Rivo!" Naomi demanded as she took a step toward Vickie.

"Nothing like that! I don't like him that way!" Vickie replied as she squared up to face Naomi.

"Then why are you always around him?" Naomi pressed as she bawled her fists.

Upon seeing the rage in Naomi's eyes, Vickie's own scowl changed into a sinister smile.

"What's so funny!?" yelled Naomi.

Vickie threw her head back and let out a booming cackle.

Naomi's eyes darted back and forth. "What in the stars' name are you doing? Have you lost your mind?"

"Oh dear Naomi," Vickie said through her laughter. "You haven't been watching Rivo at all this whole time, have you?" she asked as her laughter subsided into a smirk. "You've been too focused on me instead."

"What!? Of course I've been watching him!" Naomi retorted.

"Oh, really? Then where is he right now?"

"Getting firewood like we asked him to," Naomi said with a puzzled expression.

"Oh yeah? And who's he with?" asked Vickie as she raised her eyebrows.

"What does that matter? He's with—" Naomi froze as the realization finally hit her.

"Who's been right at his side the whole time, ever since you came to Rhemilia?" Vickie pressed as she took a step toward Naomi. "Who's been the one that's been taking him away from the rest of the group at every opportunity, Naomi? Was it me or was it—"

"Renee..." Naomi whispered in disbelief.

"You've been so focused on me that you haven't seen what's been going on this whole time. Right... in plain... sight," Vickie said as she leaned toward a wide-eyed and confused Naomi. She leaned in further, "I wasn't hanging around Rivo because I wanted to be with him, I was there because my sister was there. But now, thanks to you, I'm not there to keep an eye on them. So all I know, Naomi, is that Renee and Rivo are out there in the woods somewhere," her tone got deeper and softer as Naomi's heart sank, "and they're *all* alone..."

Naomi stood speechless. Vickie began to laugh hysterically at the sight of it.

"No way," Naomi rasped. "She's been doing this the whole time, right under my nose...this whole time," she fell silent for a moment. "I've been focusing on the wrong sister," she muttered.

Naomi stood stunned that she somehow never noticed, all to the sound of Vickie's laughter. She had just made a fool of herself, and Vickie was relishing every second of it.

Chapter 17

From the Buttcrack of a Rock

"You know the deal, Vick, you distract, I act," said a young Renee, who was all of 10 years old.

"Renee," replied Vickie, "Please look out for yourself, okay?"

The two sisters walked down the bustling market street like they had a thousand times before in towns all across Wyverly. The boys working the stands would all have their eyes set on Vickie, and never noticed Renee sneaking in to fill her sack with whatever goodies she could get her hands on. It seemed as though when Vickie was around, Renee was invisible. This ability of hers, to be able to move freely in plain sight, became second nature after a while; it had to. For those few years, the two homeless and hungry girls were on their own; this was how they had to survive.

With those days now far behind them, Vickie and Renee would reminisce every now and then and wonder what would have happened had they ever been caught. It turned out, without them even realizing, that those days weren't as far behind them as they thought. And this time, they got caught.

***

"Would you stop laughing!" Naomi shouted to Vickie.

"Relax, Renee's harmless," Vickie replied.

"Oh, really? Sneaking off with Rivo into the woods? Hanging around him this whole time, right under my nose? Doesn't sound harmless to me," she said with her brow furrowed. "Who does she think she is?" Now that her focus was off of Vickie, Naomi began to recall all the times Renee and Rivo would stray from the rest of the group, grabbing his elbow and leading him away, much like she would grab a loaf of bread or a block of cheese to fill her sack when she was young.

"Oh, stop that. She just enjoys his company. It's not her fault you didn't notice."

"Just wait 'til they get back. I'll straighten them out!" Naomi huffed.

"Look, Naomi," Vickie said calmly. "I'm sorry I provoked you like that. You kept implying that I was some sort of seductress who was trying to use Rivo, and I messed up and said too much," she let out a weary sigh. "Renee is gonna kill me," she said as she rubbed her forehead. "Please calm down, don't take this out on her."

"Hey, guys!" hollered Rivo as he and Renee walked in, each with an arm full of wood.

"What in the stars' light is going on with you two? Where were you!?" snapped Naomi.

"What do you mean? We gathered firewood like we were told?" answered Rivo defensively. Naomi marched up to him and pinched him on his side. "Ouch! What did you do that for?"

"You know what I mean! The two of you, going off on your own, doing stars know what. Bet you think you're real clever, Renee!" Naomi said as she turned her attention to Vickie's startled sister.

"I don't know what you're talking about!" Renee said sharply.

"Oh, I bet. Why exactly did you feel the need to go separately from everyone else, you little sneak!?" Naomi barked.

"I. Don't know. What you're talking about!" Renee bit back indignantly, with a sassy tone she had only ever used with Vickie.

"Naomi, cut it out!" snapped Rivo.

"Shut up, Rivo!" she said as she pinched him on his side again, "I'm gonna straighten you out next!"

"Stop doing that to him!" Renee chided. "He's not a toddler."

"That's enough!" Vickie exclaimed as she jumped in between the two irate young women. "Naomi, please stop. I'm sorry I made you so upset. Please just try to cool down." Vickie turned to Rivo, who stood with his nostrils flared, and Renee, who was looking off to her side with her jaw clenched. "Renee, Rivo, could you two please just give us some space? Lake Thorndale isn't too far away; maybe you two can head there and catch some supper."

"Yeah, that sounds good," Rivo growled as he glared at Naomi.

"Fine!" Renee yelled as she dropped the firewood at her feet. "Come on, Rivo, let's go." She scowled at Vickie as she backed away. "What did you say this time?" she hissed.

As Renee stomped off, Vickie closed her eyes as she sagged her shoulders. *Perfect*, she moaned to herself. *Me and my big mouth. I'll never hear the end of this.*

Naomi sat down on a basket nearby, putting her face in her hands as Rivo grabbed some fishing gear and headed after Renee without looking back.

Once they were out of earshot, Vickie tried to clear the air with Naomi.

"Naomi," Vickie said calmly. "Renee isn't whatever kind of woman you think I am. She's a sweet girl and always just wants to do the right thing." She drew a deep breath. "And I'll tell you this nicely once, you can mouth off to me, but don't ever speak to my sister like that again," she said firmly.

It was then that Naomi realized that maybe she and Vickie were more alike than she thought. Vickie was only concerned about taking care of her little sister, kind of like Naomi was with Rivo.

Naomi rubbed her eyes and nodded. "Okay," she replied with a sigh. "I'm sorry for snapping at her like that. I'll talk to her when they get back. And Vickie, I'm sorry for the things I said about you and how I've been towards you today. You didn't deserve all that."

"Thank you. Now, let's go ahead and finish up here," Vickie replied as she went back to prepping the vegetables, and Naomi got back up to help. "Oh, and Naomi?" Vickie added.

"Yes?"

"I would apologize for saying Rivo was an idiot. But...it's true," she said with a sly grin.

Naomi tried to stifle a little giggle that turned into an outburst of laughter between the two of them.

"Why is that funny?!" Spirit Rivo asked, irritated.

"So, Renee, how does she feel about Rivo, really?" Naomi asked as she was chopping the last of the carrots.

"She doesn't talk much to me about stuff like that. But I can tell, she really admires him and obviously enjoys his company." She gazed thoughtfully in the distance. She had already run her mouth enough and didn't want to betray her sister's confidence any further. "I don't think I've ever seen her act this alive off stage. As much as I want to help her, she's gonna need to sort this out herself. Poor girl," said Vickie as she looked down and shook her head in resignation. "She'll never work up the courage to really open up to him... That Rivo...he really is something special, isn't he?"

"Yeah...he really is," replied Naomi. "But I can promise you one thing, though. Whatever it is she feels towards him, he's completely oblivious. When it comes to girls, he's beyond clueless."

"I don't know what they're talking about," Spirit Rivo said dismissively. "Renee and I weren't like that at all. And I'm not *clueless.*"

"That doesn't surprise me one bit," Vickie said, chuckling as she chopped the last of the onions. "They do make a good team, though. They're similar in some ways and different in others. And their similarities and differences can work well together."

"How do you mean?" asked Naomi as she placed the last of the carrots in a pot.

"Well, they're similar in that they both have good hearts and want only to help and do the right thing, and they're different in that Renee is hesitant and overthinks things while Rivo is more reckless and just jumps right in," Vickie said as she went to grab some of the firewood Renee had dropped. "If nothing else, maybe they can learn a thing or two from each other."

"I see," Naomi replied as she got the fire going.

Looking at the glowing flame of the campfire reminded Vickie of what she had seen in the woods outside of Rhemilia. The look in Rivo's eyes as he killed Drokner, how they glowed amber with fury. She had tried to put it out of her mind, but the image kept haunting her. Renee was there too; she saw it, but neither said a word to each other or anybody else.

"Naomi," Vickie said as they both crouched by the fire. "There's something I've been wanting to tell you. It's about Rivo."

"What is it?" Naomi asked as she drew her attention away from the fire and looked at Vickie expectantly.

"Did you...see what happened when he killed Drokner?" Vickie asked, her eyes fixed still on the fire.

"Not really, everything happened so fast," Naomi replied as she haphazardly tossed some twigs in the flame. "I know he got hurt pretty bad. Did something else happen?"

Vickie's breath quivered, and she gave a nervous sigh. *Is she gonna think I'm crazy?* "It was his eyes, just before he killed that thing. I'd never seen anything like it before...they were—"

"Were they glowing amber?" Naomi asked earnestly.

Vickie gasped as she jerked her head to look at Naomi. "You knew?"

"No, not exactly," Naomi replied as she closed her eyes and grabbed the bridge of her nose. "Pearce told me he thought he saw something when they were sparring once, years ago."

Vickie breathed a sigh of relief, now knowing she and Renee weren't alone. "Does Rivo know?" she asked.

"No, I don't think so," answered Naomi. "As far as I know, us and Pearce are the only ones who have seen it. I've never mentioned it to anyone else."

Vickie looked at her, puzzled. "Wait, you said *us and Pearce.* Have *you* seen it before?"

"Yes," Naomi answered somberly. "But...it wasn't with Rivo," she said as her voice trailed off.

***

As Vickie and Naomi were reconciling, Rivo and Renee were making their way to Lake Thorndale, about half a mile northeast of the campsite. The muggy heat of the forest was weighing them down almost as much as Naomi's outburst.

Renee was trudging along with her arms crossed, not saying a word.

"Please don't let Naomi get under your skin too much. Whatever that was, it wasn't about you," he assured her.

"Well, it sure seemed like it. She just doesn't like me."

"No, Renee, she's just like that. When she's mad, she just lashes out at people, usually me," Rivo said as he kicked a pinecone in frustration. "I'm sorry you had to see that. Naomi really is a good person," he explained. "Besides, you heard Vickie. It sounds like they had a little argument before we got there. I'm sure we were just in the wrong place at the wrong time."

"Yeah, you're probably right. Vickie will do that to people."

There was a long silence between them as they were walking. Rivo noticed some daisies and dandelions growing in a rock crevice nearby. Renee watched puzzled as he scooped them up, then knelt down on one knee beside her, using a trick his father would use with his mother to cheer her up.

"Rivo, what are you doing?" she asked with a giggle.

"For you, my dear," he said in a pretentious nobleman's accent as he handed her the flowers. "Perhaps this will raise your spirits, milady."

Renee gasped as she played along, placing a hand to her chest in mock flattery. "Dandelions and daisies, my stars!" she exclaimed. "And from the buttcrack of a rock, no less!"

"Only the best for you, my dear."

"Well, I must say, I'm truly honored, m'lord," she replied as she took the flowers, placing a daisy in her hair.

"Marvelous, my dear," he remarked as he stood to his feet and started toward the lake. "Now let's go catch some fish for the peasants."

"I tell you what," he said as he brushed the leaves off his pant leg. "We can race to the lake, whichever one loses has to gut the fish while the other puts them in the basket."

Renee couldn't help but smile back, "Sounds good. On three. One... two...three!" she shouted as she stepped on his foot, tripping him up just like she did at the rushball game in Rhemilia, and off she went.

"Cheater!" hollered Rivo as Renee sped off. "Well, I guess I'm on fish guttin' duty today," Rivo muttered to himself.

***

With the fish cleaned and gutted, Rivo and Renee made their way back. Renee smirked as she felt the daisy still in her hair. "You know, Rivo, I think that's the first time a boy's ever given me flowers."

"Really?" he remarked as he hauled their catch back through the woods. "Well, I guess that's fitting. You're the first girl I've ever given flowers to, other than my mother, of course."

"Of course," Renee responded. "Dandelions and daisies, I presume?"

"From the buttcrack of a rock!" he proudly replied.

The two shared a laugh, and Renee nervously bit her lower lip. "Rivo." She paused anxiously, "Have you ever thought about what you're going to do when this is all over?"

Rivo looked up thoughtfully and shrugged, "Probably just work with Pearce or as an apprentice for one of the tradesmen back home. I haven't given it much thought, really."

Renee huffed sharply in frustration. "No, I don't mean that," she said as she shook her head. "I mean, like family. What are you planning for the future? Is there a special somebody waiting for you to come home?"

Rivo had a puzzled expression on his face. "Family? No, I hadn't thought about that. There is this girl, Leena, I always thought she was pretty, but she won't have anything to do with me anymore, not sure why. It doesn't matter, I'm a soldier now. That stuff's the last thing on my mind."

Renee rolled her eyes as they approached the campsite; it appeared by their friendly demeanor that Vickie and Naomi had come to terms with each other. "We're back!" Rivo announced as he and Renee walked up. Rivo set down a bucket of fish and came up to Naomi to give her a hug before she had a chance to apologize. She gladly embraced him back, grateful for how forgiving he was.

Naomi looked over to Renee, who set her basket down and stood, arms crossed, intentionally looking away from Naomi. She knew Renee would need to hear it from her.

Naomi calmly walked up to her. "Renee, I'm sorry for what I said. I was out of line. Please forgive me." Naomi said with humility.

"Thank you. It's okay," she replied with a timid smile.

"And Renee, I'm really sorry...that you're stuck having to babysit Rivo all the time," she added.

Vickie tried but failed to hold back a giggle, and Naomi smiled at Renee.

"Wait! What?" exclaimed Rivo.

"It's fine," Renee said with a chuckle, appreciating Naomi trying so hard to make her feel better.

"Okay, let's get everyone together and get some food," Vickie announced aloud.

"Unbelievable. So the thing that brought them together was them being in agreement on how dumb I am?" Spirit Rivo remarked.

His ghostly hand rubbed his face. "Well, either way, I wish this light-hearted moment could have lasted," he said as his nerves were set on edge. "But nothing could prepare us for what was coming next."

As the newly reconciled group enjoyed a moment together, with the tension behind them, Pearce and Judd returned. Both of them were sweaty and out of breath, with a look of panic in their eyes.

"Pearce! What's wrong?" Naomi asked as she ran up to him, grabbing his arms.

Pearce looked into her eyes. "Naomi," he gasped between breaths. "We've got trouble."

Chapter 18

The Good, the Bad, and the Reckless

"What trouble? What happened?" Naomi pleaded.

Pearce glanced at Judd, who, by the looks of it, had been crying, then back toward Naomi. "We came across Thorndale," he sighed wearily.

"What happened? What did you see?" Vickie asked desperately. "And Judd, why were you crying?"

Pearce took a deep breath and sighed again. "The villagers, they're dead, all of them."

The group collectively gasped at the news. Rivo's heart sank. "That's horrible," he lamented, "the Haundo?"

"Yes," answered Pearce.

"Every last one of them!" Judd sobbed, "They didn't spare a soul!"

Pearce closed his eyes and bit his lip. "Judd," he said, heaving. "We don't know that for sure. Some may have escaped."

"What about the recruits? Murphy, Myra, and the others?" Renee asked frantically.

"We saw Murphy and two others among the dead." Pearce's eyes were downcast. "There were a couple of dead Haundo among them; they must have fought while the rest escaped."

"That's terrible!" Renee gasped as she covered her mouth.

The group stood in complete silence. Pearce rubbed his face in distress, "It gets worse," he added.

"What could possibly be worse!" cried Naomi.

"There were Haundo still in the area," Pearce replied. "They were smaller than the others we've encountered, which tells me they're scouts."

"Well, did they spot you?" asked Vickie.

"No, I didn't give them a chance!" Judd cried, "I killed those two monsters with my bare hands!"

"Well, I can't say I blame you," Vickie remarked.

Pearce began rubbing his eyes in frustration. "I'd rather we'd just left the area safely without confronting them," said Pearce as he shot the strongman a sideways glance, "but Judd over here lost it and went after them instead."

"I wasn't about to let them get away with that!" Judd hollered.

Pearce was about to respond when a horrific howl was heard in the distance. He closed his eyes and clenched his jaw, "Great," he said sharply.

"Was that the Haundo?" asked Rivo. "What does that mean?"

Pearce anxiously rubbed his chin. "It means we should have left when we had the chance, like I said. They probably just found their dead comrades and are calling for backup." He then turned to glare at the strongman, "Stars be damned, Judd. Listen to me next time," he said as he looked away and shook his head. "Everybody get your weapons and follow me," he announced. "We're gonna have to kill every last one of them now, before they have time to send word to their pack leader. The last thing we need is to run into another freak like Drokner."

The group gathered their gear and set off to hunt the rest of the Haundo. Following Pearce's lead, they traveled a good mile through the woods before coming across the small village. What was once a quaint and cozy little town was now a desolate wasteland. The ground was littered with the mangled remains of its residents, along with Murphy and two other recruits, all having suffered a horrific end, no doubt a surprise attack.

Rivo's eyes welled up at what he was witnessing. "I don't care what Pearce says," he whispered through his sobs as he turned to Judd, standing nearby, "I would have done the same thing if I were you."

Rivo had to catch himself as his knees began to buckle, bile and rage filling his heart. *This—this is what could have happened to Rhemilia*, he thought, overwhelmed by the sight of the carnage and the stench of dead bodies.

Pearce and Naomi went ahead to get a closer look. She could tell that her husband seemed out of sorts since he and Judd delivered the news.

"Are you okay, Pearce?" she asked.

"It's my fault, Naomi," he moaned as he looked at the forest floor, "I sent them off by themselves, and it cost three of them their lives."

"Oh, Pearce," she said softly as she put her hand on his shoulder, "we had no way of knowing. Besides, if we had been here, it could have easily been us who got killed along with them. It wouldn't have made a difference."

It was then that the other Haundo were spotted. The group was hiding behind bushes and trees, watching the beasts roam about the village they had previously decimated. Six in total were spotted, two of them appeared to be investigating their recently killed comrades.

Pearce came back to the rest of the group, having gone to the far end of the village to check for potential escape routes. "So it looks like the backup has arrived. If I had to guess, going by how they're built, I'd say five fighters and one scout." He turned to Rivo, "Rivo, you, Renee, and Vickie go to the far end of the village, that's their most likely escape route. When we attack, the scout will run that way. If I had to guess, it'll be fast, real fast. I'm betting its job is to run, not fight. So take that thing out quickly. Remember the Creed, Rivo. *Assess, but don't hesitate. Act, but not rashly...* It means, *don't be reckless.* And don't forget to stick together. Got it?"

The three all nodded as Pearce grabbed Judd's shoulder. "Big man, this is gonna be me and you leading this. We're gonna charge in on those other five with Naomi backing us up. That rage you have over this, now's the time to use it. Let's take 'em down."

Judd looked him in the eye and nodded, trying to fight back any tears. It was obvious that he was relieved to see Pearce wasn't upset with him anymore.

Rivo, Vickie, and Renee all swiftly made their way to the escape route. Once they arrived, they waited for Pearce and the others to launch their attack.

It didn't take long for Pearce to make his move. He and Judd charged in, each killing a Haundo before they knew what hit them. The other three fighting beasts attacked while the scout fled, as predicted.

Vickie and Renee both shot their arrows with deadly aim and took the scout out long before it made it out of the village. But what the group had missed was the other Haundo who were waiting in the bushes for just such an attack.

After the scout fell, three other Haundo emerged from hiding and bolted for the escape route.

"Damn the stars, they were waiting for us to come back!" growled Vickie as she and Renee both went to nock another arrow.

Having been caught off guard, they were each only able to get one shot off, killing one Haundo and severely injuring another with an arrow to its hind leg. The third beast, along with its hobbled comrade, tackled Vickie and Renee, then went off running instead of trying to finish them off.

Pearce was right, their job is to run, not fight, Rivo thought as he saw them run off.

As much as he wanted to check on Vickie and Renee, he knew he had to get that scout. *Pearce isn't gonna like this, but if that thing makes it out of here, we're in deep trouble.* So off he ran to track the other two Haundo through the woods by himself.

"That was a dumb move," Spirit Rivo said, as he hovered nearby. "I should have checked on them and brought them with me. I should have listened to Pearce. Guess Naomi was right about me being reckless and stupid."

Rivo ran and ran, the fog getting thicker as he went. He had been following the sounds of breaking branches and snapping twigs that were made by the fleeing Haundo, but the sounds had become increasingly faint and were getting harder and harder to *pinpoint. They're way faster than me,* he thought. *I'm not sure if I can catch them, but I have to try. Our lives are on the line.*

He started to slow his pace. He had gone so deep into the woods that he wasn't sure if he'd be able to find his way back. *Dammit, they gotta be around here somewhere.* As he kept making his way to where he thought they might be, he remembered to feel every shrub and branch, to see if a blood trail had been left behind.

It wasn't long before his strategy paid off, just as it had before when they were hunting Drokner and his hounds. There it was, dripping from some brush.

Fresh blood.

"Got 'em," he whispered.

He kept following the trail, being careful not to make a sound. It wasn't long before he heard the grunts and growls of the Haundo. They were close.

I wonder why they haven't howled yet, he thought. *Maybe this means there aren't any reinforcements close enough to hear them. Perfect.*

As he kept creeping along, the grunts and growls kept getting louder. *I wonder if they stopped to rest. They must not know they're being tracked.*

As he crept along, peering through the brush, he saw them, two scouts. The injured Haundo had pulled the arrow out of its leg, letting out a quick yelp as he removed it. The other scout was pacing around him, as if to watch for any threats.

Rivo was hiding behind some brush as he watched, a good fifty feet away. *If only I had some long-range weapons.* It was at that time that he wished he had gone to check on Vickie and Renee back at the village. The three of them could have still caught up with the scouts had he done so. *No time to second-guess myself now,* he lamented. He pulled his swords out of the scabbards on his belt and made his move.

Charging at the two Haundo, Rivo swung his sword at the uninjured scout, thinking it would be his best option. The scout quickly jumped back, dodging the attack. *These guys are fast!*

The injured Haundo lunged at Rivo's leg, biting down hard and not letting go. He began hacking away at the beast, cutting the creature, but not bad enough to make it let go of his leg.

The other Haundo tackled him to the ground, biting, clawing, and pounding his head and sides. Rivo was able to raise one of his swords and slice the beast across its chest, enough to make it reel back, giving him just enough time to deliver a fatal strike to the Haundo biting his leg on the back of its skull.

As that beast fell over dead, the other one attacked again, grabbing Rivo and body-slamming him. As the scout lunged toward him to continue its offensive, it fell over dead. An arrow in the back of its head.

Rivo looked over to see Renee standing there, bow in hand, Vickie coming up just behind her.

"Damn the stars, Rivo," Vickie snapped, sighing as she walked toward him. "What did you run off like that for? You're lucky we were able to find you."

Rivo, breathing heavily and shaking nervously, didn't respond. He was covered with scratches, bite marks, and welts from the Haundo's beating.

"Oh, Rivo," Renee sighed, "are you alright?" she asked as she and Vickie went to help him to his feet.

"Yeah-yeah, I'll be fine," he gasped.

A loud, shrieking voice was heard through the fog, "Where in the stars' light is he!"

"Oh no," Rivo moaned as he hung his head.

There stomped Naomi, with Pearce and Judd following behind her.

"Rivo!" she barked, "what in Wyverly's name were you thinking, running off by yourself like that!?" She looked as if she was about to pinch him, or worse, but held back when she realized how roughed up he was.

"Naomi, I'm sorry," he moaned as he lifted his head. "I saw those two scouts run off, and I didn't wanna take a chance of them getting away."

"That was—stupid!" she yelled as she grabbed the collar of his vest. "That was reckless and stupid!"

"One of these days," Pearce interrupted from behind, his arms crossed, "you all are gonna learn to actually listen to me," he snapped.

Pearce paused for a moment and rubbed his face in agitation. "But, Rivo's okay and the Haundo are all dead," he remarked calmly. "In a way, we're lucky they tried to fight instead of run. Maybe they felt there was no escape."

"Whatever," replied Naomi as she let go of Rivo's vest. "I'm just glad everyone's okay." She put her hand on Renee's shoulder. "And Renee, thanks for babysitting him," she added as she shot a glare toward Rivo, "again."

"Okay, everybody," Pearce announced, "everyone is accounted for and the Haundo are gone. Let's head back to camp. Looks like Rivo's got a nasty bite on his calf, we'll have to bandage him up."

"I'll do it," Renee volunteered grudgingly as she and Naomi each got under Rivo's arm on either side to help him along. Though her tone may have sounded reluctant, the smirk on Renee's face showed otherwise.

"Rivo of Greencourt," she whispered mockingly, "who told you to play hero?"

Spirit Rivo couldn't help but chuckle as he looked on, "Renee again, you always had my back. I don't think I ever even thanked you for that."

Chapter 19

My Favorite Place

As they all arrived back at the campsite, the group ate supper, and all the tensions of the day had long since subsided. They were eating the trout Rivo and Renee had caught earlier. The familiar, earthy smell, along with the slightly sweet and savory flavor of the tender meat and seasoning, made Rivo think of his father, and how fresh trout was his favorite meal when they went fishing together. It had been seven years since the two last went out into the woods together.

He couldn't stop thinking of all the time he had spent in the forest with his father. He held the star pendant that was given to him the evening his father passed away. Maybe it was the trout, or maybe it was seeing so many lives taken before their time in Thorndale, but for some reason, it was hitting him hard that night. As everyone else retired to their sleep sacks for the evening, Rivo waited until they were all asleep, then headed out for a nighttime stroll to clear his head and reminisce about days gone by.

***

"The fish can sense if you're desperate or impatient, Rivo, and it's like a repellent to them," Frank said to his ten-year-old son. They were fishing together in a lake deep within the woods by Rivo's home back in Greencourt. A warm glow was cast over the water, the sun was setting, and the fish were biting on this cool summer evening. "The thing with fish is, it's almost like they'll let you know when they're ready to get caught, or maybe I should say, they're waiting for *you* to be ready to catch them."

"Huh?" young Rivo replied, wearing a puzzled expression.

"You see, Rivo, the fish are always in the water, even if you don't see them," Frank said as he extended his hand out toward the lake. "If you go out and you aren't ready, it's like the fish aren't even there. But when you get comfortable, when you make *them* comfortable, it's like the right one just kind of shows up. And if it is the right one, it's as if it's looking for any opportunity to be around you; like it wants to be caught, like it doesn't want to be just anybody's fish, it wants to be *your* fish," he added as he looked expectantly at his son, who still had the same dumbfounded look on his face.

"You see, Rivo," he said, pausing for a moment to gaze thoughtfully at the sky. "Women are kind of like fish in that way," Frank said, trying desperately to share words of wisdom with his young son, but struggling immensely.

"Father, I don't know what you're talking about," said a wide-eyed young Rivo.

"Maybe...uhh... you're not ready for this talk," Frank said, nervously rubbing the back of his neck.

There was a long moment of silence between them.

"Maybe that's not the best analogy," he continued, as he vigorously rubbed his chin. Frank decided to take another stab at it. "You see,

Rivo, women are like... uhh... they're like these crickets!" he exclaimed, frantically grasping at some way to get through to his son.

"Like the one you've got on your hook?"

"Well, no...uhh...maybe...uhh," Frank sighed in resignation. "Maybe *I'm* the one not ready for this talk," he concluded as he rubbed his eyes.

Frank pursed his lips together, thinking for a moment. "I think we've had a good catch today, son. Let's head back home," he remarked as he grabbed their basket of freshly caught trout, and Rivo nabbed the fishing poles.

He lifted the basket in one hand and held young Rivo's free hand in the other. Suddenly, he dropped to his knees, clutching his chest and coughing intensely.

"Father! What's wrong!" Rivo hollered.

Frank coughed into his handkerchief, his eyes widening as he noticed blood. "It's... It's fine, Rivo... let's just get back home," he replied, his voice quivering.

As they made their way back to their family cabin, Frank—typically eager to share stories and life lessons with his young son—was completely silent. The chirps of crickets, the hoots of owls, and the sound of the wind blowing through the trees are the only noises to break the stillness.

"Father," Rivo said with a concerned expression, "are you sure you're okay?"

Frank stopped to look at his son, "Yes, Rivo," Frank replied, bending down to eye level with him and placing a hand on his son's shoulder. "Please, don't ask me again," he said sternly. "And Rivo," he paused for a moment and sighed, "don't say anything to your mother. Understood?"

The boy nodded, on the verge of tears.

"Why don't you take the fish and go inside first, Rivo? I'll be there in a minute," Frank said as they got back to their cabin.

Rivo nodded once and walked in to help his mother prepare supper. He couldn't resist looking out the window to try and see what his father was doing out there by himself. The young boy's stomach twisted in knots at the sight of something he had never seen before.

His father was crying.

There, on the front steps, sat Frank, sobbing with his hands over his face. Rivo knew this had to be something serious. He had never seen his father, his hero, in this condition before. He had no clue what it meant, but he knew it was bad.

Frank stood up, took a deep breath to compose himself, and opened the front door.

Rivo backed up as his father walked in, desperate to see some sign that things were okay. Frank walked in with a smile beaming on his face. He approached his wife, Gwen, embraced her, and gave her a kiss on the forehead. He walked up to Rivo and did the same.

"C'mon, son, let's get the fish ready," Frank said with a smirk as he patted Rivo on the shoulder.

Rivo's mind instantly settled at the sight. *Things are back to normal*, he thought. *Father was just sad for a bit, but he's better now. Everything's fine.*

But it wasn't fine. That, it turned out, was the last time the two ever went into the woods together.

A few days later, any hope the boy had crumbled. Frank had become very ill. The town doctors could do little to help. His condition kept getting worse, and before long, it became clear that he wasn't going to make it.

As he lay dying in his bed, Frank called his son to his side. The boy came and sat next to his father. He handed him a round gold and silver pendant with a star engraved on its face. "Rivo, I want you to have this. It's a star pendant. My father made it for me when I was about your age. It's yours now, son. May the stars watch over and protect you always."

"Thank you, Father. I'll keep this close for the rest of my life," the boy said, choking back tears.

"Rivo," Frank said, struggling to get the words out, "do you remember the last time we went out fishing together in the forest?"

"Yes, Father," the boy replied, tears streaming down his face.

"When I collapsed and coughed as I did, I knew I didn't have much time. I had gotten a deadly sickness. I didn't tell you or your mother at first. I wanted to enjoy the moment... Do you want to know what I found when I got home, son?"

"What did you find, Father?"

"I found my favorite place, Rivo," Frank rasped as he turned his head to look into his son's eyes, clasping the boy's hand.

"Your favorite place?" Rivo asked in bewilderment, "What's your favorite place, Father?"

"Well, it was when we got back to the cabin, our tiny, simple cabin. As your mother was singing while cooking the beans and corn, and you and I were cleaning the fish, that's when I realized it. For a moment, I was there," Frank said, his voice strained, using the last of his strength.

"I don't understand, Father. What do you mean?"

"It means, Rivo, that I realized I had found that place I'd been looking for my whole life—my favorite place. It was there, in our tiny little cabin...with you...and your mother." his voice faded to a whisper. "Thank you, Rivo...for helping me find my favorite place." His voice trailed off, and his hand went limp.

Rivo's father, Frank, breathed his last breath and passed away quietly into the night.

"Father," Rivo whimpered as he knelt by, tears streaming, his mouth dry, and the lump in his throat making him feel he was about to vomit. Gwen stood behind him, wrapping her arms around his chest, sobbing. His father's last words echoed in his mind, *My favorite place.*

***

Rivo sat perched on a ledge high above the trees overlooking Lake Thorndale, where they had fished earlier. He stared blankly at the lake's surface stretched out below, the water reflecting the nighttime sky like a mirror. *How many of them had a lifetime of memories at this small lake?* he wondered, grieving for the lives lost. *And Murphy, he gave up everything. I can only hope Myra and the others are okay, that his sacrifice was not in vain, and that some of the villagers were able to escape along with them.*

The night had grown cold, with a biting breeze that stung his skin. His calf was still throbbing from the Haundo's bite, though Renee had managed to bandage it up quite well.

Despite the day's chaos, the forest brought Rivo a strange sense of peace. It reminded him of the woods outside of Greencourt: the scent of pine, the chirping crickets, and the earthy taste of trout still lingering on his tongue. He couldn't help but reminisce about his last fishing trip in the forest with his father, the illness that had overtaken him so quickly, and his dying words to his son. "My favorite place," Rivo whispered, clutching the star pendant his father had given him.

Spirit Rivo sat beside him quietly, sharing the same memories. "Father really was something, wasn't he?" he remarked.

Just then, a voice startled him from behind, "Rivo? Rivo, are you okay?"

He turned to see who was calling for him. It was Renee, slightly hunched over with her arms crossed, shivering. She hadn't thought to bring her cloak and wore only a thin nightgown, perhaps not realizing how cold the nighttime air was away from the warmth of the campfire.

"Renee again," Spirit Rivo chuckled, "looking out for everyone else, as usual."

"Oh, Renee, you scared me," Rivo said, rubbing his eyes and shaking off the vivid memory he'd been reliving. "What are you doing out here?" he asked.

"I should be asking you," she replied. "I woke up and noticed you weren't in your sleep sack. I was just worried because it's the middle of the night. Rivo, you're still hurt. Do you really think you should be out here by yourself?" Her voice carried a note of both chiding and concern.

"Uh, yeah. I'm good. We can head back," he said as he arose from the ledge, brushing off the seat of his pants.

As he stood there, he saw stars shooting across the sky. "More shooting stars," he remarked thoughtfully. "Seems like there've been a lot of those lately. Just about every night, it feels like. Guess they must really want people to make a wish."

Renee arched her eyebrows, looking at him expectantly. "Well, did you make a wish?" she asked teasingly.

"You only get one wish, right?" he replied with a slight smirk. "I already made mine, a long time ago."

"Do you really believe in that stuff?" she asked. "That we can wish upon a shooting star and it'll come true?"

"I don't know. I used to," he said with a shrug, his eyes still fixed on the sky. "I remember my parents telling me about it when I was a kid. They said people really used to believe in all that. They told me how people would spend their whole lives studying the stars. I remember one time at the Festival of Celestial Lights, my father did a performance. He did some sort of amazing maneuver with his sword. He laughed when I called it a magic trick. Looking back, I'm not sure if there was something real to it or if it was just a trick of some sort. Either way, I feel like there might be something to it." He turned to Renee. "What about you, Renee? Did you ever believe that?"

She shrugged and looked down, "Maybe when I was small," she answered, "but not anymore. I made a wish that my daddy would come back, and it didn't come true." She sighed and walked up to the ledge beside him, gazing over the lake, rubbing her arms with her hands to try and keep warm. "Vickie says that if wishing upon a star really worked, we wouldn't need so many of them."

"Yeah, maybe," he remarked with a quick chuckle, then turned toward her. "Renee, can I ask you something?"

She turned to him, her mouth slightly agape. "Umm...sure."

"What...what's your favorite place?"

She blinked, caught off guard by the question. "My favorite place?" she asked, bewildered.

"Yeah, do you have a favorite place?"

Her eyes darted around as she thought it over. "Umm...I don't know, we've been to so many. I don't really have a home like most people. All I've ever really had has been Vickie. So I guess it would be wherever she is. But sometimes, I do need a break from her," she said with a nervous laugh, unsure of what kind of response he was expecting. "What about you?"

Rivo looked back over the cliff and drew a deep breath as he thought it over for a moment. "My father used to take me out to the forest practically every day," he replied, "he taught me everything I know in those woods. How to fish, how to hunt, how to use a weapon. How to be brave. Everything I learned about life, my father taught me there." he paused to let out a weary sigh, "So that's my favorite place, the forest."

Renee nodded slowly. "Wow," she murmured, "it sounds like he really loved you."

There was a long pause between the two. The only sounds to be heard were the crickets chirping and the frogs croaking, along with the nighttime breeze. Rivo stood on the ledge, still looking over the woods.

Renee broke the awkward silence. "Rivo, there's something I've been meaning to share with you. The other day by the lake, I got you to tell me all about your parents, but when you asked me about mine, I cut the conversation off. I'm sorry I did that."

"That's okay," he said gently. "You don't have to talk about that kind of stuff if you don't feel comfortable. I get it."

"No, I want to," she said, her voice trembling. "Well, like I said, my daddy died in a work accident when I was seven. I told you we lost our mother shortly after, but she didn't die...she left us." Renee's anxiety rose. She started shivering, unsure if it was her nerves or the cold night air.

"She left you?" Rivo asked, his eyes widening as he looked over at her.

"Some nobleman came right after daddy died and asked for her hand in marriage. She accepted. Next thing I knew, she was getting in a wagon to leave. Vickie told me to stay inside the house. I could hear the three of them arguing about something. I remember Vickie screaming something about how they had to either take both of us or neither of us. After that, she came back into the house crying as they rode off. I never saw my mother again."

"That's awful," he replied.

"Poor Renee," Spirit Rivo murmured. "She deserved so much better."

"It's just been me and Vickie ever since; the mysterious beauty and the invisible girl." Renee paused, sniffling and wiping away a tear—she'd never shared this story before. "The only thing I can think of is that they offered to take Vickie with them and leave me behind. She must have refused to leave me, so they just left us both. She won't tell me exactly what was said; she gets mad whenever I try to bring it up." Renee sighed, her voice cracking with emotion, "I'm sure she's just trying to protect me from the truth."

Rivo turned sharply to face her. "That's not the truth!" he snapped. "And that was no nobleman, that was a thief!" He stepped toward her. "And I can't think of a single reason for someone to leave you like that, Renee, not one!"

Renee stood frozen, her eyes wide. She could have been knocked over with a feather at that moment. No one had ever spoken like that to her before.

He took a few deep breaths to calm down. "Let's get back to the campsite, Renee. You look cold," he said as he placed his cloak over her shoulders and turned toward the camp a couple of hundred paces away.

"You're giving me another one of your cloaks?" she asked with an awkward laugh. "Rivo, I'm sorry. I'll give it back when we get back to camp."

"That's fine," he said as he started walking toward the campsite. "Thanks for coming to check on me. Sorry you felt you had to do that."

As Rivo was walking, Renee lingered by the ledge, gazing out at the lake. She took a deep breath. "The streams," she blurted out.

He stopped and turned toward her, eyebrows furrowed. "The streams? What about them?" he asked.

"You asked about my favorite place. It's the streams," Renee said with her back to him. She could feel his blue eyes staring at her from behind.

"Why the streams?" he asked as he stepped toward her.

She drew a deep breath and closed her eyes. "My parents didn't have a very good relationship. Daddy would be gone for weeks at a time, and when he came home, he'd usually go off to the streams a little ways from our house. I would go with him." She sighed sharply and brushed her bangs from her eyes, "Mother gave Vickie all of her attention...But I had Daddy when I was with him by those streams."

Rivo nodded thoughtfully as he listened. "Tell me more about your father and the streams," he said softly.

Renee took another deep breath to stifle her emotions. Her chest tightened as she spoke—she'd never in her life told this to anyone, not even Vickie. "It felt like the one thing in the world that was mine. He used to have a nickname that he'd call me, but I can't for the life of me remember it, almost like my mind has blocked it out. But everything else, I remember so clearly: the way his shirt felt when I snuggled up against him, the smell of tobacco smoke from his pipe, how his beard would tickle the side of my face when he'd kiss me on the cheek, how he would toss me up in the air and catch me. All my memories with him are by the streams. That's my favorite place." There was another long pause. "I know it sounds childish and silly, but that's my answer—the streams."

The conversation fell silent—she was almost too embarrassed to look at him. As she finally turned to meet his gaze, her eyes went wide, and she gave a loud gasp.

Rivo was crying. Tears streamed down both sides of his face, making his eyes glisten like blue sapphires.

She could hardly muster a word at the sight, "Rivo..." she whispered, her voice barely audible.

"That's not silly at all, Renee," he said through the tears, his voice raw and trembling. "The streams... I like that."

Renee stood speechless, not knowing what to do or say. A storm raged inside of her, a combination of longing and excitement, panic, and terror. She wanted to run and hide, yet hold his hand and never let go—all at once. She stepped back and crossed her arms, keeping them pinned to her body, despite her desperate urge to reach out and wipe the tears from his eyes.

"C'mon, Renee, we should head back now," Rivo remarked as he turned to make his way back to camp.

The silent hike back felt like an eternity to her; she couldn't think of a thing to say. Not a word was spoken between the two as they approached the camp.

The real Rivo didn't notice it at the time, but hovering behind them, Spirit Rivo's eyes widened as he watched Renee. She had kept a couple of paces behind him, at one point reaching to grab his hand, but then recoiling at the last moment, just as their fingers were about to touch, her face wincing from her inner turmoil. "Renee?" he gasped.

Once they finally arrived, she quietly handed Rivo his cloak without looking at him and briskly walked toward her sleep sack.

"Renee," he said as she kept walking, "thanks for coming to check on me."

She turned her head to the side and offered only a quick nod as she kept walking. He went to lie down on his sleep sack, about twenty feet from hers and Vickie's.

"Goodnight, Renee," Rivo whispered.

She wanted to say something, but couldn't come up with the words. Unbeknownst to her, Vickie, lying on her side in the sack right next to hers, was still awake but with her back facing them.

"Rivo," Renee said, sitting up in her sleep sack.

"What is it, Renee?" he replied as he sat up as well.

Go ahead, Renee. Tell him how you feel. Vickie thought to herself.

Spirit Rivo hovered over them, taken aback by Vickie's thoughts. "*Tell him how you feel?*" he asked, perplexed.

Renee just couldn't bring herself to say what she really wanted. Her heart screamed, but her courage faltered. "Goodnight," she uttered.

He smiled at her. "Thanks, you too," he said as he lay back down and fell soundly asleep.

She lay with her back to him, her shoulders trembling with silent sobs, the ache of her cowardice clawing at her chest for letting the moment slip away.

Vickie lay still, a quiet tear rolling down her face, crying over her sister. Renee was suffering, and she was helpless to comfort her. *Oh, Renee,* Vickie thought with a silent moan. *You've fallen for that boy, haven't you? And now you're beating yourself up because you don't know what to do about it. Please don't do this to yourself. I'm so sorry... Damn you, Rivo, look at what you've done. What in the stars' light did you say to her out there?*

"Renee?" Spirit Rivo said, bewildered as he watched. "I had no idea she liked me that way. Why didn't she just talk to me about it?"

Chapter 20

A Very Exclusive Club

The group was now nearing the tail end of their journey. The hiking formation had shifted slightly. Pearce and Judd were at the rear with Rivo, who couldn't move as quickly due to his injury from his fight with the Haundo at Thorndale. Vickie and Naomi had overcome their previously tumultuous relationship and were now getting along quite well, traveling together at the front of the group. Renee was traveling with them.

Rivo had just assumed that Renee had repositioned herself to be closer to Vickie and thought little of it. Renee, however, had done it to get away from him. Every moment she spent near him since that evening in the forest was like a punch in the gut.

Spirit Rivo found himself toward the front along with them.

Renee was hiking a few steps ahead of Vickie and Naomi. She walked with her hood up and her arms crossed the entire time. Vickie saw her angrily kick a small stone off to the side of the trail. She could tell Renee was bothered by something and knew it was over Rivo.

"So what did that dope do this time, Renee?" asked Vickie as she sped up to her sister's side.

"I don't know what you're talking about, Vick. Nobody did anything," Renee replied evenly.

"Renee, your voice sounds angry, but your eyes look sad," Spirit Rivo said as he floated in front of her. "Was this because of our talk by the cliff? Because you didn't tell me how you felt?"

Vickie let out a loud, exaggerated sigh. "Do I need to get him over here and—"

"No, Vick!" she snapped. "Just leave me alone. I'm sick of you."

Vickie was the only person Renee ever spoke to that way. She closed her eyes and tightened her jaw. "Fine," Vickie replied curtly to her sister's outburst. She slowed down to give her some space.

Naomi had been walking a few steps behind the two and couldn't help but overhear. She walked up to Vickie as she backed away from Renee. "Did something happen between her and Rivo?" she whispered, hoping Renee wouldn't hear.

Vickie grabbed Naomi's elbow and lingered a few paces farther back from Renee. "Something happened between them last night after everyone else fell asleep," Vickie whispered back. "I'm not sure what exactly, she won't tell me."

"Oh no. I can talk to him. If he said something that hurt her, I'm sure he didn't mean to."

"That's not it." Vickie paused for a moment to look toward Renee, then back at Naomi. "Naomi, I think Renee...is in love with him."

"Really!" Naomi blurted out as she quickly covered her mouth, realizing she'd spoken too loudly. "So why does she seem so upset?"

"She's never felt this way before, Naomi," answered Vickie. "That girl doesn't even believe in love. She doesn't really like even talking to boys. But here she is, she's fallen for your cousin and has no idea what to do about it."

"And she doesn't want to hear about it from you, right?"

"Especially not from me. Renee feels she's been living in my shadow her whole life. She never believed she'd find love; she's told me that. I think subconsciously, she blames me."

"That's too bad," said Naomi. "I guess it's like you said before, she's gonna need to figure it out for herself."

Vickie was right, Renee never really believed in love, but she had to face the fact that her feelings towards Rivo were beyond just admiration and friendly affection. Her feelings had grown past that for some time now. The events of that evening by the forest ledge forced her to face the fact she'd been avoiding. She had fallen for him. Part of her wished that she'd never gone to check in on him that night, but the truth was, she'd been lying to herself about her feelings for him long before that night.

Vickie was wrong about one thing, though. Renee *had* felt this way before. It was the same feeling she had when she and Vickie were homeless, wandering the streets and she would watch happy, innocent children playing with their parents, or she would look through a shop window and see a beautiful dress that she knew she'd never be able to afford, nor did she feel she would ever have the kind of figure to wear one. Those luxuries weren't for nobodies like her. Love wasn't for her; it was just another unattainable pleasure that somebody like her would never be lucky enough to enjoy. It was like flaunting a delicious treat in front of a hungry child who would never know its taste.

Renee, Vickie thought, *you won't tell me what's going on, but I know what you're doing. You probably considered being mean to him, to push him away, but you just couldn't bring yourself to do it, could you? So now you're putting some distance between you and him, hoping that will help. But that's just causing yet another conflict within you, isn't it? Part of you wants to run away from Rivo, while the other part of you wants him to chase after you.*

"Is Vickie right, Renee? How could I have not seen any of this before?" asked Spirit Rivo. "Renee...you were in love with me? Why did you put yourself through all this instead of talking to me? Renee...I'm so sorry that you went through all of this just over me. I feel terrible."

***

It was late morning, a few days later, when the group had finally arrived. The outpost was in an abandoned estate that had been converted into a makeshift military complex, most likely owned by a noble family sometime in the distant past. The estate had all the infrastructure of a small town. There were multiple large guard towers built of big gray stone blocks around the edge of the massive campus.

In the center was the main building, a large two-story brick mansion, which had the infirmary, along with some officers' living quarters, some meeting rooms, and who knows what else. Next to it was a slightly smaller building with the same architecture that appeared to serve a similar purpose. Scattered throughout were numerous small buildings along with some makeshift wooden buildings and tents that had just been built; likely, these were living quarters for some of the other soldiers.

As they checked in at the main guard tower, they were led through the grounds to the main building by one of the guards. As they made their way in, the group got to see all they had up close. Rivo had heard of horseless wagons before, but had never seen one until now. They ran on coal and could ride much faster than a horse-drawn wagon. It was claimed that you could go as far in one day as you could in ten with a regular wagon. They looked almost like a regular horse-drawn wagon, but with four wheels and a steering wheel for the driver. Some of the cars were open wagons, while others had a closed cabin for riders. It looked like most could only fit a handful of people at a time.

"That would have been useful to have had from the start," Rivo mumbled under his breath as he walked by.

"Yeah, but who would drive it, you?" whispered Pearce.

"Sure, why not?" Rivo replied in a snarky tone.

Pearce scoffed loudly and shook his head. "No way."

There were several tents scattered throughout the entire estate grounds, with children playing around them.

"What in the stars' light are children and their families doing here?" Rivo asked. "Could they possibly be refugees from Thorndale?"

"That they are," answered the guard. "And we have you all to thank for that. It was your recruits who brought them here."

Rivo's eyes welled up with both sadness and pride. He looked over at Pearce and could see the same expression. *Murphy,* he thought, *your death was not in vain. These people lived because you guys fought.*

Just outside of the main complex, they noticed a series of large iron tubes sitting on wheels. "Those are cannons, we just got them," announced the guard. "They shoot out large iron balls; they can destroy any structure or wall, even something like one of our guard towers."

They were finally brought to the main building. The entrance brought them to the Atrium, with hallways branching off to either side and staircases ascending to the second story. The group was in awe at the sight of it all.

"Renee! Vickie! Naomi!" an excited and familiar voice called out from the far hallway. The group looked over to see Myra running towards them, tearfully embracing the three young women.

"Myra, I'm so sorry about everything," Renee's voice cracked as she spoke.

"Thank you, Renee," Myra replied with a bittersweet smile. "It was horrifying. Murphy and the others fought while we rounded up as many villagers as we could and escaped. They—they were heroes."

"You're all heroes, Myra," Naomi interjected as she placed her hand on the grieving young woman's shoulder.

"Thank you. It doesn't feel that way sometimes," Myra said as she wiped a tear from her cheek.

They could hear footsteps approaching. Myra gave the group one last hug and went back to her assigned duties, as they promised to catch up again later.

"Well, I see you brought us some recruits. Well done," said a familiar, gruff voice from down the hallway as the footsteps got closer. It was Captain Tremlee.

"Captain Tremlee, good to see you again," said Pearce. "They came from Rhemilia. More wanted to join, but we felt they should stay to help defend the town. You see, when we were there—"

"The town was attacked by the Haundo, led by the one named Drokner," Captain Tremlee interrupted.

"I see they must have filled you in," remarked Naomi.

"We knew before they even arrived," he said. "We have scouts traveling all across Wyverly, sending back reports regularly. Some of them visited Rhemilia not too long ago. It was said that the townspeople told of how you fought the Haundo off, hunted them down, and killed Drokner. That, my young soldiers, is quite an accomplishment." Captain Tremlee paused for a moment. "Tell me, which one of you is Rivo of Greencourt?" he asked.

"Uh...that would be me, sir," Rivo spoke up, taken aback by how the Captain knew all this information.

"Is that so? I do vaguely remember recruiting you in Greencourt," Captain Tremlee said, looking closely at Rivo as he stroked his mustache. "You know, young man, you are in elite company. Everyone here knows your name. Rivo the Beastkiller."

"What do you mean?" asked Rivo. He'd only ever heard that word from the Forest Folk.

"You see, Rivo, you killed a Greater Haundo. A feat only one other soldier has accomplished thus far. We call this very exclusive club the Beastkillers," Captain Tremlee stated.

"Wow, I didn't realize that. Who's the other soldier?"

"He's chosen to keep a low profile on the whole matter. He's here today, and I think you two should meet," Captain Tremlee told him. "But first, we need to get things in order with the new recruits." He motioned to an officer standing nearby. "You all can follow him, and he'll go through some instructions on your training." Vickie, Renee, and Judd followed the officer down the left hallway to a large room lined with weapons and maps for their orientation.

"Now, you two, Pearce and Naomi, I'd like to take you to my office and discuss your next recruiting trip. It's just up these stairs to the right. But first, I'd like to introduce Rivo to our other Beastkiller, he's waiting in the first room down the hall," the Captain said as he pointed down the right hallway.

"Here it is," remarked Spirit Rivo with a sigh. "My first meeting with the only other man to kill a Greater Haundo...Cade."

Chapter 21

Like Two Little School Boys

It was a small meeting room. Perhaps used when a small group of officers wanted to gather and didn't want to occupy the larger war room upstairs. There wasn't much to it: no artwork or decorations to speak of, a couple of lamps, a few bookshelves, and a small square wooden table with four chairs. There was a small carafe of whiskey or some such drink that sat open. And in one of the chairs, there sat who could have been none other than Cade, the Beastkiller.

Cade had taken one of the chairs and turned it towards the large window, which was on the wall opposite the door. He was lounging in the chair with his back toward Rivo, holding a glass of whiskey, not drinking it, but twirling the glass, gazing at it as if lost in thought.

Rivo cleared his throat. "Umm, excuse me, sir," he said politely.

"What do you want?" Cade asked bluntly, still looking at his glass.

From behind, Rivo couldn't get a good look at him. His head was shaved around the sides and back; the blond hair on the top of his head was long and braided, long enough to reach about the middle of his back. He wore dark leather armor and gauntlets, along with matching cloth pants and boots.

"Uhh...Captain Tremlee told me to introduce myself—"

"Tremlee," Cade scoffed. "Why? Because we're the *Beastkillers*? What, did he think, we'd be best friends or something? Like two little school boys on the first day of class?"

"Well, I'm not sure. I guess he just felt like it would be a good idea," Rivo replied nervously.

"You guess," Cade mocked. "I already know more than I want about you, Rivo of Greencourt...*the Beastkiller.*"

"You do? How—"

"You idiot. Everyone here knows. Your name's been spreading like wildfire. You killed Drokner. Even the Haundo know. You just put a bullseye on your back, kid. You don't know the first thing about war and survival."

"I made it this far, didn't I?" Rivo said defensively.

Cade shook his head. "Tuval."

Rivo darted his eyes from side to side in confusion. "Tuval?"

Cade gave out what sounded like a mix of a grunt and a snort. "That's who hunts you."

Rivo raised an eyebrow and turned his ear towards Cade to make sure he was hearing him right. "What do you mean *hunts me*?"

"Unbelievable," Cade groaned as he rubbed his forehead. "You don't know anything, do ya?" Cade took a frustrated sigh and went on, "Tuval, the leader of the Haundo. He's also Drokner's brother, or at least sees Drokner as his brother. Or should I say he *saw* Drokner as a brother, however, in the stars' light that works with them. Anyway, Tuval is the one who's going to kill you. You killed Drokner, so he'll kill you. It'll be a miracle if you live another week."

" I-I hadn't heard about any of this," Rivo paused to process what Cade had just said. "What about you? You killed one, too, so why don't you have a target on your back?"

"Watch your tone with me, boy," Cade said sharply. "Because I'm not an idiot, I didn't let my name get spread all over. In fact, I wish Tremlee didn't even know. This is a war for the kingdom of Wyverly, not for personal glory."

"I didn't do it for glory. I didn't have a choice," Rivo replied sharply.

"I don't wanna hear it, kid," Cade replied as he waved his hand dismissively. "War is a place for men. It's for the strong and the noble. It's not for brats with a hero complex. What do you know of war? How many real battles have you actually been in?"

Rivo was about to reply, but realized that Cade had no interest in hearing his opinion.

"I've been in more battles than I can even count. Even before those monsters arrived. I've seen a lot of good men die on the battlefield. My comrades, brave soldiers, men and women I'd known my whole life. Yet they're gone, and here you are, getting praised as the Beastkiller, like you're some kind of hero, like you and I are on the same level." Cade finally paused and took a sip of his whiskey. "Those men and women I lost, my brothers and sisters in arms, I'd take any one of them over some kid like you. But they're dead, and you're still alive. Doesn't seem right to me."

Cade stood up to set his glass on the table and walked up to Rivo. He couldn't have been much more than thirty years old, yet he somehow looked older. His face was weathered, and he had scars on his cheek and both knuckles. He had a streak of dark blue paint going from the middle of his forehead on either side, down over his eyelids, stopping just above his jawline. He stood about a head taller than Rivo, and probably outweighed the boy by almost a hundred pounds, all muscle, no doubt. He looked like he could give Judd a run for his money in the strength department. This man had an intimidating presence; it was obvious that he was no stranger to battle.

His neck is thicker than my waist, Rivo thought.

He wore a snarl on his face, and Rivo couldn't tell if he looked like that because of him or if he always looked that way. He stood face to face with Rivo, just a few inches away. He studied Rivo's vest, looking at the golden embroidery in disgust.

"Stars be damned, who told you you could wear that vest?" he demanded.

Rivo's jaw clenched as he glared directly into Cade's eyes. "It belonged... to my *father*," he replied, his voice low yet sharp.

Cade stared him down for a moment, then pointed his finger in Rivo's face. "You know what I've noticed in my years on the field, in *real* battle? Kids like you, who think they're signing up to play commando and be a hero, always die first. You've got no business being here." He stood silent and looked back at Rivo's vest before meeting his eyes again. "And you've got no business wearing that vest," he growled, shaking his head as he walked past Rivo and left the room.

Rivo stood in stunned silence, his mind reeling. *I wonder if he's just saying out loud what the other soldiers are thinking?* At that point, he just wanted to find Pearce, Naomi, and the others so they could go on to their next mission and get out of that place.

"My stars, that was rough, even watching it again. I remember standing there, just glad it was over, and hoping to never have to deal with him ever again. But boy, am I glad I met Cade. For better or worse..." said Spirit Rivo.

Chapter 22

Eating then Meeting

A couple of days later, the group gathered together in the dining hall for lunch. Pearce, Naomi, and Rivo had been told by Captain Tremlee that they had earned a few days to rest before they went on their next recruiting trip. He felt Rivo's moniker as *The Beastkiller* would be an excellent recruiting tool.

They sat down to eat their daily serving of chicken with potatoes and beans. The tables in the dining hall seated only four each; Rivo sat with Pearce and Naomi, while Vickie, Judd, and Renee all sat at a separate table. Though Rivo was oblivious to Renee's feelings for him, he had grown used to her company throughout their journey. He quickly scarfed down his food and excused himself from the table to go sit with Renee and the others, much to Renee's unease.

"Well, I don't know about you all, but I've been bored to tears in this place. Nothing but meetings and studying maps," he said to the three. "How has your orientation and training been going?" he asked.

"Good," replied Judd, stuffing his face with chicken. "Kind of boring, but the food's good."

"I suppose I can't complain. They're talking about making us scouts," Vickie remarked.

"Really? Sounds interesting," said Rivo as he turned to Renee. "So, Renee, how have you been liking it here? It's been weird not having my travel buddy around lately."

"Hello, Rivo," Renee replied solemnly with a nod, not looking at him directly.

"Renee was trying to put on her best face, and I was completely clueless," Spirit Rivo said as he watched her.

Vickie chimed in. "So, Rivo, do you know if we'll be traveling together moving forward, or will you be on a different assignment?" she asked, glancing at Renee for a reaction. Renee was picking at her food with her fork, pretending as if she wasn't listening.

"Looks like they're gonna keep us on recruiting duty. We'll be leaving in a day or so," he answered. "It sounds like we'll be parting ways at that point. I'm gonna miss you guys."

"Really?" Vickie replied with a pretentious gasp. "So I guess if anyone here has something they want to say to each other, they'd need to say it soon, right, Renee?" Vickie remarked, gazing at Renee with a wry grin.

Renee slammed her fork down and stood up. "I think I'm done. I'm heading back to the training grounds," she said, shooting a sneer toward Vickie before stomping out of the room abruptly.

"Renee...I'm sorry you were dealing with this, and I had no idea. Man, I wish I could make it up to you..." said Spirit Rivo.

"Is she okay? What was that about?" Rivo asked as Judd reached over and took the rest of Renee's food off her plate.

"I heard you had a little meeting with the other Beastkiller yesterday. How did that go?" Vickie asked to change the subject.

Rivo gave a disgusted sigh. "Ugh, not my kinda guy at all," he said, rubbing his eyes. "He was real stuck-up and thought he was better than me. I never get along with those types."

"He didn't like you?" Judd asked in surprise. "Do I need to talk to him?"

Rivo chuckled, "Oh no, Judd. Please don't," he said, holding the bridge of his nose. "But thanks for the offer."

"Well, the good news is, it doesn't sound like you'll have to deal with him much longer," Vickie remarked, leaning back in her seat as she propped her feet up on the chair Renee had been sitting in. "Rivo," she added, "please do come find us and say goodbye before you leave. Judd and I would appreciate it after all we've been through. And I'm sure Renee would as well."

"Oh, of course. I'm gonna miss you three," he replied as he slapped Judd on his shoulder.

The group finished their meals and went their separate ways. Vickie and Judd joined Renee and the others at the training grounds. Rivo, Naomi, and Pearce went to the large meeting room on the second floor to meet with Captain Tremlee and make their final plans.

As the three entered the meeting room. They saw a large round table in the center with a marked map of Wyverly. A couple of other officers stood at the table with their backs to Rivo and the others, along with Cade, who stood facing them. Cade saw Rivo and the others walk in and gave Rivo a narrow-eyed scowl before giving his attention back to the two officers and the map on the table. Rivo pretended not to notice and instead looked to Captain Tremlee, who was standing to the left of the table, closer to the entrance, waiting for them.

"Excellent, you're all here. Let's take this over to the smaller planning table and go over everything one last time." Captain Tremlee told them, gathering some papers.

He led them to a small square wooden table by the windows, opposite the doorway. They had to walk past Cade and the officers. Rivo could feel the hostility emanating from Cade as he walked by.

"Well, I trust you feel you've been treated well during your visit here. We're certainly glad you made it." Captain Tremlee said casually while he rifled through the papers. "Now," he said as he took a deep breath, "down to business—"

It was at that point that the conversation came to a halt. Some sort of loud siren had gone off, accompanied by sounds of screaming and howling.

"What is that!?" exclaimed Naomi, clutching Pearce's arm.

"It can't be!" shouted Captain Tremlee as he ran to look out the window. "We're under attack. It's the Haundo!"

Chapter 23

No Going Back

They all ran to join Tremlee at the window. The guard tower at the front gate was surrounded by the Haundo; there were hundreds of them. At the front, facing the main complex, was a large Greater Haundo, even larger than Drokner.

"Tuval?" Rivo whispered.

The Haundo had overrun the guard tower. The bodies of both Haundo and Wyverly guards lay scattered on the ground around the tower. All the Wyverly soldiers who were standing outside ran to meet them in a standoff.

The Greater Haundo that stood at the front roared in a horrifying growl, "Silence! We have hostages!" At that, the Wyverly soldiers and Haundo alike all fell silent at his command.

Captain Tremlee opened the window and hollered back, "Haundo, I am Captain Tremlee of the Kingdom of Wyverly. What do you want?"

"I am Tuval, leader of the Haundo. I want the Beastkillers. Rivo, of Greencourt! I know you're here somewhere. I know you killed my brother, Drokner. I also demand to know who killed Brooner. Come out and fight me, and I'll leave this place. And don't lie to me, I know Rivo is here. We've been tracking him—his trail stops here!"

Rivo gasped as his heart raced. "How?" he rasped, breathing sharply and anxiously running his hands through his hair. "How does he know?"

"Stars be damned, boy, I told you," grunted Cade, standing behind him.

Rivo glanced over at Cade. *Brooner—that must be the one Cade killed*, Rivo thought.

Pearce turned to glare at Cade, visibly bothered by his attitude. "Who are you?" he demanded.

"None of your concern, boy. Besides, we have bigger problems to deal with right now," replied Cade.

Captain Tremlee leaned out the window. "We can't do that, Tuval," he hollered.

"You will!" Tuval hollered back. "I have a thousand other hounds on their way here, ready to attack. If Rivo isn't out here in ten minutes, we'll tear this place apart. And when we're done, we're going to Greencourt to kill every last one of your kinfolk, Rivo!" growled the giant beast.

The room fell silent. Rivo looked at the tower as Tuval walked inside it, followed by three other Greater Haundo. They weren't taking any chances; they brought their best.

"We're going to need to arm up and attack. We're badly outnumbered; all we can hope is to take down as many of them as we can," Captain Tremlee announced to the others in the room. "This is it for us, this is what we train for. To defend the Kingdom of Wyverly."

Captain Tremlee, the other two officers, and Cade all began to leave the room to inform all within the complex of their plan.

As they opened the door to leave, Rivo lingered by the window, unable to stop thinking about what Tuval had said. About how he was going to attack the outpost. And then, Greencourt. "I'll go. I'll go fight him. Just me. That's all he wants," he told them, still looking through the window at the guard tower.

Naomi stopped in her tracks. "What? Absolutely not!" she shouted. "He'll kill you."

"She's right. By no means are you to go fight by yourself. That's not how we do things here. I don't believe in suicide missions," Captain Tremlee barked.

"Really? You just said we were outnumbered and our only hope was to take out as many of them as we could. Sounds like a suicide mission to me either way," Rivo retorted. "Besides, you heard what he said. He called me out by name. He said he'd kill everyone here and everyone back in Greencourt. Maybe he's planning on doing that anyway, but it's the only chance we've got."

"Rivo, stop! We're not doing this," Pearce said bluntly.

Captain Tremlee's lip curled as he jabbed his finger toward Rivo. "Rivo, you are not to go out there. That is a direct order," he stated firmly.

"Fine," Rivo replied evenly. "Didn't you all need to get ready? We have less than ten minutes, right?"

"Alright, let's get going," replied the Captain as he and the other officers left the room, followed by Pearce and Naomi.

Cade lingered behind, glaring at Rivo. "Quit trying to play hero, boy," he grumbled. "It's too late for that now." He started to head out with everyone else, but stopped when he felt Rivo grab his arm. "Meet me in the small meeting room downstairs, where we first spoke," he whispered in Cade's ear.

Cade scowled at Rivo and jerked his arm out of Rivo's grip and walked out without acknowledging the request. But glanced back at him and gave a quick nod before leaving.

As they all made their way downstairs, Captain Tremlee ordered all soldiers to prepare for battle. They responded and began to rush to get their gear.

Rivo made his way back to the room he had been sharing with Pearce and Naomi. Every step he took felt heavier than the one before. *Tuval said he had thousands more hounds. We wouldn't stand a chance against those numbers. Was he bluffing? Is it worth finding out?*

He quickly got his gauntlets on and grabbed his two short swords. "Pearce, Naomi, I'll be right with you. I need to get something out of the meeting room real quick. I'll be right back," he told them, as he bolted out of the room.

He slipped inside the small meeting room and was both surprised and relieved to find Cade waiting for him.

With his arms crossed, Cade stood wearing his signature scowl on his face. "What, Rivo?" he grunted as he uncrossed his arms and balled his fists, almost as if he was about to pummel the young Beastkiller. "We have nothing to talk about. You messed up and caused all this," he snarled.

"I'm going to fight Tuval myself," Rivo blurted out.

"What? No way, kid!" Cade snapped, heading for the door.

"Cade, wait!" Rivo said as he grabbed Cade's arm again.

He violently swung his arm free of Rivo's grasp. "Get your damn hands off me!"

Rivo pulled his arms back and glared at Cade intently. "Cade, please just listen!" he pleaded.

"No!" Cade growled as he turned toward the door again.

"We can end the war now, Cade!" Rivo bit back.

Cade sighed as he sagged his shoulders and rubbed his forehead in exasperation. "What?"

"I can fight him, just me," Rivo said plainly. "Nobody else needs to get killed."

"Stop deluding yourself, boy," Cade chided. "You can't beat Tuval."

Rivo nervously swallowed. "I don't have to," he said. "I just need to get him and those other Greater Haundo in the guard tower. I tell him I'll only fight if he releases the hostages. Once the hostages are freed, you fire a cannon to take down the tower."

"Killing the Greater Haundo," Cade said, his voice unimpressed. "And you."

"Ending the war," Rivo corrected him emphatically. "Just one casualty."

"You," Cade replied.

Rivo stood silently. It felt so real hearing someone else say it. *Is there any possible way I can make it out alive?* he pondered. *I beat Drokner; maybe I can beat him too.*

"So eager for glory that you're willing to die for it," Cade said as he shook his head, his back still facing Rivo.

"It's not about that, Cade," Rivo pleaded. "All those Greater Haundo in one place. We'll never have another opportunity like this. They won't see it coming."

"Tremlee would have our heads."

Rivo held his breath, *I think he's starting to see my point,* he thought. "Since when did you care what he thinks?" he asked, almost daring Cade to answer.

"How do I know you won't change your mind at the last second?"

Rivo knew he had to answer without hesitation. Otherwise, he might be tempted to change his mind. This was his life that he was putting on the line. "On my Father's honor, I won't back down," he swore, his heart racing and his breathing getting heavier. *I just did it, there's no going back now. I have to go through with it; there's no running away.*

Cade let out a deep and disgruntled sigh, then turned his head slightly. "I'll make my way to the cannons," he said grudgingly. "I'll fire as soon as I see the hostages leave, and when they leave, you try to make a break for it too. There's still a slim chance for you to make it out of this."

Rivo's breathing didn't relax in spite of Cade agreeing to the plan. *It's settled. This is it. I'm going, and I won't make it back.*

Cade made his way out and turned his head in Rivo's direction one last time. "Oh, and by the way," he added, "this talk never happened. We both acted on our own. I shot at the tower when I thought all our men were gone, and I didn't know you were inside. Got it?" he said firmly.

"Yeah...yeah, I got it," Rivo replied, hoping Cade couldn't hear what he felt was a noticeable trembling in his voice.

Cade left the meeting room. Rivo stood alone, his mouth dry, his breathing shallow and shaky. "I'm—I'm scared," he whispered as he braced himself against the cold stone wall of the meeting room.

He struggled to make his way out. He knew if he went out the door, there was a chance Naomi or Pearce would spot him and put an end to his plan. He would have to climb out the window. Part of him was hoping there was a way out of this, but it was too late. *That was stupid. I just threw my life away,* he thought. *And now it's too late, Cade's already agreed to do his part. On top of that, I swore on Father's honor that I would follow through. Dammit,* he lamented. *I got caught up in the moment, said what I felt I had to in order to impress that bastard.*

Rivo slowly rubbed his face. "No!" he said adamantly. "It was the right thing to do. For the people here at the outpost. For Greencourt. It was the right decision... I'm doing it."

He slowly opened the window and climbed out, careful to make sure nobody saw him. Once outside, he collected himself as best he could and made his way toward the guard tower.

Rivo of Greencourt, Rivo the Beastkiller, was heading out to meet his fate.

"That was without a doubt the most terrified I'd ever been in my entire life," said Spirit Rivo.

Chapter 24

Like a Smith's Hammer

"It's a simple question, Renee. Why can't you just answer it?" a young Vickie asked her sister.

"Because it's childish and dumb, Vick," Renee replied.

"Well, we *are* children, Renee," Vickie retorted, wagging her head. "You're eleven, I'm fourteen. This is the kind of thing kids our age talk about."

The two young girls were chatting in the woods on a sunny afternoon while eating a pile of food Renee had stolen from some street vendors.

"It's just dumb, Vick," Renee replied with a mouth full of bread. "Besides, it'll never happen to me."

Vickie paced back and forth, throwing her hands up in frustration. "Why can't you just give an answer?" Vickie pressed. "If a boy you loved was in danger, and you had to risk your own life to save his, would you?"

Renee dropped her shoulders and rolled her eyes. "Vick, love like that is a fairytale. It's not real—at least, not for people like me."

"Oh, Renee," Vickie groaned as she leaned against a nearby tree. "Stop selling yourself short like that. You're a cute girl, cuter than you think. You are *my* sister after all." Vickie said, holding her chin up proudly with her eyes haughty.

"That's just it," Renee responded, shaking her head. "Not cute compared to you. Boys all just go for gorgeous girls like you. I'm invisible to them," she sneered.

Vickie sighed and rolled her eyes. "Why can't you just answer the question, Renee?" she pleaded, leaning in Renee's direction.

Renee stood up straight. "I already told you, Vick," she said sharply, stepping toward her big sister, her eyes wide, the irritation on her face showing. "It. Will. Never. Happen!"

***

Rivo approached the large stone tower, his heart racing, breathing heavily. It had a door in the side and open windows every few feet around; the tower stood over twenty feet tall. As he got close, the guards, in a standoff with the Haundo, saw him walk past.

"Kid, what in the stars' light are you doing?" one of them asked.

Rivo, still looking straight at the tower, ignored the guards' question ."Haundo!" he shouted.

The door slowly opened. Tuval, the massive beast, walked out, glaring at Rivo. "Don't waste my time, boy," he snarled. "I'm waiting for Rivo of Greencourt. Now, go back to your pack before I eat you alive."

"I am Rivo of Greencourt. The one you're looking for." He was so shaken that he was barely able to get the words out.

Tuval looked at Rivo and laughed. "This is a joke, right? You're telling me this puny runt killed my brother?"

Rivo's chest was heaving, his forehead covered in beads of sweat. "Yes. It was me," he replied, hoping Tuval didn't notice his legs shaking.

The Greater Haundo studied Rivo up and down, panting heavily. "Well, come to think of it, you do match their description. Though I thought you would be a little older and bigger."

Upon hearing this, Rivo thought to himself, *Whose description?*

"So, after all you've done, this is the place you die, huh?" Tuval remarked.

Rivo's heart was pounding like a smith's hammer. "Inside the tower," he said flatly. "And you have to release the hostages," he added, trying to keep his words few, worried that Tuval might sense any signs of fear in his voice.

The beast laughed again. "Fine," he scoffed. "Whatever you say." Tuval gestured for Rivo to follow him and walked back to the tower.

As Rivo walked in behind the giant beast, another Greater Haundo walked up and shut the door, then placed the wooden beam used to keep it locked so nobody else could come in. Rivo scanned the room. As he thought, there were three other greater Haundo inside with Tuval, all looking at Rivo with sinister grins. He looked for the hostages, but all that was there were a few dead Wyverly guards. The Haundo had already killed their hostages.

Dammit, he thought. *What a monster, they didn't have to kill these men.* Then his blood ran cold as another thought occurred to him. *The hostages' release was supposed to be Cade's signal to fire the cannon.*

Rivo grimaced at the sight of the dead soldiers. "I see you killed your hostages," he said as he gripped his swords. "I'm going to let you know that I won't go down without a fight."

"Of course," Tuval scoffed. "It's always more fun when the food fights back," he replied. "But before I kill you. I have one question," he said, taking a step toward Rivo. "Who killed Brooner? Tell me, and I promise to kill you quickly."

Rivo's eyes met Tuval's—he clenched his teeth and tightened his jaw. "I'm not telling," he replied firmly, raising his swords.

"Have it your way," Tuval growled. "If he's here, we'll find him and kill him."

With that, Rivo charged.

Tuval effortlessly swatted him to the side, laughing as he did.

Rivo was jarred but kept going at him. He was getting a few hits in, cutting the beast's arms as he blocked, but the Haundo showed no signs of pain. He then grabbed Rivo around the torso with one hand and slammed his back hard against the wall. Rivo let out a shout of pain and collapsed to the ground, the wind knocked out of him, and his back was throbbing. He was simply no match for this massive beast.

Tuval taunted him as he lay face down, struggling to get up. "Well...I need to keep my word on something," he said as he walked to the corner of the room where there on the ground, lay a familiar-looking cloth sack.

Rivo was able to lift himself up enough to see what Tuval was doing. He pulled out a long, wooden tube. Rivo had seen this strange-looking piece of wood before. It was the bamboo shaft that Bon had used to hold his drawings. His heart sank as he noticed that it was covered in blood spatters.

***

As the fight was going on in the tower, there was chaos in the complex.

Vickie, Judd, and Renee were all getting their gear together, trying to figure out what exactly happened. They heard Captain Tremlee screaming at the soldiers.

"Stars be damned, find Cade! Somebody better find him! Damn those two!" he shouted as he marched frantically around the complex, barking out orders.

The three took the opportunity to check on their old friends and find out what was going on.

As they all ran to the room Rivo, Pearce, and Naomi had shared on the second floor. They walked into what looked like a warzone. Naomi was throwing things across the room and screaming.

"Damn you! Damn you! Damn you, Rivo!" she shrieked as Pearce made futile efforts to calm her.

"Naomi! Pearce! What's wrong!?" hollered a frantic Vickie.

Naomi now sat on the floor, leaning against the bed with her head in her hands, sobbing.

"Pearce, what is going on?" Judd pleaded.

Pearce sat on the bed across from Naomi, staring at her and not registering the question.

As Judd went to sit beside Pearce, Vickie knelt by Naomi and gently brushed her friend's hair with her fingers. Renee scanned the room, noticing through all the knocked-over chairs, clothing, and bedding Naomi had thrown, Rivo was nowhere to be found. "Guys...where is Rivo?" she asked cautiously.

Naomi was finally able to speak to them through her tears. "Rivo," she sobbed, "is in the tower, getting killed by those monsters. He left to fight that thing all by himself."

The room went completely silent, aside from Naomi's sobbing. They all stood in disbelief. Vickie's eyes went wide as she covered her mouth. She looked over at Pearce, who was still staring blankly at his wife. "He couldn't have," she gasped. "Naomi," she said softly as she placed her arm around Naomi. "I'm so sorry."

"Oh man, I caused them so much grief. I feel terrible," said Spirit Rivo.

In addition to Naomi's crying. Another sound could now be heard. Renee was breathing fast and loud. Vickie looked at her. Renee was still standing, with her fists clenched, tears going down her cheeks. She looked at the second-story window facing the tower, with a wild look in her eyes.

Vickie got up to talk to her, holding her hands out, trying to calm her sister. "Renee," she said with her voice low and soft, "I know you have feelings for that boy. Whatever you're thinking of doing right now. I promise it won't help anything. Please, Renee. There's nothing we can—"

Vickie was interrupted by Renee, who grabbed a nearby stool and hurled it through the glass window. Before anyone could react, Renee bolted and jumped out of the second-story window, to the cries and screams of Vickie.

"No, Renee! No!" Vickie shrieked. She ran towards the window but was held back by Judd. "They're gonna kill you! Renee! Renee!" Vickie screamed helplessly.

"No way. Renee? What on earth are you doing!" gasped Spirit Rivo.

Renee had jumped out of the window and landed on the ground; her adrenaline was pumping so much that she didn't even register the pain from the impact. She ran at full speed to the tower, broken glass crunching underneath her feet as tears streamed from her eyes. She ran so fast that the guards and even the Haundo standing outside couldn't stop her in time. All to the sound of Vickie screaming for her sister from the room.

Chapter 25

An Amber Glow

Back in the tower, Rivo's eyes opened wide, and he started breathing heavily, his lip quivering at the sight of the blood-spattered bamboo. "Where did you get that?" he asked, still struggling to get his breath back.

"Oh, I think you know where I got this," Tuval said with an evil smirk.

"What—What did you do?" Rivo asked, his facial muscles twitching.

"I did what I had to do to get the information I sought," Tuval replied, holding the bamboo shaft in one hand, waving it in front of him.

"What. Did. You. Do to them?" Rivo growled.

"You see," Tuval replied calmly, "We had been tracking your scent for quite a while. But we always just seemed to be a couple of steps behind you. What made it more difficult is that I thought we were looking for some brave and mighty warrior, not some child."

Tuval began pacing back and forth. "I sent some scouts to find Drokner's body so they could pick up your scent." He began tapping the bamboo shaft against his palm like a club. "As I met up with them, a strange thing happened. Your scent trailed off into two different directions."

Rivo's eyes darted back and forth, his mind racing to piece together what he had just heard. *What! How?* He thought, perplexed.

"I sent a small group of hounds one way, ordering them to slaughter any and all humans they came across. But," Tuval went on, "they never returned. I'm guessing they must have run into you and your pack."

He must be talking about the Haundo we encountered in Thorndale. Rivo realized.

"But I just so happened to lead the pack that followed the other path with your scent."

My scent? Rivo thought, *How did it lead them in two different directions?* Rivo's heart nearly stopped. *Oh no!*

"Here you go, boy. I think this belongs to you." Tuval snickered as he dropped a red handkerchief in front of Rivo. It was the same handkerchief he had given to Bon earlier.

Rivo grabbed the handkerchief and tucked it in his vest. His breathing grew erratic, and his eyes welled with tears. "What did you do!" he screamed.

"Well, we finally found some valuable information. We stumbled across these disgusting forest humans. I couldn't get any information out of them at first. So I decided to persuade them a little," Tuval said, chuckling.

"Tuval...you're gonna tell me what you did to them—now," Rivo replied through his clenched teeth.

"I noticed there was a young boy among them. I figured he'd be a valuable resource for obtaining some information."

"Bon!... No!" cried Rivo.

"Oh, don't worry, I didn't have to kill that filthy little runt. Once I... *persuaded* them, they started talking. The younger redhead wouldn't talk—it was the older one—that weasel ratted you out!" Tuval started laughing with a wicked cackle. "Just when you thought you had a friend. Right, Rivo?" he scoffed.

"Zim...Zon...I'm sorry," Rivo cried.

"Oh, you'll get your chance to apologize to them, don't worry."

"What are you talking about?"

"So after they told me who you were and I found those damned drawings, I decided to thank them for their cooperation."

"Damn you, Tuval. What did you do!?" demanded Rivo.

"So I took this piece of scrap," Tuval said as he waved the bamboo in front of Rivo's face, "and I bashed those two red-headed bastards' skulls in with it."

Rivo started trembling with fury. His eyes wide open, his breath shaking. "You..."

"As the rest of them ran away screaming and crying, I made sure to promise them that I was gonna use this to bash your skull in too," Tuval added with a wicked chuckle.

Rivo hoped that the same power that came to him when he fought Drokner would help him now. He felt it for a brief moment, his eyes flickered bright amber, then faded, along with the surge of power.

Tuval stood still, staring intently at Rivo. "Was that the glare?" he whispered in a low growl. "With this child? It can't be... But that would explain how you defeated Drokner." A smile crept back across his face. "Either way, it appears you no longer possess it."

Though the mysterious power never came to him, Rivo's rage took over nonetheless. "You...," he said, grabbing one of his swords and gripping it so tight, his knuckles turned white. "I'm gonna kill you!" he shouted as he leaped to his feet and delivered a deadly blow, putting a deep gash across the Greater Haundo's throat.

This sent Tuval reeling back, but he didn't fall down. He looked at Rivo and smirked. Rivo stood stunned that the fatal blow didn't kill the creature. He noticed a light underneath the fur on Tuval's chest began to glow a bright amber, and the wound that Rivo had dealt healed completely.

Rivo stood in shock at the sight. "How?" he muttered.

He hardly had a chance to take in what he had just seen when he was clobbered across the side of the face with the bamboo shaft by Tuval. Rivo fell on his back as he rolled over and tried to get up The beast struck him again, this time in his back, between the shoulders. He struggled to rise, only to be struck again in the same spot on his back. Rivo began to lose consciousness.

Tuval raised his hand again to strike, this time aiming for Rivo's skull, but was interrupted by Renee, who had jumped in through the window and stood between the monster and an unconscious Rivo. She stood with a knife in each hand, glaring at the beast furiously.

"Renee? That was... Renee, who ran in to save me?..." Spirit Rivo said in disbelief.

"What is this?" Tuval scoffed as he swatted her to the side. She sprang right back up and ran between them again, knives still drawn. Tuval paused, his yellow eyes narrowed. "So, you wanna die first, huh? Fine by me!" the beast shouted as he raised the shaft like a club towards Renee, who didn't flinch.

Just at that moment, a massive explosion erupted in the tower. Despite not receiving Rivo's signal, Cade had fired the cannon. Knowing that he was about to get caught by Captain Tremlee and the others, Cade took a chance and opened fire. He could only assume the hostages had been killed and was unaware that Renee had run in.

The explosion sent Tuval and the other Haundo flying. The tower was beginning to collapse. Renee grabbed an unconscious Rivo and dragged him out of the window she had come in through.

Once she got outside of the tower window, she screamed for help, "Somebody get him, please! He's badly injured!"

By then, Pearce, Vickie, Naomi, and Judd had made it outside. They ran to grab the two and get them away from the tower as it collapsed on Tuval and the other Haundo trapped inside.

The rest of the soldiers thought that this was part of the plan. The tower had collapsed, and all the Greater Haundo were thought to be dead. They used this moment to attack. The remaining Haundo backed away as the Wyverly forces attacked.

Tuval roared as he emerged from the rubble. He was the only survivor of those in the tower; the other Greater Haundo inside had been crushed in the collapse. The amber light on Tuval's chest glowed bright; his injuries were beginning to heal, but it appeared that he would need time to fully recover.

Tuval barked some indecipherable orders to the remaining hounds as they fled from the outpost.

The Wyverly soldiers had sustained heavy casualties but were ready to pursue until ordered to stand down by a furious Captain Tremlee.

"Renee...you loved me so much...that you risked everything," Spirit Rivo groaned, lamenting over the trouble his actions had caused, as he again found himself being carried away to his next destination.

Chapter 26

A Living Nightmare

Spirit Rivo found himself in the infirmary on the first floor of the complex, looking over his past self lying in bed. It was nighttime now, and Rivo had been there for almost eight hours at that point. He was still unconscious but kept under guard due to his earlier actions. He was going to face trouble whenever he woke up. Captain Tremlee was still furious with both him and Cade, who was confined to his room, effectively under house arrest. Rivo was to face the same fate. Captain Tremlee was torn on how exactly to handle them. "Their actions did save the outpost and, no doubt, hundreds of lives," he said. "But they disobeyed a direct order, and something has to be done."

Renee sat in a chair next to Rivo's bed the whole time. She hadn't left his side for a second, despite the pleas of Vickie, Judd, and the others. Her eyes were red and puffy from crying over Rivo and her nerve-racking encounter with Tuval. She sat in a huddled position on the chair, hugging her knees. It was the exact way she sat when she learned her daddy had died, and later when Vickie told her that their mother wasn't coming back.

"Renee," Spirit Rivo whispered, "how long have you been here watching over me?"

Vickie walked in again to try to reason with her sister. "Renee, I told you when we first met him. He's a fool. He's going to get himself killed and take you down with him. I should have never let that boy within ten feet of you."

Just then, Naomi walked in, and Vickie was careful not to speak ill of Rivo around her. "Renee, Pearce, and I are beyond grateful for saving Rivo like you did. You almost got killed. I'm sorry you felt like you had to do that for him. But thank you," Naomi said as she walked up to Renee and patted her on the shoulder.

"It's okay. It was my choice," Renee replied softly, looking at the ground.

Naomi then turned to Vickie. "I'm sorry she got dragged into this. I know how you feel. Believe me," she said as she glanced toward Rivo.

"I'm just glad Renee is okay," said Vickie. She then turned back toward her sister. "Please don't do anything like that again, Renee, especially over a boy."

Spirit Rivo turned his focus to the real Rivo, lying in bed, still unconscious. He saw his face twitching and grimacing. "This must be when I had that horrible nightmare," he said as he looked on.

***

Rivo found himself in a dream...or was it a dream? This felt different from any other dream he'd had—he was both there and yet not there.

It was nighttime in a forest somewhere. There were some campfires spread about. He heard screams and hollers...and growls.

What is this? he wondered. He scanned the area and saw bodies scattered about. And there were the Haundo, chasing and killing people.

Then he saw a boy on his knees, crying and watching helplessly as those around him were slaughtered. "Bon!" Rivo shouted. "Bon, what's happening?" he asked, to no response.

He can't hear me, Rivo realized as he looked around frantically.

"Help!" Bon cried as a Haundo was approaching him. The beast was about to pounce on the boy when it was stopped in its tracks by a spear thrust through its side.

Rivo looked over to see Zon marching up to the creature and pulling his spear from its body.

"Flee!" he shouted desperately to the remaining forest folk, "flee!"

As his people fled, more Haundo came to pursue them. Zon fought them off with his spear, killing one, then another, and another. Out of the darkness, a horrifying growl could be heard.

"Black Fang!" a voice shouted. A wave of black energy struck Zon, and he collapsed to the ground, writhing in pain.

"Zon!" shouted Bon, as he watched his brother fall. The boy ran to aid his older brother when he felt a hand grab him by the back of the neck and lift him off the ground.

The boy's eyes filled with terror as he came face to face with a giant Greater Haundo, its menacing yellow eyes striking fear in the child.

"Tuval, no!" Rivo shouted.

The beast growled at the boy, staring him down, "I smell his scent on you, boy. But you aren't him." Tuval directed his attention to the red handkerchief wrapped around the boy's arm, "I'm looking for the one this rag belongs to. Where is he?" the Haundo asked the quivering boy.

Bon was speechless, his breath shaking with fear.

"Answer me, you little runt!" Tuval shouted as he shook the boy.

"You get your hands off him, Tuval!" Rivo hollered.

Bon's bamboo shaft fell off his back, and his drawings spilled out as it hit the ground. Tuval looked down to see drawings of a man in a blue vest stabbing a large Haundo.

"What's this?" Tuval asked, as he knelt down to study the drawings, letting out a low growl. "Is this the one who killed Drokner?"

Bon remained silent, still in the beast's firm grip. Tuval stood and let out a loud roar, "Somebody answer me or I'll break this runt's neck!"

"Aye!" Zim shouted, running toward Tuval. He set his spear down on the ground as he knelt before the massive Haundo.

A sinister smile crept across Tuval's face as he gazed upon the cowering leader of the forest folk, "Talk," he grunted.

"No, Father," groaned Zon as he lay on the ground, moaning in pain.

"Rivo..." muttered Zim, his eyes welling up in tears. "Rivo of Greencourt."

Tuval chuckled as he dropped Bon and grabbed the bamboo shaft. "Perfect," said the beast, as he walked past Zim and made his way toward Zon. "Was that so hard? You just saved your worthless life."

The Greater Haundo hovered over Zon and raised the piece of bamboo over his head, "You, on the other hand, just threw your life away."

"No, Tuval, there's no need to do this. He's defenseless!" Rivo shouted.

Tuval brought down the bamboo shaft like a hammer, striking Zon across the skull again and again. The crack of the impact echoed through the woods. Zon lay on the forest floor, dead.

"No!" cried Zim as he charged the Greater Haundo.

Tuval glared at Zim. "You fool, I was actually going to spare you," he said as he struck Zim across the head with the bamboo.

Zim fell to the ground, alive, but struggling to move. Tuval raised his arm again, delivering a final blow that ended Zim's life.

"Damn you, Tuval!" screamed Rivo, as he watched helplessly.

"Zon! Papa!" Bon shrieked as he fell to his hands and knees, sobbing.

The boy then sat up as he noticed the other Haundo surrounding him. He scooted back, his eyes full of terror.

As the hounds approached, Tuval intervened. "Halt!" he shouted. "Don't waste your time. That runt doesn't have enough meat on him to be worth it, you'd be spitting out bones for a fortnight," he added, as he approached Bon and knelt in front of him.

"Boy," he growled, "if you see Rivo of Greencourt before I do, you tell him Tuval is coming." The beast looked over at the two dead bodies of Zim and Zon, "And tell him that he'll meet the same fate as those two," he added, standing back up, barking a command to his hounds. One of them grabbed Bon's cloth sack, the last of his possessions, and left the camp.

Bon knelt on the ground, his head in his hands, as he cried over the bodies of his brother and father.

"Zim, Zon...Bon, I'm sorry," Rivo cried. "Tuval...you're gonna pay for this."

***

Spirit Rivo looked upon his past self in the infirmary, slowly stirring himself awake. "That was a terrible dream, wasn't it?" Spirit Rivo remarked somberly. "I wish there was something I could do to help you right now."

The real Rivo started to moan and slowly opened his eyes. "Zim... Zon...Bon...I'm sorry," he groaned, shifting in his bed.

"Rivo! You're up! Thank the stars!" Naomi shouted.

Renee stood up, wide-eyed, covering her mouth with her hand. Rivo was going to be okay.

"Naomi?" asked Rivo faintly.

"Rivo! I'm so glad you're awake," Naomi said with tears in her eyes as she bolted toward him. "Oh, Rivo," she moaned. "That was stupid, what you did. It was stupid and reckless!"

"I'm sorry. I didn't see another way," he said, rubbing the side of his face. "Did we get them, the Haundo?" he asked.

Renee was quietly sobbing, stepping back in hopes that Rivo wouldn't notice.

"It looks like three of the big ones were killed," Naomi replied, kneeling beside him as she gently ran her fingers through his hair. "That really big one, Tuval, survived somehow. But they all fled."

Vickie stepped toward the bed. "Your foolish plan worked, Rivo. Somehow," she added with a bite to her voice.

"Okay, good," Rivo said, not catching her scolding tone. "Where's everyone else? Are they okay?"

"Pearce and Judd are back in our room. They've both been crying their eyes out over you," Naomi said, shaking her head with a light laugh. "They didn't want anyone to see them that way."

"And Renee has been here the whole time. She's the one who—" Vickie was interrupted by Pearce busting through the door.

"The Haundo are back already. They're after the armory!" he shouted. "They were spotted by the guards. It's not all of them, and there's no sign of the big one. But they're heading towards the armory and definitely look like they're coming to attack."

"Oh, no!" Naomi said, jumping to her feet. "Let's get ready. We have to move quickly."

"We can take them. Like I said, it's not a large force. The Captain thinks they must be trying to destroy the cannons. There aren't enough of them to make a run at the complex." He looked at Rivo and nodded, "I see you're up, Rivo. Glad you're okay." He then looked over at Naomi and the others, "I think someone should stay here with him."

Naomi and Vickie both looked at Renee. "I'll stay," Renee told them.

As the others left to prepare. Rivo, forgetting the condition he was in, started to sit up.

"Just lie down, Rivo," Renee said as she looked out the window.

"I need to help," Rivo groaned as he struggled to get up.

She quickly turned toward him, "I SAID *LIE DOWN!*" she shrieked in a voice so loud and shrill it could have shattered the windows.

At that, Rivo quickly lay back down. He had never heard a scream like that come out of her before. "What's wrong, Renee?" he asked gently.

Renee sat back down in the chair, bent over with her head in her hands, quietly sobbing, "Just lie down, please."

An exhausted Rivo slipped in and out of consciousness over the next couple of hours as the others went to defend the armory. Renee sat in the chair next to his bed, relieved that he was going to be okay, but still feeling overwhelmed by the events of the day. She wasn't ready to talk to Rivo about what happened in the tower just yet.

***

Pearce and the others returned, the expression on their faces frustrated and dejected.

Renee stood up. "What happened?" she asked.

Pearce ran his hand through his hair in frustration. "We didn't get there in time," he said flatly. "By the time we arrived, the guards had killed all the beasts, but not before they destroyed all our cannons." He drew a deep breath and sighed. "Evidently, this was a suicide mission for them."

"Why the cannons?" Rivo asked, sitting up in his bed. He stood up briefly but then noticed Renee had turned around and shot him a vicious glare, so he quickly sat back down.

Pearce walked to the window, bracing one hand against the wall. "The cannon blast that destroyed the tower earlier must have really scared them. I bet they've never seen anything like it before," he replied. "We just ran into Captain Tremlee. He thinks this must mean their base of operations is in a similar stone structure. They must have been afraid we'd find them and blow it apart."

Naomi leaned against the wall by the foot of his bed and stared blankly at the floor. "They got the cannons, but the Captain says they overplayed their hand," she said as she crossed her arms. "He wants to meet with us to discuss possible locations for their hideout and a counterattack."

"What do I need to do?" asked Rivo.

Naomi quickly turned toward him, her forehead wrinkled. "I'm sorry, Rivo, but after that stunt you and Cade pulled, Captain Tremlee has you both under house arrest," she said firmly. "You aren't to leave this room. Pearce and I will be the only ones from our group joining them."

Rivo slowly shook his head and rubbed his eyes in irritation. "I should have figured," he sighed.

Vickie went up to her sister. "Come on, Renee, they've got a guard stationed outside the door now. We need to go back to our room. Visiting hours are over." She shot a glance over at Rivo, "Stars be damned, Rivo, you have no idea how lucky you are right now."

Rivo nodded as Vickie turned and left the room. Before following her, Judd walked over and put his hand on Rivo's shoulder. "I'm glad you're okay, too, Rivo. Real glad."

"Thanks, Judd," Rivo replied as he gently patted the big man's hand.

Renee walked up to the bed. "Rivo, I'm really glad too." She placed her hand on his arm and bent over to kiss his forehead. "Please be more careful, okay?" she added before she turned to leave.

"I will. Thank you, Renee."

As the room emptied, only Pearce and Naomi remained. Rivo began to think about his battle with Tuval. How he hit him with what should have been a fatal strike. But Tuval healed himself right in front of his eyes. *Could it be that I was just seeing things? Did I somehow miss him?* he wondered. *No, I'm sure my strike landed. It was something to do with that amber light on his chest. What sort of magic is that? And then,* he thought, *he somehow survived the tower collapse. How is this possible?*

Rivo turned to Pearce and Naomi, who were getting ready to retire for the evening themselves. "Can you tell Captain Tremlee something for me?" he asked.

"What is it?" asked Pearce.

Rivo rubbed the bridge of his nose, worried that they wouldn't believe him. "I think Tuval...is invincible," he said, almost in disbelief as the words came out of his mouth.

Pearce and Naomi both looked at each other, confused, then at Rivo.

"What makes you say that?" asked Naomi.

"Is it because he survived the tower collapse?" Pearce interjected. "Those things have an incredible pain tolerance, Rivo. And I'm sure that one's much stronger than Drokner or the others. I wouldn't read into it too much."

"It's not just that," Rivo replied, shaking his head. "When I was fighting him in the tower. I slashed him across the throat, hard. I thought for sure that I had killed him; there's no way anything could have survived that. But his wound healed up, right in front of me."

"Rivo, are you sure you saw that?" asked Pearce, with his eyebrows furrowed.

"Positive," he replied. "There was something under his fur on his chest. It was a light, like a gem or something. It lit up as he healed, almost like whatever that thing was, was restoring his body."

"Was it an amber colored light?" asked Pearce.

Rivo nearly jumped out of his bed. "How did you know?" he asked.

Pearce and Naomi both looked at each other, then back at Rivo. "Some of the soldiers by the tower said that they swore they saw a glowing amber light coming from Tuval's chest when he rose from the rubble," said Naomi as she paced back and forth. "Nobody was sure what to make of it, but it looks like now we might know."

"This definitely changes things," Pearce remarked, anxiously rubbing his chin. "We'll make sure to tell them all about this. You just get some rest, we'll tell you what we come up with later."

As Naomi and Pearce said their goodbyes. Rivo, now all alone with his thoughts, began to reflect on the battle with Tuval. *He survived the tower collapse. How can he possibly be beaten?* He wondered. Then another thought occurred to him, one that hadn't crossed his mind until just then. *How...did I survive the collapse?* As he lay in his bed, he began racking his brain, trying to remember what had happened before the tower fell. He had been beaten badly by Tuval and was slipping in and out of consciousness. *Somebody was there. I remember now, but who was it? I could hardly see them, but they were definitely there. They must have carried me out of the tower as it fell. But who?* Rivo rubbed his eyes in frustration; he never got a good look at the person who pulled him from the collapsing tower. *It had to have been one of the soldiers in the area,* he concluded. *I guess that's not a question I can get an answer to right now. I'll just have to find out who it was and thank them later.*

Rivo sighed in resignation and picked up his copy of *Tales of the Star Sage,* flipping through it again. He stopped at *The Battle in the Star Temple,* one of the tales his parents would read to him as a child. The story where the Star Sage defeated the Demon King Garel with the power of the Guardian's Glare and then sealed him away. *The orb that Garel had taken,* he thought. *It made him invincible. It was placed in his chest.* Rivo grew uneasy as he started noticing some shocking similarities.

They hunted humans for food and sport, the story would say.

Rivo's heart started pounding as he broke out in a cold sweat. His thoughts began racing. *The orb. The amber light on Tuval's chest, how they hunted humans...the Glare...Tuval mentioned it when we were fighting. How did he know about that? What made him think that I had it?*

Without realizing it, Rivo had dropped the book on the ground. He rolled out of his bed, his legs started shaking, and he fell to his knees. "It can't be," he gasped. "It's a fairytale—it can't be real!" His breathing became erratic as he tried to reason with himself. "Even if it was real, he was sealed away. Forever."

The nursery rhyme that the children of Wyverly Kingdom were all taught came to mind. *Nobody knows how the shooting star hears, but a shooting star's wish can last ten thousand years.*

"Ten thousand years," he whispered. "No. That's just a silly song for kids. And the stories—they were just fairytales."

He thought about the Guardian's Glare, and how even Tuval seemed to fear it. It was said that the Glare could give a burst of supernatural power to its wielder if their loved ones were in danger. He thought of his battle against Drokner, how he was somehow able to get up after being attacked by the monster, and killed the beast with one strike. He remembered when he was a boy, how he almost knocked Pearce's head off his body in a sparring match one time, after his father told him to act as if his family was in danger.

Rivo sat there on his hands and knees on the cold stone floor of the infirmary, his breathing heavy as his mind began to piece everything together. "That was the Guardian's Glare," he gasped. "That's how I beat Drokner. That's how I nearly killed Pearce that time when we were kids."

He sat against the side of his bed, his hands atop his head and his eyes wide. "But how? How come the Glare didn't work when I fought Tuval?"

The nursery rhyme echoed in his mind again. *Nobody knows how the shooting star hears, but a shooting star's wish can last ten thousand years.*

"The nursery rhyme," he said. "But what does that have to do with the Guardian's Gl—"

He stopped himself as he thought of another passage: *Wyverly's Wish.* "Wyverly the Star Sage made a final wish while on his deathbed," Rivo remarked as he looked at the book lying by his side. "He died shortly after his battle with Garel. Before he passed, the Star Sage called his children to his side and made a final wish...his secret wish...must have been to pass the power of the Guardian's Glare onto his descendants..."

Nobody knows how the shooting star hears, but a shooting star's wish can last ten thousand years.

"That's it," he muttered in disbelief. "It all makes sense now. How the Haundo came out of nowhere, and how I can no longer summon that power."

Rivo grabbed *The Tales of the Star Sage* and looked upon it with awe. "The ten thousand years are up, and the power of Wyverly's wishes has faded. Garel is back, the seal is no longer in place, and the Guardian's Glare is no more." He felt his hands shaking and a lump form in his throat as he had an epiphany. "Tuval...is Garel...and I...am a descendant of the Star Sage."

Chapter 27

An Agreement of Sorts

As Rivo lay in his bed, pondering this revelation about Tuval, about himself, there was a knock at his door.

"Come in," he said wearily.

In walked Captain Tremlee, holding a stack of parchment papers. "Rivo. Glad you're doing better," he said as he walked past Rivo and stared at the nighttime sky. "I suppose you felt that was awfully noble, what you and Cade did—Working behind my back and disobeying a direct order."

Rivo did his best to collect himself and focus on the Captain. "I'm sorry, sir," he replied as he sat himself up. "Aren't you supposed to be meeting with Pearce and Naomi?"

"I just saw them," Tremlee responded, "I told them to wait in the small meeting room for me. I wanted to have a word with you first."

He continued, "I overheard what you mentioned to your cousins before they left. You believe Tuval to be invincible, is that right?" he asked.

"I don't see any other explanation," Rivo replied.

"The eyewitness reports we received before he fled, along with intel we've received from our scouts, seem to point in that direction as well," The Captain stated as he turned back toward Rivo and held up the papers.

Rivo saw that the papers were mostly drawings. "Sir," he asked, "are those drawings from the scouts?"

"They are," answered the Captain. "We've made an agreement of sorts with the Forest Folk; they've been providing some valuable intel."

"You know, the first time someone called me a *Beastkiller*, it was them. Is that where you got that from?"

"It is. Very astute," the Captain replied with a nod.

Rivo immediately thought of Bon and the others. *Bon, I can't help but wonder what you're going through right now,* he thought. *I'm so sorry for all of this.*

"Well, what are we going to do now?" asked Rivo.

"We've been trying to find out this whole time where exactly these creatures came from. Thanks to the latest intel, we believe we have the answer," he said as he thoughtfully stroked his mustache. "The scouts found an old abandoned druid star temple deep in the woods, about half a day's journey northeast. It likely hasn't been used for centuries, maybe longer."

Rivo began to recall again the old fairytale his parents used to read to him. About how Garel was defeated in a temple and sealed away. *Should I mention Garel and the ten-thousand-year wish?* He wondered. *No, not now. There's no way he'd believe me.* "You want to attack?" he asked.

"According to our intel, Tuval stays inside the temple. His minions patrol the outside; there are about a thousand of them at that outpost. We know there are thousands more across Wyverly, but they have no leader, no Greater Haundo to guide them," Tremlee said as he took a breath to calm himself for his next remark. "Thanks to your and Cade's reckless actions," he said, shaking his head.

Rivo cracked a smile, "So this could be it? Taking out this base could basically end the war?"

"As irate as I am over your and Cade's actions, the Haundo were dealt a devastating blow, losing three of their leaders. So in a word, yes. But," said Tremlee as he began anxiously rubbing his chin. "The problem is," he paused to draw a deep breath, "Tuval isn't going to just stand by and let us wipe out his hounds." Tremlee paused again and looked Rivo directly in the eye, "We need to keep him from the battle on the field, or else he'll just cut us down. Rivo, there's only one person that he'd allow to distract him," the Captain hinted as he placed his hand on Rivo's shoulder.

Rivo's heart sank; he knew where this was going. "Me," he replied flatly, beginning to realize the point of this one-on-one visit, "you want me to go and fight him so the others can battle the Haundo without having to deal with him, right?"

"Not just you, Rivo. Cade will fight alongside you," the Captain told him as he patted him on his shoulder, "We're sending in the Beastkillers."

"Rivo's stomach turned as he looked to the ground. "Me and Cade against an invincible opponent in a fight to the death," he said, his voice stoic and low.

"Not a fight to the death, not if we can help it," Captain Tremlee replied as he walked back to the window. "I told you before, I don't believe in suicide missions. You just need to hold him off as long as you can. We've already sent for help from all the nearby outposts. With these numbers, we believe that we have a chance to take them out." He turned back to face Rivo. "You and Cade do what you must to survive, just keep Tuval occupied in the temple. Once we've defeated them on the outside, we'll join you and figure out some way to restrain him."

Rivo let out a weary sigh, "I don't see any easy way around this. You're right, the Beastkillers are the only ones that can do this...Besides, I wouldn't mind taking another shot at Tuval. I owe him one," he said as he felt Bon's handkerchief still tucked in his vest.

He saw Captain Tremlee crack a smile for the first time. He walked back towards Rivo and gave him another pat on the shoulder, "I like that spirit, soldier," he said as he turned to leave. "Oh, and get some rest, young man," he added before walking out the door. "I'd like for you, Cade, and me to get together in the war room first thing in the morning.

We'll do our preparations tomorrow, then the following morning, we march."

Chapter 28

A Promise

"I will watch out for him, Aunt Gwen, I promise," young Naomi sobbed as she knelt beside the bed, holding her aunt's hand.

"So will I, Miss Gwen. I'll treat him like my own brother," a tearful Pearce promised.

Rivo's mother, Gwen, lay dying in her bed, just a few months after losing her husband. "I'm so glad to have you two. Rivo is such a lucky boy to have such a loving cousin like you, Naomi. You've always been like a big sister to him, ever since the day he was born." Gwen said faintly, her time was almost up. She struggled to take a deep breath, "I would like to speak to Rivo one more time. Could you bring him in?"

"I'm here, Mother," Rivo said as he entered the room. He had been listening the whole time.

"Oh, Rivo. I'm so sorry you've had to deal with all of this at such a young age." Gwen said as she touched the side of his tearful face. "You know something that your father and I never told you? You were such an easy child to raise. Such a good-natured boy. And with an adventurous, fearless spirit, what others see as danger, you see as opportunity." Her breathing was labored as she wheezed for more air. "Oh, Rivo. You were my shining star. I always wished I could just hold you up for the whole world to see your light. Please, don't ever lose that light."

With that, Rivo's mother, Gwen, breathed her last breath. Rivo stood frozen at the sight, as Naomi fell to her hands and knees, sobbing.

She stood and hugged her young cousin. "From now on, Rivo, I'll be looking out for you. And I promise, I will *always* keep you safe."

***

The sun had barely risen when Rivo was awakened by a knock on his door. "Rivo, it's me and Pearce. Can we come in?" asked Naomi.

"Yeah, c'mon," said a groggy Rivo as he shuffled to gather his thoughts.

"How could you possibly sleep?" she asked, her forehead wrinkled, "Pearce and I hardly got a wink."

"Rivo, we spoke with Captain Tremlee last night," Pearce said as he followed her in. "He told us everything."

"He said you and Cade were going to fight Tuval. Do you understand what that means?" Naomi asked as she sat next to him on the bed. Rivo could tell from her red and swollen eyes that she had been crying. "Rivo, that's a suicide mission."

"Not if we can hold him off long enough, or if we can beat him," Rivo answered.

"Beat him? Rivo, he's invincible. You said so yourself," Pearce remarked as he threw his hands in the air. "Aren't you hurt? Can you even fight, Rivo?" he asked.

"I'll manage, I have to," he answered, "this is our best shot to end this once and for all."

"Rivo," Naomi said as she stood up, closing her eyes as she drew a deep breath, "do you remember what I promised your mother the day she died? I promised that I would keep you safe." She winced to choke back her tears. "I feel like by you going out to fight Tuval, I'm breaking that promise."

Rivo stood up to give Naomi a hug and put his hands on her shoulders, "Naomi," he said, "you *have* looked out for me. And thank you for that. Thank you for everything. Today...I'm releasing you from your promise. You don't owe me or Mother anything anymore. Do you understand?" Naomi nodded silently as she sat back down.

"Naomi, Pearce, I'd like to ask you something, and I know it may sound strange," Rivo said as he walked up to the window.

Pearce and Naomi exchanged glances and swallowed nervously, awaiting Rivo's question.

"Pearce, remember how we used to always spar when we were kids?"

"I do," Pearce nodded slowly.

"You would always win," Rivo said wearily. "Except, one time. Father had you strike me, then told me to retaliate. He tried to motivate me by telling me how everyone was in danger if I didn't step up to fight."

Pearce's heart began to race as he remembered all those years ago, the look in Rivo's eyes, glowing with amber fury as he rose to attack. "Yes," he answered hesitantly, "I remember."

"Did anything about me seem different to you? Did you notice anything in the way I looked?"

Pearce grimaced as he dug the memory back up, a memory he had hoped was false. "Yes, Rivo, your eyes, I swear I saw them glow bright amber, for just a moment."

Rivo turned to face him. "So, that must be it," he realized.

"*That must be* what?" Naomi asked as she stood up.

"The Guardian's Glare," answered Rivo as he stared blankly at the ground. "Did you see me when I killed Drokner? Did I have the same look in my eyes?" he asked.

"We couldn't see, but Vickie told me she saw the same thing," Naomi said nervously.

"Then that must settle it," Rivo concluded as he paced the room.

"Rivo, that stuff's just a fairytale for kids," Pearce remarked.

"I thought so too, but it's the only thing that makes sense right now," Rivo replied. He went on to tell them everything that occurred to him the night before.

"I remember that," said Spirit Rivo. "I told them everything: about Tuval being Garel, about the Star Sage's wishes, the Guardian's Glare, and the ten thousand-year power of them, all of it."

"So, you think this is all connected?" Pearce asked as he shook his head. "You think you're a descendant of the Star Sage?"

"That's what I'm starting to believe," Rivo replied as he turned to Naomi. "Naomi," he asked. "Did you ever see or hear about the eyes of the Guardian's Glare with my Father? This would mean he had it too."

Naomi's chest began to heave as she swallowed, her lip quivering. "Not with Uncle Frank, Rivo, but I have seen those eyes before...it was Aunt Gwen."

Rivo spun around and walked up to her. "My Mother?" he gasped. "When did you see this? How come you never said anything about it?"

"I guess I wasn't sure if I was just seeing things or not. I was so young when it happened," she said as her voice trailed off.

"When, Naomi? When did this happen?" asked Rivo.

"When you were still a toddler. You were too young to remember."

Rivo's eyes went wide. "The coyote," he whispered.

"Yes. When that coyote showed up, I was petrified and started to scream," Naomi recalled. "Then out ran Aunt Gwen, her eyes lit up like fire. Rivo, you were told she swatted that thing and chased it away, but that's not quite how it happened." She continued, "When your mother charged that coyote, she swatted it like a bug, and I swear it flew thirty feet in the air before falling to the ground, dead."

Rivo stood frozen. "I can't believe it. Mother," he said as he braced himself against the wall. "I got the Glare from her."

The three stood in silent disbelief. All the things Rivo had told them about Tuval and the Star Sage it was a lot to take in.

"Rivo," Pearce said as he mulled everything over, "it sounds like this Guardian's Glare was how you were able to take down Drokner. But you said the power is gone now." He looked at Rivo and rubbed the back of his neck. "So if you don't have it anymore, how do you expect to be able to fight Tuval?"

"I don't know," Rivo replied as he ran his fingers through his hair. "I inherited a power I didn't know was real until after it was gone." He shook his head in resignation. "A lot of good that does me now."

The more they talked, the more the reality of the situation began to set in. This could very well be the last time they ever speak to Rivo. "Please, Rivo," Naomi said as she walked up next to him, "Promise me you'll do whatever you have to do to survive."

Rivo didn't want to make her a promise he couldn't keep. He knew that his survival wasn't the main goal; it was to occupy Tuval. "Thank you, Naomi," he said as they embraced for quite possibly the last time.

Pearce didn't want to get emotional in front of him, so he just gave Rivo a one-armed hug and some words of encouragement, "You'll figure this out, Rivo. I know you will," he said as he gave Rivo a firm pat on the shoulder, "I'm proud of you, kid. You've done well for yourself, real well."

"We love you, Rivo. Please always know that." Naomi said as she and Pearce began to walk out.

"I love you too, both of you," Rivo replied.

Pearce was about to tell Rivo he loved him, but held back at the last second when he realized he was about to cry. He and Naomi quietly left the room.

The silence in the small bedroom, which served as both his hospital bed and holding cell, was deafening. The reality of his upcoming battle with Tuval was beginning to weigh on him, and now he had to get ready to discuss a plan with Captain Tremlee and Cade. Rivo was a little nervous about facing Cade yet again after yesterday's renegade attack that landed them both in trouble.

Chapter 29

Five Seconds

As Rivo left his room and made his way upstairs, he saw Renee standing at the top, waiting. She was wearing his mother's cloak, which he had given her after their encounter with the Forest Folk several weeks earlier. With her hood up and her bangs covering her eyes, he could only see the bottom half of her face. From what he could tell, there was no expression, almost as if she had numbed herself to any emotion.

This was the first time he had ever really studied her face before. He was caught off guard when he noticed his heart race slightly upon looking at her. Her small mouth and nose, her pointed chin, and smooth, tanned skin, *I never noticed how pretty her face is,* he thought, *like a porcelain doll.* "Renee, is everything okay?" he asked.

"I ran into Pearce and Naomi last night," she replied in a low, stoic tone that almost sounded accusatory.

"Oh, so what did they—"

"They said you're going to fight that monster again. Is that true?" she interrupted.

Rivo wasn't very good at reading people, especially girls, but he could tell she was upset about something. "Yeah, it is. Cade and I, we—"

"Do you have a death wish or something, Rivo?" she asked, her voice still low and almost eerie. "Why do you always feel like you have to play the hero all the time? Who are you trying to impress?"

"I'm not trying to impress anybody, Renee," he replied defensively. "I'm a soldier for the kingdom, I don't really have a choice."

"There's always a choice, Rivo," she countered. "You know, you don't have to do this. We could..." her voice faltered as her words failed her.

Rivo stood in place, uncomfortable and confused by her demeanor. He leaned his face toward her expectantly. "Could what?" he asked.

She stood silent for a moment. "Forget it," she snapped. She paused and let out a frustrated sigh. "Just be careful. And come back safe, please," she added as she stepped in to give him a quick hug, wrapping her arms tightly around his chest. Then, just as quickly, she turned and walked away without looking back.

He didn't know exactly how to respond. "Uh, okay, thanks. You too," he stammered. She kept walking away, ignoring his words. *Man, what's gotten into her?* He wondered.

"Hug her back, you idiot. Talk to her...thank her...say something," Spirit Rivo muttered in frustration as he watched the scene unfold.

He made his way down the hall and walked into the war room, the door already open. As promised, there stood Captain Tremlee and Cade. Cade still wore his military-issued scowl on his face, but it seemed somehow slightly less hostile towards Rivo than before.

"You finally done saying goodbye to your woman?" Cade asked in his gruff voice.

Rivo looked at him in bewilderment. "What are you talking about?"

"What are you, an idiot? That girl you were just talking to. Isn't she your woman?" Cade asked.

"What do you mean, *my woman*?" That's Renee, she was just being nice."

"Oh, that's right, she was just in here giving me and the Captain a hug before you came up," Cade said dryly.

"Really?"

"No," groaned Cade as he rolled his eyes.

"Gentlemen, let's get to the business at hand," interrupted Captain Tremlee, "what are your plans to occupy Tuval while we fight off his beasts?"

Cade drew his attention back to the Captain. "You said we've reached out to some nearby outposts for help," he responded, "do any of them have cannons? Can't we just meet him in the temple and bury the bastard again?"

"Unfortunately not," answered the Captain. "Ours was the only outpost with that kind of weaponry. You're going to have to fight him head-on."

Cade rubbed his chin and sighed. "Then that settles it. Kid," he said, looking at Rivo. "You follow my lead. I'll fight him one-on-one. I'll hold him off as long as I can. If he kills me before I buy our men enough time, that's when you come in. Keep him on his toes for as long as you can. Ya hear me?"

"What?" Rivo objected, "You want me to just stand there and watch?"

"Yes," Cade replied, "I don't need you getting in my way."

"What about that orb on his chest?" Rivo asked. "Can we try to break that? Maybe that will kill him."

"That's gonna be my goal," Cade responded. "But if that thing is a weak spot, I wouldn't count on him letting us get a shot at it. We need to plan for a prolonged fight to the death."

"No way!" Rivo replied, "I can't just sit there while that monster tears you apart. I can help, I won't be in the way."

"This isn't a debate, kid," Cade said, leaning toward Rivo. "We came here to go over a plan, and that's the plan."

"Listen, Rivo," said Tremlee, "We appreciate your willingness to fight—"

"I don't," interjected Cade.

The Captain continued, "But Cade has been fighting for the kingdom almost as long as you've been alive. If he says this is the best plan, then that's what you need to do. Understood?"

"He's only saying that because he doesn't think I can help," Rivo retorted.

Cade pounded his fist on the table so hard it nearly shook the room. "Listen, kid," he said sharply as he pointed his finger at Rivo, "I've been holding back with you, but now I'm just gonna come out and say it. You killing Drokner was dumb luck; it was a fluke, nothing more. You're not a true warrior, and you haven't seen real battle. I said it when we first met, and I'll say it again—you don't belong here."

"I never said I was a true warrior, but the battle with Drokner and his hounds was a real battle!" Rivo bit back. "And I've been practicing how to fight with weapons since I was a kid. I'm not the best, but I know how to fight," he shouted.

"You and your friends playing hero and slaying make-believe dragons in the woods when you were little isn't training, boy," Cade scoffed as he walked up to Rivo and stood in his face, poking his finger in Rivo's chest. "You listen to me. Your job is to follow my lead; you hold back until after he takes me out. If that isn't enough time, then you can jump in," he grunted. "Your job is to make sure the battle lasts as long as it can, even if you only survive five seconds against him. I'm your senior officer on this mission, and you follow my orders. Got it?"

Rivo kept his eyes locked on Cade's, but knew he wasn't about to convince either him or the Captain. "Fine. But I'll last longer than five seconds, Cade," he said sharply.

Cade grabbed him by his vest. "Let's just hope it doesn't come down to that, kid."

"Let. Go," Rivo said firmly as he pulled Cade's hand off of his vest.

Cade snarled at him and then examined the vest's golden embroidery. "Nice vest, boy," he scoffed. "It's a shame your daddy isn't gonna be the one fighting in it."

Rivo clenched his fists and glared at Cade, who waved his hands dismissively at him as he left the room.

Rivo hissed through his teeth after Cade walked out. "Captain," he said, rubbing his eyes. "If we're done here, I think I'd like to take a walk to clear my head."

"I'll never forget that," said Spirit Rivo, "I was so mad that I had to go outside and just walk around the grounds of the complex for a bit to cool off. Pearce, Naomi, and the others were busy preparing. I think Tremlee wanted to keep them away from me anyway, so I wouldn't be tempted to have second thoughts. I was fine with that; it was good to be by myself and clear my head."

Interlude

The Festival of Celestial Lights

Part 2 of 2

T he sun was setting, and candles were being handed out to all, along with lanterns. Everyone was to light their own and send it floating out into Lake Rhemilia, causing the lake to resemble a starlit sky. The gesture symbolized the people's reaffirmation of their wishes.

As the evening set in, it was time for Frank to prepare. The closing ceremony was about to begin.

Torches were set in a large circle as the crowd hushed, drums began to play, and Frank sat kneeling in the center. He remained kneeling as he turned his gaze up to the heavens, his arms spread out to his sides, a symbolic way of showing reverence to the stars and seeking their guidance, honoring Wyverly lore. He muttered a prayer, asking the stars to lend him their power, then bowed before grabbing the sword he had set in front of him. Meanwhile, an effigy of large logs was carted into the circle not far from him.

As he rose, he looked upon the large wooden effigy, meant to resemble the Demon King, Garel, or rather, what the people thought he looked like. What was supposed to be the demon's head had a fiendish-looking face carved into it with large horns protruding from the top.

Frank began performing maneuvers with his sword that dazzled the crowd, especially his young son. He would swing his blade and do rolls, lunges, and spins that looked immaculate, like an acrobat with a blade—every movement was performed with purpose and precision. He looked upon the demonic wooden statue and, with his voice booming, said, "I am ready." He paused for dramatic effect and then bellowed out, "Blade of the shooting star!" His sword lit up with a holy white flame, and he lunged toward the effigy, effortlessly plunging his blade into the log, its tip protruding through the other side. A violent crack was heard as the massive log was cut clean in half from top to bottom as if he were cutting through paper. The excited crowd all gasped collectively as Frank's blade then faded back to its normal state, and the effigy of Garel fell to pieces. He put his sword back into his scabbard and took a knee before the stunned gathering. Thunderous applause erupted throughout as fireworks were set off and the festival was concluded.

With the closing ceremony now over, Rivo looked with excitement at his mother, Gwen. "Mother, how did Father do that?!" Rivo asked eagerly.

Gwen leaned down to be eye level with her son. "Your father is a very special man, Rivo. Didn't you know that already?" she answered as she brushed the back of his head with her fingers.

"I know, but I've never seen anything like that!" the boy gasped.

Frank approached his wife and son, giving Gwen a peck on the lips before lifting Rivo up and cradling him with one arm.

"What did you think of my performance, son?" Frank asked as he smiled at the boy.

"That was the best thing ever, Father!" the boy exclaimed. "How did you do that magic trick with your sword?"

Frank chuckled at the question. "A magic trick? Is that what you thought that was?"

The boy's mouth hung open. "Wait, was that real?!" he asked in disbelief. "How did you do that? Can you teach me?"

Frank and Gwen looked at each other, their smiles fading before looking back at their son. "Rivo," Frank said with a sigh. "You're far too young for that. Maybe when you get older, if I feel you're ready. We can talk. For now, let's go enjoy my favorite part of the festival—The meal!" he said with a grand gesture towards the food tables as he set the boy back down on the ground and kissed him on the forehead. Young Rivo couldn't help but look back in wonder at the massive log his father had just split clean right down the middle.

Chapter 30

Stay Back Together

Before Rivo knew it, the afternoon was approaching. He decided he was going to retire for the day. They all had to get up early for the battle tomorrow. His nerves were growing more and more unsettled. As he made his way back to his room, he couldn't help but think to himself over and over again, *Tomorrow might be the last day of my life.* As nerve-racking as the thought was, he was trying to find a sense of peace about it all.

As Rivo walked down the first-story hallway to his room, he opened the door and walked toward his bed. He didn't notice that somebody was waiting for him. He heard the door shut behind him. He turned to see Vickie standing in his room by the door, her back leaning up against the wall.

"Rivo of Greencourt," she announced mockingly, "or should I call you Rivo, the Beastkiller? Which do you prefer?" she asked as she studied her nails, not even looking in his direction.

"Vickie? What are you doing in my room?" he asked.

"Waiting for you," she said, rolling her eyes. "What else?"

Rivo narrowed his eyes. "For me? What for?"

She pursed her lips and gazed up at the ceiling. "So you're fighting that beast tomorrow, I hear."

"Yeah, me and Cade are," Rivo remarked, his forehead wrinkled.

Vickie let out a quick sigh, her thoughts on her sister, but not wanting to say too much. "Rivo, haven't you thought at all about what you're going to do if you make it out of this? There are people here who care deeply about you."

Rivo's shoulders sagged as he gave out an exhausted sigh himself, the stress of the day mounting on him. "Not this again. I don't know what's gotten into everyone." He turned to look out the window. "You and Renee are both starting to sound like Naomi. I have bigger problems to deal with right now."

Vickie shot him a menacing glare, though he didn't see it because his back was facing her. *Did he just mention Renee?*

"Vickie, that sounded colder than I meant it to," Spirit Rivo remarked. "I didn't mean it like that."

She stood behind him with her jaw clenched. Rivo's thoughts kept drifting to Cade and Tuval. He couldn't get past how they were supposed to defeat that monster when they couldn't even stand each other's presence.

Vickie began pacing his room, her arms crossed and her anger kindled. "I've tried to keep out of this, ya know. But now I'm speaking up." She stopped, grabbed him by his shoulder to turn him around, and looked directly at him, her eyes full of an anger he had never seen before. "I'll say this once, Rivo," she hissed, pointing her finger at him. "You better not break her heart, you understand?"

"What!?" he asked, furrowing his eyebrows. "Break whose heart? I don't know what you're talking about," Rivo replied sharply as he pushed her hand off his shoulder.

Vickie rolled her eyes and gave a frustrated sigh as her nostrils flared. "Ugh," she grunted. "Just don't die, you idiot!" she snapped as she opened the door and stormed out of the room.

"Well, you could always wish on a shooting star for me!" he shouted, wagging his head sarcastically as she slammed the door.

After she left, Rivo sat, flabbergasted. "What in the stars' light is wrong with that woman?" he groaned, rubbing his face.

"She was talking about Renee, you dope," Spirit Rivo said, shaking his ghostly head in embarrassment. "How could I not have realized that?"

Rivo sat in his bed, waiting for the day to end. Waiting for the knock on his door to let him know it was time to go. He looked down at his bag and saw his father's star pendant. "I'm definitely putting this on," he said, placing it over his head. He reached into his vest, and there it was, the red handkerchief. "Bon. I'm so sorry for all the harm this caused you," he whispered as he clenched it tight. "He's gonna pay, Bon. Even if I have to tear that cursed orb off his chest with my bare hands, he's gonna pay for what he's done. I promise."

He wrapped the handkerchief around his arm one last time, reciting the old motto of Wyverly lore, the same words spoken to him when he first received it, now with a whole new meaning to him. "Red," he said, his voice quivering, "for the blood that's been shed under the stars that guide us."

As the evening slowly began to approach, Rivo thought back on that day when he was a boy at the Festival of Celestial Lights. How his father had put on that amazing performance, his sword lighting up with a white flame as he cut through the effigy of Garel. He recalled how his father had told him that he would teach him that technique someday when he was older—a day that never came.

Rivo got out of his bed and knelt before the window, laying one of his swords on the ground before him. He gazed up at the evening sky, arms spread out to his sides as his father had done. "Please," he said to the stars softly as he began to weep. "Please, lend me your power for just this one battle. I used Mother's power to defeat Drokner; now I need Father's power to defeat Tuval. I may not be anywhere near the man or the warrior that my father was. But, for the people I love, for Wyverly. I beg you, please," he sobbed.

He then briefly felt something like a soft heat stirring in his gut, pulsating for a moment before dissipating. The fleeting sensation was so quick and subtle that Rivo wasn't sure if it was in his head or not. He repeated his prayer over again before lifting himself up and retiring to his bed.

"I didn't think much of it at the time," Spirit Rivo remarked. "But something told me back then that the stars heard my plea."

As the real Rivo lay down, gazing at the ceiling, Spirit Rivo was whisked away to another room in the complex. It was Vickie and Renee's room. Renee stood looking out the window, still with her hood up over her head and an expressionless look on her face.

Vickie slipped in after her talk with Rivo. She froze as she saw Renee standing there. *Damn, she must know*, she thought, her stomach twisting.

Her eyes darted around the room. "Renee," Vickie said with a nod as she sat on her bed.

"What have you been up to, Vickie?" Renee asked, her tone still low and stoic, as it was when she last spoke with Rivo.

Vickie's chest tightened; she knew right then that she was in for it, as Renee never called her by her full name unless she was really upset. "I was just taking a stroll," she answered plainly.

"You were talking to *him*, weren't you?"

"I don't know what you mean," Vickie replied, feigning ignorance.

"What did I tell you after your antics in the dining hall the other day?"

"Renee—"

"What! Did I tell you?" Renee's voice cut like a blade.

Vickie closed her eyes and took a deep breath to compose herself. "You said you didn't want me talking to Rivo anymore."

"And here you are, talking to him."

"He's my friend too, Renee," Vickie bit back, defensively.

"Don't give me that!" Renee snapped. "You can't stand him. You can't stand that I like him."

"That's not true, Renee. I never said I didn't like him," she retorted as she stood up. "I just don't want to see you get hurt more than you already are. That boy doesn't see you, Renee."

"Just butt out, okay!" Renee screamed as she turned around.

Vickie took a step back, her eyes wide. She blinked and bit her lip, trying to calm herself. "Fine," she replied sharply.

As Vickie sat back down on her bed, Renee gathered up her backpack. Vickie looked at her, puzzled. "Renee, what are you doing?" she asked.

"I'm going to room with Myra," Renee snarled. "I already spoke with her. And when this is over, I'm going to stay in Rhemilia. She said I can work at her family's bakery."

Vickie's heart sank; she felt a lump in her throat. "Renee?" she groaned. "All this over a boy?"

"I'm sick of this, Vick!" exclaimed Renee. "And I'm sick of you. I'm sick of you feeling like it's your duty to protect me from myself."

"Renee, please," Vickie pleaded, her eyes watering. "Don't do this. Not over a boy. Have you even told him how you feel? Have you even told yourself?"

Renee slammed her backpack on her bed and turned toward Vickie. "Fine, I'll say it! I'm in love with Rivo, okay?" she shouted. "There, I said it. And I'm going to tell him when this is over."

"Whoa, Renee..." Spirit Rivo gasped.

"And what if he doesn't love you back, Renee?" Vickie's voice quivered through her tears.

"I don't know, Vick," Renee barked as she turned to pick up her backpack, "but at least he'll know how I feel. Besides, that's my business, not yours." She walked past Vickie and reached for the door to leave.

"Please don't leave me, Renee!" Vickie cried. "I'm sorry, I was just trying to protect you."

Renee turned back toward Vickie. "I'm a woman now, Vick!" she shouted. "I don't need you to protect me from everything. Not from Rivo, not from Mother, not from anything."

Vickie's eyes widened as she gaped at Renee. "That's what this is really about, isn't it? It's about Mother."

Renee stood speechless for a moment. "Yes, that's part of it," she said, "I know what really happened back then, Vick. But you won't talk to me about it because you don't think I'm strong enough to handle it. Isn't that right?"

Vickie closed her eyes. "Renee, you don't know," she replied. "It's in the past, it doesn't matter anymore."

"It matters to me, Vick," Renee said, leaning towards her. "I want to know. I want to hear you say it. Her and that man—they said they wanted to take you with them and leave me behind, didn't they?" she asked, her eyes welling up with tears.

"Renee," Vickie sighed wearily.

"Tell me the truth, Vickie!" Renee snapped. "I heard you arguing with them. I heard you tell them that we had to go together or stay back together. They wanted to leave me, didn't they!"

"Renee," Vickie said as she closed her eyes again, her voice trembling, "they did want to leave one of us behind. But it wasn't you," she swallowed hard, the lump in her throat burning, "it was me," a tear slid down her cheek.

Renee took a step back, her eyes went wide as she gasped in disbelief, "Vickie?"

"That man. He said I looked like a little tramp and that there was no place in a nobleman's house for someone like me. But you—you could come along." Vickie's lip began to quiver as tears streamed down her face. "I was scared, I didn't want to be alone. So I told them we had to be together. Then they just left. I was being selfish, Renee. I didn't want to lose you, too. I kept you from Mother, I'm sorry...that's the truth."

Renee stood in shock, tears running down her cheeks. "Oh, Vickie," she said, her voice breaking, "I'm so sorry." She sat next to her sister, pulling her into a tight embrace. Vickie sobbed as she let out more tears, each one bearing the weight of ten years of pain. "Vickie, I'm sorry. You've been holding on to this for so long."

"I'm sorry, Renee," Vickie choked out, "I was the one not ready for the truth, not you." She lay her head in Renee's lap, sobbing. "Please don't leave me, too, Renee," she pleaded.

"Oh, Vickie," Renee said gently as she ran her fingers through her sister's hair. "I'm not gonna leave you. You did the right thing back then. There's nothing wrong with you, Vick, you're perfect. And that man, he was no nobleman; he was a thief. He and Mother were wrong; they were wrong about you, they were wrong about everything."

The two embraced, comforting each other.

Spirit Rivo watched on, heartbroken for Vickie as her truth came to light. "Vickie...that's terrible...I'm so sorry you had to live with that for so long."

Chapter 31

Just Keep Marching

"Do you ever get scared, Mother?" a young Rivo asked.

"Oh, sure, I do, everybody gets scared sometimes," his mother, Gwen, replied. "We may not all be scared of the same things, but we're all scared of something. Anybody who says they aren't is lying."

"What kind of things scare you?" Rivo asked.

"Well, lots of things, I suppose," she answered with a thoughtful expression on her face. "The thought of something bad happening to you or your father scares me. Losing what I have and what I love would scare me."

"So...what should I do when I'm scared, Mother?" the boy asked.

"Well, the next thing, of course."

"The next thing?"

"Yes. You do what you have to do. Keep living your life, don't let it change who you are," she replied. "Put one foot in front of the other, keep marching, and hope for the best. It's all you can do sometimes. You see, Rivo, you can't stop fear, but you can keep the fear from stopping you. Remember, Rivo, no matter what, just keep marching."

***

There had been an almost surreal silence all day, ever since his wake-up call. It was a knock on his door, without a word spoken. As Rivo walked out to meet the rest of the troops in the yard, he noticed they were all wearing cloaks as ordered by the captain, the main goal being to hide Cade and Rivo's identities.

Just keep marching, those words went through Rivo's head over and over as he trekked through the middle of the formation. This was the Captain's idea; he felt it was best to have the Beastkillers in the middle of the pack. There was hardly a noise to be heard save the sound of the feet stomping on the leaf-covered ground.

Throughout their march from the outpost and through the forest, Rivo couldn't help but wonder where exactly Pearce, Naomi, and the others were in the formation. He briefly saw Pearce and Naomi that morning when they were all gathered together on the outpost grounds, but it was at a distance. *They're probably towards the back*, Rivo thought, assuming the more experienced fighters would be closer to the front. Captain Tremlee had assigned a lieutenant to every group of about a dozen or so soldiers who would silently position their troops in the formation, likely based on battle abilities. The previous day had been reserved for these lieutenants to meet with the soldiers assigned to them and go over the attack plan. It was hard to say, but between the soldiers from Captain Tremlee's outpost and the ones nearby, there had to be a few thousand soldiers.

Is this enough? Rivo had asked himself. There was no telling how many Haundo were truly out there. The Forest Folk had given intel that showed there were six greater Haundo, including Tuval, Brooner, Drokner, and the other three that were killed in the tower collapse. There were untold thousands of their smaller hounds. No one knew how many were really out there and where they even came from to begin with. Regardless, this abandoned druid star temple served as some sort of home base, taking this out and neutralizing Tuval would effectively end the war as they knew it, though it would no doubt take months or even years to hunt down every last Haundo.

As they kept moving, Rivo couldn't help but feel alone despite being surrounded by his fellow soldiers. *I have no clue where Naomi and the others are among all the rest,* he thought. Then he noticed something. It had been in front of him the whole time. There, wrapped around the sleeve of a soldier just ahead of him, was something he hadn't seen since he was in Rhemilia—his blue headband. *Renee,* he thought as his heart leaped, *you're just letting me know that you're close by. Thank you.*

"Renee," Spirit Rivo said softly, "looking out for me as always."

After marching for some time, they came to a stop. The lieutenants signaled their respective troops to break off from the main group and head into action. *This must mean they're expecting to run into Haundo soon,* Rivo realized. *I bet they're dispersing to spread out the attack and come in different directions.* He could only guess, as the plans for the other troops were never discussed with him; his only responsibility was to follow Cade into battle.

The further they marched, the more troops would break off and go into action. In the distance, Rivo was starting to hear the clang of swords and the howls of soldiers, and Haundo, the battle had begun. Cade turned to Rivo. "We're getting close. Remember, follow my lead," he whispered. Rivo nodded in response.

The formation pressed forward. The howls and sounds of battle became louder and more frequent, with more and more troops breaking off to engage. It was then that Rivo felt a hand grasp firmly on his arm. It was Cade; he abruptly pointed off into the distance. There stood the large, intimidating ancient stone structure.

The temple was built with massive gray stones stacked on top of each other, with moss and vines covering the once sacred structure and filling every crack and crevice, as if nature had reclaimed the site as its own. It was round with four spires like giant talons sticking out of the ground around its outer wall. There were massive stone monoliths scattered outside, no doubt serving as some sort of sacred landmarks to the druids in ages past. Rivo couldn't help but think of the irony; they all wore cloaks as they approached the structure, much like the druids from long ago had perhaps worn when they would come to perform their worship ceremonies to the stars.

The fear was surging through Rivo's whole body, almost paralyzing him. He remembered his mother's words, *Just keep marching. You can't stop fear, but you can keep fear from stopping you. No matter what, just keep marching.* He held on to these words as he anxiously kept walking forward.

The battle was in sight now; he could see soldiers and Haundo fighting each other, killing each other, but he had to keep marching. Cade grabbed his arm again and pointed. There he saw the entrance, a black opening in the side of the building that reminded Rivo of the mouth of the wolf den he saw in the forest outside of Rhemilia, where Drokner and his beasts had been. There was an old stone bridge that led to the entrance, spanning an old, long since dried out moat. The bridge was well guarded by a large pack of Haundo.

Tuval had to be inside, he thought.

"Once our men break their guard, we charge. We need to move quickly before Tuval comes out," Cade whispered, leaning in close to Rivo.

Just then, Captain Tremlee gave his order to the rest of the troops, "Charge!" he shouted as the remaining soldiers sped directly into battle with the Haundo guarding the bridge. As they threw off their cloaks, Rivo could see that Pearce, Naomi, and Judd were among them. Arrows began flying from nearby, and he looked to see Vickie next to Renee, firing shots. The sight of his old group and knowing they had been so close to him the whole time did give Rivo an ounce of comfort, but it didn't last long.

Having the massive and powerful Judd among those who would clear the way to the entrance was a wise choice. Even unarmed, Judd was a force to be reckoned with, as Drokner and his beasts found out, but now he was armed with a mace and wore armor to protect him from the bites and strikes of the beasts. He bashed the hounds guarding the bridge left and right, with Pearce, Naomi, and the others fending off any creature that tried to stop him, aided by Vickie and Renee pelting any approaching enemy from a distance with arrows.

Before long, the bridge was clear. "Now!" shouted Cade as he ran toward the entrance. Rivo charged in right behind him. His legs felt wobbly, but he wasn't going to let that stop him. He couldn't. They crossed the bridge and entered the temple—now it was time to battle Tuval.

Chapter 32

A Fool's Fate

The air in the clearing was filled with the sound of wood knocking. "You're getting better, Rivo," said young Pearce, "but not. Good. Enough!" he said as he swatted the wooden staff out of Rivo's hand, then performed a spinning strike to knock him to the ground.

Rivo fell to the dirt with a thud and a groan. "Dang it!" he cried as he lay face down on the ground. "I'll never be as good as Pearce!"

"Oh, cut it out, Rivo!" Naomi chided him as she stood with her arms crossed. "Not only is Pearce older than you, he's the best fighter in Greencourt."

Pearce reached his hand out to help Rivo up, but Rivo slapped his hand away in anger. "Leave me alone!" he snapped as he got up by himself. If there was one thing young Rivo wasn't good at, it was admitting someone else was better.

"Rivo!" Naomi shouted as she stomped toward him, preparing to give her young cousin a much-needed attitude adjustment.

"Everybody hold on for a moment," Frank said calmly as he stepped between them. "Naomi, I'll take care of Rivo." He walked up to his young son and began dusting him off. "Rivo," he said, brushing dirt off the boy's pants, "that's not how gentlemen behave. I raised you better than that." He knelt down to be eye-to-eye with the young boy. He could tell by the look in Rivo's eye that he was upset that he had disappointed his father. "Now, you go over to Pearce right now, shake his hand and tell him *good match*, you hear me?"

Rivo nodded and did as his father told him. Pearce graciously accepted the gesture, and they parted ways shortly afterward, Frank and Rivo heading home one way while Pearce and Naomi went the other. "I'm sorry I acted that way, Father," an embarrassed young Rivo whimpered. "I just don't feel I'm getting better at fighting, and I don't think I'll ever be as good as Pearce."

"Rivo," Frank said as he walked with his arm around his son's shoulders, "life isn't about always being the best. There may always be someone better out there. Being a good warrior is about more than that; you don't have to be the best or the strongest. In fact, admitting that you aren't can be a strength in its own way."

The boy looked at his Father, confused. "How can that be a strength?"

Frank thoughtfully scratched his scruffy chin. "Well, son, not only can it keep you from picking a fight you can't win by yourself, but it can also keep you humble, and a humble warrior is the most dangerous of them all."

"I don't understand, Father," Rivo replied, scratching his head.

Frank leaned toward his son as they kept walking. "A humble warrior isn't blinded by his ego, so he can better see and understand not only his own strengths and weaknesses, but also those of his comrades and his opponents," he added, wagging his finger. "Rivo, that's what makes someone a good warrior, understanding these things and knowing how to use them to your advantage. Knowing when and how to attack."

Rivo rubbed the side of his face as he mulled over his Father's words. "But what if they don't have any weaknesses?" he asked.

Frank shook his head. "Everyone has a weakness, Rivo. For some, it may be their pride, and a prideful warrior is just as dangerous as a humble warrior, except he's only a danger to himself. His pride will make him do something like turn his back on an opponent he perceives as being lesser than him. That, Rivo, is when you strike."

"Attack them from behind? That doesn't sound very noble, Father," the boy said with a bewildered look on his face.

"Rivo," Frank stopped and knelt down to look his son in the eye. "Any warrior who turns his back on his opponent in battle like that isn't a noble warrior. He's an arrogant fool, and he deserves a fool's fate." He grabbed Rivo by the shoulders and lifted his eyebrows. "Remember what I told you today, Rivo. It could save your life someday...or someone else's."

***

Cade charged through the temple entrance with Rivo right behind him. Once inside, they slowed to a snail's pace. The entryway was a long, wide hallway that led to a stone stairway about eight steps high. The stairs were low enough so they could see the arched doorway, though there were no doors.

They could see enough of the doorway to notice that it led to a large sanctuary of some sort, but from their vantage point, they couldn't see what, or who, was inside. There was a small set of stairs to the right of the main stairway that appeared to lead down, possibly to an old storage cellar. The doorway to the cellar stairs looked like it could barely fit a grown man, let alone a Haundo. "He's got to be up there," Cade whispered, "you ready, kid?"

"I'm ready," Rivo whispered back. As Cade faced the stairs, Rivo patted his arm. "Cade," he said, "may the stars watch over you. I'll be ready whenever you need me." He held his hand out to shake Cade's.

Cade hesitated for a second, then gave Rivo a quick nod, stood up straight, and shook his hand by clasping forearms. "You're alright, Rivo," he replied. He stood silent for a moment as he looked at Rivo's vest. "And kid," he added, "I'm sorry for what I said earlier about your father. You go in there and make him proud, okay?"

"Thanks, Cade, I will," he replied as he softly smiled and bowed his head slightly. Just then, he felt that same fleeting sensation stirring inside of him that he had felt the evening before when he prayed to the stars for strength. It quickly vanished just as it had before. *What is this?* he wondered to himself.

They slowly made their way up the stone stairs; Rivo could feel his knees shake with each step. He didn't have the aid of the Guardian's Glare as he had when he fought Drokner, nor did he have Pearce, Naomi, and the rest of his crew to fight alongside him. But he did have Cade, the only other Beastkiller in all of Wyverly.

As Cade slowly made his way up the stairs, he pulled out his weapon, a single-bladed battle axe, small and light enough to be carried with one hand. He also held a small wooden shield in his other hand. Rivo pulled out his two short swords. They each had a knife holstered in their belts in case they dropped their weapons in battle.

The two Beastkillers made their way into the large sanctuary. It was larger than it appeared from the outside, wide enough for over fifty men to stand side-by-side, with the ceiling looking immeasurably tall. The room had dirty, bare gray brick on the floors and walls, with some worn-out carvings that could barely be seen; they appeared to be different star constellations with words etched underneath in an antiquated language that few could read anymore. Anything sacred or of value in that temple had long since either rotted away or had been taken by scavengers. There were enough missing bricks in the ceiling and walls to make the room well-lit in the daytime. They could see rays of sunlight shining throughout the vast sanctuary.

As they scanned the room, there at the opposite end stood Tuval. The beast hadn't noticed they were there yet; he was busy digging through an old wooden crate, growling as he pulled out a large wooden club. "Those fools think they can attack and live to tell about it?" he growled, "I'll kill every last one of them!"

"Tuval of the Haundo!" shouted Cade.

The beast whipped around with a vile snarl. "Who the devil are you?" Tuval barked as he slowly approached them.

"I am Cade, the Beastkiller," he announced as he squared his chest.

"*Beastkiller*, huh?" Tuval remarked, glaring at Cade with his yellow eyes. "So, you must be the one who killed Brooner."

"I am," Cade proudly replied. "And I enjoyed every last second of it."

Tuval smirked at Cade's attempt to elicit a reaction. He looked over at Rivo. "I see you brought your pet along as well. Perfect, now I get to kill you both."

"I'm the one you need to worry about right now, Tuval," Cade said as he took a step toward the beast.

Tuval paced sideways, keeping his eyes fixed on the Beastkillers. "Oh, I'm not worried about either of you. At least you look like a real warrior and not a pup," he remarked mockingly as he looked at Rivo.

Rivo stiffened up and brandished his sword. "I was enough to take down Drokner," he sneered. "And you couldn't finish me off last time, could you, Tuval, or should I call you...Garel?"

Tuval stopped in his tracks. "*Garel*," he scoffed. "I haven't been called that in ten thousand years. Where did you hear that name?"

Rivo paced back and forth as he spoke; he felt it helped calm his nerves slightly. "It's an old fairytale in this land. Garel, the demon king who stole the magical orb from the heavenly realm, that made him invincible. Until he was sealed away by the Star Sage for ten thousand years," he explained. "It appears the fairytale was true all along."

"You humans can't even keep your folklore straight," Tuval laughed. "My name is not *Garel*, that's the name those human animals called me because it's the sound we make when we growl." He then pointed at the orb on his chest, "and this is not a magical orb stolen from the heavenly realm, it's from the Fallen Star. While you humans worshipped the Shooting Star and pursued knowledge, we worshiped the Fallen Star and pursued its power, which I was given. With this, the Fallen Star gave me the power to torment the children of the Shooting Star for all eternity."

Rivo stood stunned at the reality of this fairytale that had come to life. He looked at Tuval, puzzled. "Fallen Star?" he said with a sideways glance. He made a point of not looking toward Cade, who was slowly sneaking behind the Greater Haundo.

"It appears that old fool you call the Star Sage kept that from you," Tuval said as his eyes narrowed. "He must have feared others would have sought its power."

As shocked as Rivo was over this revelation, he had to focus on keeping the massive beast distracted. "Maybe, but its power still wasn't enough to defeat the Star Sage, was it?"

"It's more than enough to defeat you, boy," Tuval snapped. "Your Star Sage possessed a knowledge of star magic that you humans have long since forgotten." He bared his fangs as his ears went back, preparing to lunge at Rivo. "Not that it matters, it could only be cast once anyway. Either way, you could never hope to master such a—"

Tuval's rant was cut short as Cade dealt a vicious blow to the back of the hound's neck with his axe, causing the monster to howl in a mixture of anger and pain. With his axe embedded in the beast's neck, Cade quickly pulled out his dagger and began stabbing him in his side. The orb on Tuval's chest began to glow as his wounds began to heal; not even a drop of blood was drawn. He quickly recovered and spun around to give Cade a brutal kick that sent the brave warrior flying back, putting him on the floor.

With Cade on the ground, slowly lifting himself back up from the jarring blow, Tuval set his focus on Rivo. He ripped the axe from the back of his neck; it looked like a toy in the creature's hand. The beast hurled the axe like a tomahawk at Rivo, who barely dodged it in time. Tuval growled and charged at the boy at full speed, club in hand. Cade tried to jump in, but was swatted away by the Greater Haundo. Their plan of Cade engaging Tuval one-on-one was out the window; he had his sights set on Rivo.

Tuval again charged at Rivo, who could tell that the beast was going to use his club to attack him with a backswing. Rivo anticipated the maneuver and struck the hound's arm with one of his swords. This seemed to do little to dampen the blow; Tuval's strike sent Rivo reeling back, and he landed on the floor with a loud thud. Shaken from the attack, Rivo labored to haul himself back up and regroup.

"Okay, boy. I'm done toying with you. Let's see you get up from this one," Tuval puffed his chest and let out a howling scream, "Black Fa—"

Tuval's attack was interrupted as Cade jumped on his back, stabbing the beast in the neck with his dagger.

The Haundo dropped his club and pulled Cade off, then threw him to the ground. Cade quickly recovered, rolled over, and got back on his feet.

Rivo still had some fight in him and took the opportunity to charge Tuval, swinging his swords and getting a clean hit on the Greater Haundo's back.

Tuval recovered rapidly and turned around to deliver a brutal backhanded blow across Rivo's jaw, knocking him to the floor so hard that he felt sharp pain shoot through his entire body.

As Rivo lay on the ground, struggling to collect himself, Cade saw his axe lying next to the crumbled remnants of a pillar. He quickly snatched it up and ran to take another shot at Tuval. He gave out a battle cry and swung his axe with every ounce of strength he had in him, striking the beast directly on the orb in his chest.

The strike connected with such force that the blade of his axe broke off the handle. With his chest heaving, Cade stared in disbelief at his weapon, broken, along with their hopes of taking down the Greater Haundo once and for all.

Tuval smirked at Cade as he wrestled the axe handle out of the stunned Beastkiller's grasp and bashed him across the face with it. Cade fell back, and Tuval grabbed him and threw him across the sanctuary floor. The sound of his leather armor smacking the ground echoed throughout.

Tuval hesitated as he saw Cade somehow getting slowly back to his feet. "Well, you can certainly take a beating, I'll give you that," he scoffed. "But this ends now!" Tuval heaved his chest and howled.

"No, Cade, watch out!" Rivo screamed helplessly as he struggled to gain his footing. He knew what was coming, but it was too late.

"Black Fang!" Tuval hollered, and a wave of black energy shot out of the beast's mouth, striking Cade directly. He screamed out in pain and collapsed to the ground.

Rivo picked one of his swords up off the ground and lunged at the beast for one last attack.

Tuval quickly spun around. "Black Fang!" he shouted again, as another wave of black energy emitted from his mouth, this time striking Rivo.

The impact was enough to take Rivo off his feet, but as he fell to the ground, he noticed something—the pain quickly dissipated, like being hit by a strong gust of wind that died down to a meager breeze.

Renee was right! Rivo realized. *Black magic only works once.*

Tuval stood proudly between the fallen Beastkillers. "That one never failed to take even the strongest of you humans down," he chuckled as he looked upon the two of them.

He doesn't know. Rivo thought as he lay on the sanctuary floor. *He doesn't realize that I've been hit with this before.*

Rivo made sure to grip his sword tightly, waiting for Tuval to get closer so he could strike him in the chest. *My only hope is that Cade's attack may have somehow weakened the orb.*

Tuval took a step toward Rivo, then stopped. "I think I'll take the big one out first," he grunted, looking at Rivo. "Then, I'll take my time with you, boy. At least *he* was a worthy opponent."

The beast laughed and turned his back to Rivo to approach Cade, who was still paralyzed on the ground.

As Rivo looked upon Tuval, the beast's back was facing him. He gathered what strength he had left and slowly rose up, the words of his Father coming back to him.

That, Rivo, is when you strike.

Tuval loomed over Cade, still unable to move. "Did you actually think that was going to work, Beastkiller?" he asked mockingly as he stomped on Cade's leg, crushing it against the hard stone floor. "Weapons forged by man will never defeat me."

Cade howled in pain as Tuval relished every second of it.

Rivo stood and slowly walked toward Tuval, his narrowed eyes fixed on the beast in a focused fury. He felt the same mysterious energy from before flare up deep inside of him once again. With each step, his resolve grew as he felt his strength returning. Echoing through his mind were the words once spoken by a loving father to reassure his anxious and frightened son, who was worried that the monster from a fairytale would someday come to get him.

Son, don't you know anything about fairytales? When the monster comes, a hero always rises up to save the day.

Tuval stood over Cade, baring his massive fangs as he taunted his fallen opponent. "The protection of the Star Sage is no more," he growled. "The time of the Haundo has come again. This, human...is the end."

Rivo advanced on the Greater Haundo, sword in hand. "This is *your* end!" He screamed as he leaped toward Tuval, the holy power within him now surging with fury.

"BLADE OF THE SHOOTING STAR!" He bellowed out. His sword lit up with a glorious white flame as he stabbed the beast in the back, his blade sinking all the way through to the hilt. The tip of it pierced Tuval's chest, protruding through the orb, and cutting it cleanly in half.

Tuval stood frozen as he watched the amber orb split and fall to the ground. Blood spilling from his chest, Tuval gasped for air. "Star magic? It...can't be..." he sputtered as blood began to flow from his mouth.

Rivo stood behind the beast, breathing heavily as the realization hit him. Rivo, the descendant of the Star Sage, had just defeated the Demon King Garel.

The beast stumbled as his strength faltered, and he fell backward, pinning Rivo underneath him. Tuval let out one last gasp and then died, suffering a fool's fate.

Spirit Rivo looked on as Tuval perished. "As tough as this has been to watch. I'd be lying if I didn't say I enjoyed watching that bastard die again." He clenched his ghostly fists and grimaced. "I can't...really remember anything after this..."

Chapter 33

As the Rest Celebrated

Cade struggled to lift himself up, his leg badly injured from Tuval's stomp and the shooting pain of the Haundo's black magic attack. "Rivo! Rivo! Are you okay? Can you hear me?" he cried.

He slowly rose to his feet and limped toward Tuval's body. "Rivo! Stars be damned, kid, you did it! You killed him!" he shouted as he inched closer, unable to put weight on his injured leg.

"Ughhh...Cade?" groaned a delirious and badly injured Rivo as he lay pinned down by Tuval's body.

"Hey, Rivo. I'm here. You did good, kid. You got the bastard," Cade replied. He saw Rivo trapped underneath the massive beast, and he needed to find a way to get him out. "Sit tight, Rivo. I'll figure out a way to get this mutt off you."

As he limped over to grab Tuval's ankles and try dragging him off Rivo, Cade noticed the orb fragments lighting up. The amber light slowly turned red, as if emanating a dangerous heat. "What in the world?" Cade said as he reached for the orb. Just before he grabbed it, the orb exploded with a deafening blast that shook the temple walls and took Cade off his feet, planting him on his back several feet away.

He lay on the ground, stunned and groaning, with blood trickling from his forehead. He slowly rolled himself over, only to see the floor caving in. Cade crawled over to Rivo, but it was too late; Rivo had fallen into the cellar of the temple under the sanctuary.

"Rivo!" Cade shouted as he struggled to drag himself over. He looked down and saw Rivo lying unconscious on the cellar floor, his body getting pelted by pieces of falling stone, Tuval's lifeless corpse now lying next to his. As Cade tried to figure out some way to get down there, he saw something happening to Tuval. The Greater Haundo's body began to disintegrate.

Between the sounds of the stone structure giving way and the shock at what he was witnessing, Cade didn't hear the battle outside come to a complete stop. Later, it was discovered that around that time, all the other Haundo in Wyverly disintegrated along with Tuval.

The war with the Haundo was over.

None of that mattered to Cade at that moment. His only concern was saving Rivo, his brother-in-arms. As he lay there trying to think of a way to reach the cellar, the wall adjacent to him began to collapse, burying Rivo and nearly crushing Cade.

"Rivo!" Cade screamed in futility as a massive stone came crashing down, missing his head by mere inches. He could barely move, and all paths to the cellar were blocked—there was no saving Rivo.

"Rivo," he gasped helplessly. "We did it...*you* did it. At least we know that bastard's gone now." He dropped his head in resignation. "The kingdom has a chance now, kid. You and I, we'll go down as heroes...the Beastkillers," he scoffed with a faint smile.

Just then, Captain Tremlee, along with Pearce, Naomi, and Judd, entered. While Pearce and Naomi were looking frantically for Rivo, the Captain spotted Cade and motioned for Judd to grab him.

"No!" Cade shouted, "Don't save me. Let me go down with the boy!" They couldn't understand what he was saying; the sound of crashing stones made any conversation impossible. Judd grabbed Cade and ran outside.

While Pearce and Naomi called out for Rivo, their shouts were drowned out by the thunderous sound of the stone structure falling apart. More soldiers arrived, and the Captain gestured for them to get Pearce and Naomi out of the temple.

As they evacuated, all the soldiers on the outside were cheering and shouting for victory. All, that is, except Vickie and Renee.

Renee stood outside the temple, watching the others come out with Cade—and no sign of Rivo. She collapsed to her knees with her hands over her mouth as she witnessed another section of the structure come crashing down.

Vickie wrapped her arms around her sister to console her. They knelt down, crying together as the Captain and the others ran past them to safety, Cade, Pearce, and Naomi all being carried out against their will.

"Where's Rivo?" Vickie wailed. "What happened to Rivo!"

Captain Tremlee stood looking at the crumbling temple, rubbing his hand hopelessly across his scalp. "We couldn't find him. We think—"

Pearce interrupted, "We have to go back!" he shouted.

"We can't!" Captain Tremlee hollered back. "The structure isn't safe; it could all collapse and kill you all."

"We have to!" cried Naomi. "Cade, where is he?"

Cade sat slumped against a nearby tree, a defeated expression on his face. "I was supposed to go down with him," he groaned, shaking his head and rubbing his eyes.

"Cade," Pearce said forcefully, "what happened to him?"

Cade couldn't bring himself to look directly at him. "He fell...he fell underneath," he said grimly, his chest heaving. "The floor gave out, and the wall crashed down on him. I'm sorry, but he didn't make it."

Naomi fell to her knees, her hands over her face, bowing down on the ground, sobbing in disbelief. Pearce sat next to her, the look on his face stoic and numb.

Judd approached Vickie and Renee, the two young women who had become like sisters to him, his eyes swollen with tears. "I'm sorry, Renee," he said softly as he ran his hand through her jet-black hair. "There was nothing we could do."

Renee sat, hyperventilating, barely able to squeeze out a word. "He's...he's really gone...isn't he?" Renee said faintly through her tears.

Vickie held her sister tightly. "I'm sorry," she moaned. "I don't know what else..." She ran out of words to say and buried her face into Renee's shoulder.

As the rest of the soldiers celebrated, there sat the now group of five, mourning the loss of a true hero.

Spirit Rivo looked on, seeing for the first time how everyone learned of his fate. He looked upon his heartbroken friends and family, those who were looking out for him the whole time. "This is terrible. I can't stand to watch them like this... this is where it started...where I came back like this...so what happens now? Why can't I close my eyes? Why can't I look away? I still don't understand why I have to watch this...I feel like I'm being punished, like I'm having to suffer..."

Chapter 34

Go Kiss the Stars

The soldiers all made their way back to the outpost, cheers, hoots, and hollers of victory accompanying them. Pearce, Naomi, and the rest, however, lagged behind. They didn't feel like celebrating—they couldn't. The three women of the group all walked arm-in-arm, with Naomi in the middle, crying and sniffling the whole way back. Pearce and Judd walked just in front of them; Judd sobbed like a baby the entire time. Pearce, in a state of disbelief, had to step away to vomit as the temple vanished on the horizon.

Even farther back from the rest was Cade. Captain Tremlee and some other soldiers built a makeshift stretcher for him, composed of a few sturdy branches and some garments. He requested to be far enough behind to be out of sight and earshot of Rivo's comrades. He refused to speak to the Captain or anyone else about what exactly happened. If one were to look upon the gloomy scene, they would think the soldiers had lost the war, and in Cade's mind, they had.

Or at least, *he* had.

"Cade..." Spirit Rivo said as he watched his dejected comrade. "I'm sorry you're the one bearing this burden. It wasn't your fault."

***

The next day, the group all sat at the outpost together in Pearce and Naomi's room. They had hardly eaten or slept the night before. Little had changed, and few words were spoken. Naomi and Renee constantly wiped their eyes with handkerchiefs.

"It feels like a piece of my gut has been ripped out," Naomi remarked as she sat on the side of her bed. Vickie and Renee both went up to her on either side, Vickie combing Naomi's hair with her fingers, and Renee patting her on the back to console her. Judd was still sobbing, and Pearce sat silently looking out the window.

The group all wanted to know exactly what had happened in the temple yesterday, but the only person who knew was Cade, who was being treated in the infirmary, and he had refused to see any visitors.

"Maybe if I snuck into the infirmary and held a knife to his throat, he'd feel like talking," Pearce said flatly as he stared out the window.

"Pearce?" Spirit Rivo remarked. "This isn't like you. I feel terrible that my death has brought this out of you."

"I think I like that idea," Vickie muttered, raising her hand as if the matter was up for a vote.

"Just stop, both of you," Naomi pleaded. "I can't deal with this right now."

Just then, Captain Tremlee stopped by. "I feel I must bear a great deal of the burden for this," he said somberly. "I was the one who sent him in there. I wish there was something I could do or say to make you feel better." He stood silent for a moment, thoughtfully rubbing his mustache. "Please know that Rivo died a hero for the kingdom—his bravery will never be forgotten."

Nobody was offering a response, so Pearce turned his attention toward the Captain and spoke up, "Thank you, Captain," he said with a quick nod, before turning back around to face the window.

The Captain nodded back slowly as he realized he wasn't going to be getting much conversation from the group. "The war is over. You all are, of course, free to stay or leave whenever you wish. There will be an impromptu memorial service held for the soldiers who lost their lives yesterday. King Roland could not attend on such short notice, but please understand he is aware of the sacrifices made and his heart goes out to all of you." The Captain took a deep breath. "Duke Kincaid will come in the king's stead to preside over the service."

"Ugh," Vickie let out an exaggerated groan. "Duke Kincaid is a drunken lush and an embarrassment to the royal family," she said sharply. "This is an insult! Sending that drunken fool over here. They sent him because nobody else wanted to travel this far for us nobodies, isn't that right?"

The Captain raised his hands defensively. "Now hold on, I will not abide this kind of talk about the royal family," he replied firmly. "I can assure you the King holds his troops in the highest regard. The kingdom has every intention of properly honoring all the soldiers who've served. It's only been a day since the battle, King Roland and his officials are all occupied with other matters."

Vickie rolled her eyes. "Please. Spare me this nonsense, Captain," Vickie responded tersely, shaking her head.

"Young lady—" The Captain stopped himself, realizing there was nothing he could say to get through to her. He let out a flustered sigh and moved on to the next topic. "The memorial service will be tomorrow at noon. I do hope you all attend." He pulled out a piece of parchment paper and handed it to Pearce. "This is a letter from Cade. He wanted you to have it. He wrote down everything that happened in the battle with Tuval." The Captain opened the door to leave, then turned to face the group on his way out. "Thank you, all of you. I'll never forget your bravery."

After the door shut, Vickie muttered under her breath, "Go kiss the stars, you uptight bastard."

"Vick, please cut it out," Renee pleaded, her voice strained.

"Fine," Vickie snapped. She was ready to leave. She couldn't wait to get away from that outpost, but she didn't want to push Renee to do anything right now.

Pearce read aloud the letter from Cade. It said everything—everything that happened during the battle, Rivo's heroics, how he killed Tuval, and how he met his untimely end. But the comfort and closure they all had hoped to get from Cade's candid letter was not to be found. Rivo wasn't coming back, and that's all there was to it.

"Well, I'm glad he wrote that for us," Naomi said, her voice hoarse from crying. "But it doesn't change the fact that we'll be going home without him." Part of Naomi wanted to just go home, but the other part of her didn't want to face the fact that, from now on, she would only be setting up two plates at the dinner table. She thought about how all of Rivo's belongings were still in his room in the small cabin the three shared, how she and Pearce would have to go through it all and decide what to keep and what to discard. The thought made her sick to her stomach.

"Writing a letter like a little schoolboy, what a coward," Vickie remarked with a sneer.

"Vick, please just stop," Renee pleaded as she rubbed her eyes.

Vickie quickly stood up, "It's his fault!" she shouted, "he's supposed to be this great warrior and he couldn't save one boy! One boy!" She started tearing up as she paced back and forth. "That's why he's too much of a coward to face us. He was supposed to kill that thing, and he couldn't! Rivo had to do it. But now, Rivo's dead, and that fool's still alive."

"Vickie, please don't do this now," Judd replied, his voice shaking.

She glared back at Judd. "He shouldn't have made it out of there without Rivo, Judd! He doesn't belong here. He knows that's the truth, and that's why he won't talk to us."

"That's enough, Vickie!" snapped Pearce as he turned to face her.

"Well, it's the truth! We all know it, and I'm the only one who has the guts to say it," she bit back.

"Vickie, please not now," Naomi groaned.

At that, Vickie let out an exhausted sighed and sat back down. "Fine," she said, "but I'm not going to that stupid memorial service."

"Either way," Pearce said, rubbing his forehead in exhaustion, "you all can do whatever you'd like, but after the service, I'm going to go back to the temple. I'd like to try to recover his—" His words dropped off as he covered his eyes, his chest quivering, "recover his body," he said faintly, his voice shaking as he began to sob for the first time.

Naomi rushed to him and wrapped her arms tightly around his chest.

"Wow, this is tough to watch," Spirit Rivo sighed. "Seeing everyone I care about in this condition. I just wish there was something I could do. Some way I could let them know that I'm watching over them."

Chapter 35

The Cry of the Dove

Most Gracious King Roland of Wyverly,

I trust this letter finds you well. I am certain that by the time this letter reaches your hands, the good news of the Haundo's defeat has already reached your ears, and I have already been informed that the honorable Duke Kincaid is on his way to congratulate us all.

So as not to burden Your Majesty's valuable time with redundant information, I will keep this letter as brief as possible.

Wyverly has emerged victorious, and we are now rid of the Haundo threat. This victory is thanks in no small part to the countless brave men and women across the ranks of the Wyverly military, and much gratitude is also due to the invaluable intel provided by the Forest Folk.

That being said, and I say this in no way to disparage those who fought, and the many who perished throughout these strenuous months of facing this vile threat, there is one brave soldier whom I feel deserves special recognition for his contribution to our victory: Rivo of Greencourt.

It was by Rivo's blade that the Haundo were ultimately defeated. It seems that once their leader fell, the rest fell with him. It was as if their existence was tied to his somehow, though I doubt we'll ever fully understand how exactly this was the case. I am sure Your Majesty has many questions about our victory and this heroic young man from one of the smallest villages in the Kingdom. I wish I could offer more details to you at this time.

Though in many ways my heart leaps as the Kingdom is now at peace, it also aches as I must sadly inform Your Majesty that young Rivo perished in the final battle with the Haundo.

Though I am certain that Your Majesty, along with all of Your loyal subjects in the Kingdom, wish to know more about this remarkable young soldier, I am afraid there is little I can add at this time.

Even others within the ranks here at the outpost have been pressing me for more information about our young hero. They all want to know what it was like to serve with him, what kind of soldier he was, and so forth.

I wish I could say he and I were close, that we were comrades and confidants, but that simply wouldn't be true. As Your Majesty knows, I was raised never to tell a lie or even to embellish. The truth is, though I was present at key times in his journey, I simply cannot claim that I was well enough acquainted with him to give those who ask the insights they seek. All I will say on the matter is this: Rivo was like a shooting star; when it seemed the sun had set on the Kingdom and darkness came, he shone brightly. And like a shooting star, when the sun rose again and the darkness lifted, he was gone.

Please send my regards to Her Majesty the Queen and the rest of the royal family. I look forward to being in your presence in the near future.

Yours respectfully,

R. Magnus Tremlee
Captain, North Wyverly Battalion

***

Duke Kincaid had arrived about an hour before the service was to be held, alcohol on his breath, and an eye for the ladies, as usual. Vickie made sure to keep her distance. She didn't want to go, but Renee was adamant.

"I want to hear the kingdom honor Rivo," she told Vickie.

"I'm at my own funeral. I can't believe it," Spirit Rivo said, shaking his head.

They all gathered in the courtyard to hear the Duke deliver his address. His speech was surprisingly heartfelt; he choked back tears a couple of times as he described how so many lives had been lost over the course of the last several months. How so many lived in fear, and how all have lost someone they loved.

Must be the alcohol talking, Vickie thought to herself.

"Really, Vickie?" Spirit Rivo couldn't help but let out a faint chuckle at Vickie's musings.

Unfortunately, the Duke knew nothing of the individuals who were lost in the battle two days earlier—Though in fairness, how could he? Rivo's heroism hadn't yet been made known to the royal family, or to any outside a handful of people at the outpost. Duke Kincaid did the best he could with what he knew of the battle. "And we both celebrate our victory and mourn the loss of our heroes, such as that young man who battled alongside Cade," he said somberly.

"Rivo!" Renee shrieked as she wept, "His name was Rivo, dammit, and he deserves to be remembered!" She dropped to her knees as she continued to sob.

Spirit Rivo looked upon the scene, tearful and heartbroken by what his death had done to those close to him. "Renee, I'm so sorry. I wish I could just talk to you one more time."

The others in attendance turned to look at Renee, their expressions all shocked. Duke Kincaid struggled to keep his composure, while Vickie quickly came to her sister's aid, followed by Naomi. They picked her up by her arms and helped her to a shaded area under a tree away from the crowd. Pearce and Judd followed close behind.

"Renee," Vickie chided, "what was that?"

"Just leave me alone, Vick," Renee snapped through her tears. "So this is how his story ends? Forgotten by the kingdom he died for?"

"No, it isn't," replied Naomi as she held Renee close to her. "We'll always carry him with us. One day, everyone will know his story."

"He saved my life, I'll never forget that," remarked a sobbing Judd.

"He was our family, Renee," Pearce added as he knelt in front of her. "We've known him his whole life. It means a lot to us that you cared for him so deeply."

"Renee, I think we just need to get away from this place. To create some distance. There's nothing here for us anymore." Vickie told her as she knelt down and combed her sister's hair with her fingers. "I say the three of us load up and start heading back to Rhemilia. I'm sure Mr. Sundry and the people there will be thrilled to hear the news of Wyverly's victory. We'll see about joining back up with the circus troupe and going back to the way things were."

Judd stood up straight. "You two can go ahead back to Rhemilia if you want. I'm gonna stay here and help Pearce and Naomi at the temple with the recovery effort," he announced.

"Judd, are you sure?" Vickie asked. "I know why you're doing this, but you don't owe Rivo anything anymore. These things happen in war."

"She's right," Pearce interjected. "We'd certainly welcome any help, but please don't feel obligated."

Renee got up and went to stand next to Judd. "Well, I think I'll join Judd and the rest of you," she said as she nodded to Pearce and Naomi.

Vickie sagged her shoulders. "Oh, no. Renee," she pleaded. "Please stop doing this to yourself. That boy is gone."

"Renee, Judd, please listen to Vickie," Spirit Rivo said desperately. "Don't go through this for me."

Renee shook her head and looked intently at her sister. "Just let me do this, Vick. Please. You don't have to come."

Vickie dropped her head and stood silent for a moment. "I'm going if you're going, Renee," she muttered.

***

The temple structure was far from stable. When they arrived the following morning, they noticed that yet another section had already fallen, making their recovery efforts even more difficult. Day after day, they were out there moving stones until their fingers bled, with no sign of Rivo. On the last day, another part of the temple wall collapsed, nearly taking some soldiers out.

Captain Tremlee called the recovery efforts off after that incident. "It's simply too dangerous," he said in resignation. "Besides, even if he were found, the condition his body would be in..." his voice trailed off, not wanting to say what everyone knew to be true.

As much as they all hated it, they knew the Captain was right. It was approaching the end of the day, and with the structure still collapsing, it felt like they were making no progress.

"I'll do whatever you want me to, Pearce," Judd said, hunched over and dripping with sweat.

"You've done more than enough, Judd," Pearce replied as he patted the strongman on the back. "We haven't made any progress," he said, exhausted, with a look of defeat across his face as he looked at Naomi. "We tried, Naomi. It's no use. Tremlee's right. "

Naomi sat with her head in her hands. A look of initial defiance was replaced with reluctant acceptance. "I'm sorry, Rivo," she groaned, her voice strained. "We tried."

"Naomi...Pearce," Spirit Rivo muttered as he put his head in his hand. "Don't put yourselves through this any longer. I can't bear it anymore, please just get on with your lives."

Renee sat beside Naomi and put her arm around her shoulders.

"Renee, I know you probably want to stay, but it's time to leave," Vickie said as she knelt beside her sister. "I feel we're only making things worse for us all."

Renee didn't reply. But only nodded quickly, with her lip quivering and her eyes glistening with tears.

As everyone was preparing to leave, Renee stood watching the fallen temple, lost in grief. "I can't get over what it must have been like for him in those final moments," she said softly.

Vickie put her hand on Renee's shoulder. "I know, Renee," she said gently, "but whatever happened, he's not in pain anymore. Let's let his spirit rest in peace."

What was it like, Rivo? Vickie wondered. *Did you go quickly, or were you in agony? I can't imagine. I'm sure Renee will always want to know.*

"I wish I could tell you, Vickie," Spirit Rivo replied. "I wish you all wouldn't keep putting yourselves through this for me."

Renee patted Vickie's hand and closed her eyes. "Vick," she said as she still faced the wreckage, "Why don't you go on back with the rest of them? I think I may stay here by myself for a little while."

Vickie dropped her hands to her side. "Oh, Renee," she moaned. "Please don't. We need to go, it's gonna get dark soon."

Renee turned to her sister. "I'll be fine, Vick," she replied. "I can take care of myself. I'll be back before bedtime."

Vickie slowly rubbed her eyes. "Renee, please," she begged. "I don't like the idea of you being out here by yourself this late. Can I at least stay with you?"

Renee shook her head. "I'd like to be by myself, Vick," she said as she held Vickie's hands in her own. "I'll be fine. The Haundo are gone, remember?"

Vickie closed her eyes and drew a deep breath. "Okay, Renee, but I'm not going back to the outpost without you," she said with a worried expression. "I'll wait a little ways out for you. That way, you'll still have some privacy, and I'll feel better knowing you aren't too far away. And I'll make sure to ask the Captain to leave a horse for us so we can get back quicker."

Renee sighed and slowly shook her head.

"Please, Renee?" Vickie asked desperately.

"Fine," Renee replied grudgingly. "I'll meet you there in a little while."

***

After everyone else left, Renee slowly paced the grounds outside the temple. The air stood still as she heard the chirps of insects and the scurries of small critters moving about. She sat on a large rock that lay not far from the bridge, near where she had last seen Rivo, bravely charging to his eventual death.

No longer having to worry about any onlookers, Renee sank to the ground, on her knees, sobbing. Tears streamed down her face unabated, like waterfalls, her body quivering.

"Renee..." Spirit Rivo said longingly. "I would do anything to be by your side right now. I wish there were some way I could comfort you."

As Renee let her tears run freely, she looked to see some dandelions and daisies sprouting out from the base of the rock she had just been sitting on. She reached over and grabbed a handful of them. The memories of Rivo's over-the-top gesture of giving her flowers, just like those to cheer her up, play through her mind. Her sobs slowly gave way to a faint chuckle in her reverie.

She studied the flowers in her hand, slowly humming a melody. She rose to her feet and started singing an old song she had once heard in her travels:

All of the stars shine so perfect in spring
All the fools wish for the good luck they bring
They light up the sky with their beautiful glow
It's said that if you ask them, their secrets you'll know
A wish from the heart can never go wrong
So why does the mourning dove still sing her song
They sail through the air like a songbird in flight
Their brightness gives hope in the darkness of night
But I've asked, and they never brought back my lost love
So all they'll hear now is the cry of the dove

"Renee...your voice. That was beautiful," Spirit Rivo lamented.

Renee walked across the bridge leading to the now caved-in temple entrance. She knelt down and set the flowers on the ground in front of the rubble. "For you, Rivo. Maybe they'll cheer you up a bit," she said softly. She then took off her cloak, the one that belonged to Rivo's mother, and hugged it tightly to her chest before setting it down as well. "Take this too, so you don't get cold," she added, her voice trembling.

She remembered his headband was in her satchel and pulled it out. She was about to place it along side the cloak, but held onto to it tightly instead. "I'm going to keep this, if that's okay with you," she whispered, tucking it back into her satchel

She let out a heavy sigh, fighting back the tears welling up in her eyes. "Goodbye, Rivo...I'm gonna miss you," she moaned as she stood up and wearily made her way back to meet Vickie and head to the outpost.

Spirit Rivo stood facing her, tears streaming down his ghostly face. "Renee, I'm so sorry...for all of this."

The next morning, the group of five exchanged tearful goodbyes as they left the outpost and parted ways for likely the last time. They left on separate steam cars, with Vickie, Renee, and Judd heading back to Rhemilia to meet up with Mr. Sundry on the first car, while Pearce and Naomi headed back toward Greencourt on the next one, departing later that day.

Chapter 36

This Was You

"*You either get bitter, or you get better.* That's what my mother always told me," Gwen said to her grieving young son. He had hardly left the house since his father died just a few weeks earlier.

"But I don't know how to get better, Mother," replied a teary-eyed Rivo.

She ran her fingers through his hair and kissed him on his head. "Our pain, our suffering, it can either bring us closer to others or drive us away from them," she told him. "The choice is yours. When you hurt, you either want to make others hurt, or you want to do anything you can to keep others from hurting."

"I don't want anybody to feel the way I feel right now," Rivo remarked as he rubbed his tear-swollen eyes.

"I know, Rivo, me neither," she replied gently as she hugged her young son. "You know what? It sounds like you're already getting a little better."

"Really?" he asked, looking up at her, his eyes glistening.

"Yes, really." She pressed her forehead against his and closed her eyes. "Oh, Rivo," she sighed, "you have such a good heart. Don't ever lose that."

***

Rivo's spirit was again whisked away, this time to Rhemilia. It was late in the evening, several days after they all left the outpost. He saw Vickie and Renee sitting on a hill, overlooking the town. He could practically see the whole town from there: the inn where they stayed, the rushball field he and Renee had played at, and the fairgrounds where they held the circus on that fateful night.

"Why am I back here?" Spirit Rivo asked. "Can't I just end this? This is torture. I just want my life back," he groaned, rubbing his forehead in frustration. "I want to be with everyone again. Please, is there anyone who can hear me? Who's doing this to me? I want a second chance!" he shouted. "I want to see Pearce and Naomi, I want to see Judd, and even Vickie. I want...to see Renee."

As he drifted closer, he saw that Renee was lying on the ground on her side, her head on Vickie's lap, crying. "When does the pain go away, Vick?" she sobbed.

Vickie was gently stroking her sister's hair as she looked hopelessly off in the distance. "I don't know, Renee," she said as a tear rolled down her own cheek, grieving over her sister's heartache. "I'm sorry, I wish I could make it all better. I would do anything to take your pain away right now."

"Why?" Renee moaned, "Why couldn't I just tell him how I felt about him? I never told him that I loved him!"

I wish I had never let that boy within ten feet of you, Renee, she thought to herself. *Stars be damned, Rivo...you broke my sister's heart...I'll never forgive you for this.*

Spirit Rivo's translucent body collapsed hopelessly in front of them, "Renee..." he pleaded, "I'm so sorry. I'm so sorry I put you through all of this. I'm sorry I didn't see how much you loved me." He held his head in his hands as he looked at her face. "I love you, Renee. I would do anything for the chance to tell you that one time... Why am I having to suffer like this?" he cried as he looked at the nighttime sky. "Why can't I do anything about this? I just don't understand. Who is behind this? Why are they doing this to me?"

He sat despairingly as he watched Vickie help Renee up and walk her to their room at the inn. She tucked her in bed and kissed her sister on the forehead. *Oh, Renee, you were too good for that boy...damn you, Rivo.*

"Vickie, I'm so sorry. I wish you could hear my thoughts like I can hear yours," he responded. "That's what I don't understand. Why in the world can I hear only your thoughts? This makes no sense!"

Rivo's spirit lingered in the room, a faint glimmer against the moonlight spilling through the window. Vickie, believing her sister to be asleep, went out to take a nighttime stroll to clear her head. Renee, however, lay in bed still awake.

He could do little more than sigh in despair as he watched on. "Renee, I would do anything to make you feel better right now," he lamented.

Lying in bed, tears streaming down her face, Renee stared blankly out the window. "I just wish you were still here, that you would somehow return, even if you never loved me back," she whispered. "Rivo, you were my shooting star. And like a shooting star, I could always see you, even though you could never see me."

Rivo was speechless. As much as it hurt to admit, she was right. Renee had been looking out for him the whole time, and he had never truly noticed her watching over him. "I don't know what else to say, Renee. I'm sorry for not seeing you," he murmured, his voice a useless echo in the dark.

"I've been invisible to the whole world my entire life. Why should you have been any different?" She pressed her blanket to her face, muffling a sob, "Oh, Rivo. I would have been so good to you, if you only knew."

He sat on the floor beside her bed, holding his ghostly head in his hands. "I can't take this anymore. I can't stand to see her suffer like this!"

"It's my own fault, I guess. I never told you how I felt. I could have, but I was just too much of a coward."

"You're not a coward, Renee. You're the bravest person I've ever known."

"Do you remember when I kissed you on the forehead after you fought Tuval the first time? Or how I hugged you tightly the night before your last battle? Did you know that you're the only boy I've ever done that to?"

Her breath quivered through her sobs; a symphony of crickets outside was the only sound to break the silence.

"And the time I hugged you, I was so nervous. Not just about the hug, but about what I wanted to tell you."

Rivo raised his eyebrows. "What did you want to tell me, Renee?"

"I so badly wanted to tell you how I felt. I wanted to tell you that you didn't have to fight anymore. I wanted to tell you that we could just run off together, somewhere far away where nobody could find us. I wanted to tell you that I would take care of you. That I would always be by your side."

She paused to wipe away her tears with the sleeve of her gown. "I knew that would have been selfish of me. The kingdom is bigger than my heart. You were a soldier; you had a duty to the kingdom, not to me. You did the right thing."

Rivo sat by, hanging on her every word.

"Just imagine if we could have been together, Rivo. I think about it all the time. Anything you would have given me, I would have given it back to you tenfold. If you had given me land, I would've given you a garden. If you had given me a house, I would've given you a home, if you had given me your love...I would've given you a family."

"Whoa, Renee... " he gasped.

"Oh, Rivo," her voice trailed off as sleep began to overtake her, "I...would have been so...good to you." With that, the room fell silent—Renee had finally fallen asleep.

Rivo's anguish was becoming unbearable. "Whoever or whatever is behind this, show yourself! Why are you doing this to me? To Renee!" He sat with his back against the side of the bed, hopelessness and despair overtaking him. "Is this some sort of curse for killing Tuval? Some kind of black magic?"

The now-familiar gust of wind roared to sweep him away. The room slowly faded to black. "What now?" he groaned, "I've had enough of this torture."

***

As Renee lay asleep, Spirit Rivo found himself outside with Vickie, still out on her evening stroll. She walked to the place outside the fairgrounds where they had all first met. She closed her eyes and thought back to that moment, how that meeting changed all of their lives.

"Oh, great. Vickie," Spirit Rivo scoffed. "Why in stars' light do I need to listen to her now?"

"I was right about one thing, wasn't I, Renee?" she asked herself, "That fool was gonna get himself killed, and he was gonna take you down with him." She sighed as another tear ran down her cheek. "Rivo...I have the feeling that you're still out there. That you somehow pulled through. I don't know why, but I just kind of have that feeling. Then again, maybe that's just your foolish optimism that's rubbed off on me. But I certainly wish you were here, so you can look at what you've done to us all... So you can see what you've done to *her*."

As Vickie continued on her walk, she went back to the hill overlooking the town, the place she and Renee had just been sitting earlier that evening. She fell to her knees, weeping over her sister's broken heart. "Damn you, Rivo," she gasped. "You broke the one thing in this world that I loved more than anything else! That girl gave her heart to you, and you were too dumb to even realize it," she howled, pounding her fist on the ground.

It was then that she gazed up and noticed shooting stars dashing across the sky. She desperately reached out, as if to hold one in her hand, only to have it slip through her grasp.

As Vickie knelt hopelessly on the cool, wet grass, she closed her eyes, drew a deep breath...and made a wish.

***

Spirit Rivo saw the hills and the grass fade away as he found himself in an empty void. "What's happening now?" he asked, his voice quivering. He noticed that this time, he wasn't alone. Vickie stood nearby, gazing in his direction, almost as if she could see him.

"Vickie?" he asked, his eyebrows furrowed. "Vickie, can you see me?" He waved his hands desperately in front of her, but got no response. "What are you doing? Why are we here together?" he pleaded, to no response.

"I wish," she spoke softly, "that you would come back, Rivo... That you would come and give Renee the life she deserves. That you would marry her and build her the house of her dreams. That she would give you beautiful children and you would give her love and happiness." Tears were cascading down her face like a waterfall.

Vickie's tearful eyes turned angry and vindictive. "But first," she added, "I want you to suffer."

"Huh?" Rivo's eyes went wide as he took a step back.

"That's right, Rivo," she grunted through her clenched teeth, looking directly at him, almost as if she could see him. "You don't just get to come back and sweep her off her feet...you need to suffer first." She balled her fists as her eyes narrowed in fury. "I want you to see and feel the pain you've caused her. You can't look away, you can't close your eyes, you have to see it! I want your spirit to come back first, you have to relive every bit of it, all the way back—Back to the first time you put on that *stupid* headband that she thought looked so cute on you," she said sharply, a look of vengeance upon her face. "I want you to see the first time you met, to see that damned rushball game. What, did you think that was a coincidence? She had been keeping her eye on you, waiting for a chance to be around you again, Rivo."

Rivo stood frozen, gaping at Vickie.

"I want you to see how she slowly fell in love with you, and then I want you to torture yourself the way she tortured herself because she didn't know what to do about it." Her voice shook with anger as she stepped toward him. "I want you to see how she almost got herself killed saving your worthless neck from Tuval in the tower, how she watched over you the whole time you were laid up in that hospital bed. I want you to see how her heart shattered as she watched you die in that temple. I want you to see her break down again and again over you, how she screamed for you at that memorial service, how she cried herself to sleep tonight. I want you to see all of it! And I want you to hear every thought I have...so you can know how much I hate you right now. And when you find yourself screaming into the darkness for answers, I want you to know that it was *me* who did this to you." Her chest heaved in rage as she pointed toward him. "I want you to be on your hands and knees, begging for one more chance to see Renee. Then, Rivo...then you can come back." She dropped her hands to her side as her breathing slowly returned to normal.

"The last time we spoke, Rivo, you told me to wish on a shooting star for you," she said as she closed her eyes and let out a slow sigh. "Well, Rivo...this...is my wish."

Vickie slowly vanished from sight while Spirit Rivo stood with his hands atop his head, blinking his eyes in bewilderment. "I can't believe it," he gasped. "Vickie, this...this was you all along..."

Chapter 37

A Familiar Embrace

Spirit Rivo stood distraught, alone in the void, his breathing sharp and erratic. "It all makes sense now," he said, rubbing the side of his face. "That's why I could hear Vickie's thoughts. Why so much of this involved Renee?"

Rivo fell to his hands and knees. "Damn you, Vickie!" he sobbed. "I'm sorry. I'm so sorry for what you all are going through because of me. I'm sorry I didn't see how Renee loved me and was watching over me the whole time," he said remorsefully. "I need to get back, I have to!" he cried. "I have to see Renee. Can anybody hear me? Please tell me I'm not alone," he pleaded desperately.

From the dark void came a loud and familiar male voice. "Rivo... Rivo! Over here," the voice called out.

"Who said that?" Rivo asked as he jumped to his feet. "Can you hear me?" He scanned his surroundings and saw two translucent figures off in the distance.

"Yes, Rivo," answered a gentle female voice. "We're over here."

As he approached the two figures, he was able to make out their appearance. A man with sandy brown hair and a short, trimmed beard, and a woman with long brown hair tied in a low bun.

"Mother! Father!" Rivo hollered as he sped toward them. "Is it really you?"

"It is, Rivo," Frank replied as he and Gwen embraced their son for the first time since he was a boy. The embrace didn't feel like a real hug but was still warm, comfortable, and familiar.

"Yes, Rivo. It's really us," said his mother. "It's good to see you again."

His parents stepped back to look over Rivo from head to toe. "My stars, son, look how you've grown," Frank said, smiling proudly.

"And you two look exactly as I remember," Rivo replied joyfully. "I'm so glad you're here. Thank the stars, I'm so glad!" he said, wiping tears from his ghostly face. "The things you taught me when I was a boy, all the lessons you shared with me, I remember them all," he said, his hands shaking with excitement. "I held on to everything. It was your words that helped pull me through so many trials."

"We know, Rivo," Gwen replied, smiling warmly. "You want to know how we know?"

Rivo paused for a moment as he thought over her question. "How did you know? Were you watching over me the whole time?"

His parents looked at each other, then back at him. "Not exactly, Rivo," said Frank. "It was because we both made a wish when we were still alive."

Rivo took a step back, his eyes darting back and forth between the two of them. "You made a wish?"

"Yes, Rivo," his mother answered as she softly touched his arm. "Both of us did. We wished on a shooting star that if we couldn't be with you, then our words would be there to help carry you through life's storms."

Rivo swallowed hard and slowly nodded his head. "I understand," he said as he thought back to all the times their words would come to him throughout his journey. "So…what now?" he asked hesitantly. "Are you here to guide me to the afterlife?"

Frank smiled and shook his head. "No, son. We're here because of *your* wish."

"My wish?" Rivo said, confused, rubbing his forehead as he thought back to his own wish.

"Do you remember that wish you made when you were a boy, Rivo?" his mother asked expectantly. "Do you remember that? When you saw a shooting star after your father read you a bedtime story."

"Oh, yeah," Rivo replied, scratching his head in embarrassment. "I do remember that."

"Silly me, Rivo," his father chuckled. "We thought you wished to become a hero." Frank rubbed his chin, smiling broadly. "We should have known. You already knew you were going to be a hero. Your wish wasn't for that, it was—"

"It was for you to be around to listen to me tell my story," Rivo interrupted.

"That's right!" said Frank, playfully wagging his finger at his son.

"And *that* is why we're here, Rivo," Gwen added as she wrapped her arm around her husband's.

"Well, Rivo?" Frank asked, looking expectantly at his son. "We wanna hear *all* about it."

Rivo rubbed his eyes, laughing in disbelief. "I can't believe this," he whispered.

He told them everything that he had gone through: about being recruited along with Pearce and Naomi, about fighting the Haundo, the truth about Tuval and Garel, he told them of all the friends he had made and the trials he had faced along the way… He told them about Renee, and how she loved him and watched over him, and he told them about how he fell in battle after defeating Tuval.

Frank and Gwen looked at each other, their eyes filled with pride. "Amazing, son," Frank said as he looked back at Rivo. "You've truly become a hero."

"And this Renee girl, she sounds amazing, Rivo," Gwen added.

Rivo smiled faintly and sighed. "Thank you, Father. And yes, Renee is amazing. But," he paused for a moment, "I don't really feel like a hero right now."

"What do you mean, son?" asked Frank.

"After you died, I remember crying to Mother," Rivo replied. "I remember telling her that I didn't want anybody to feel the way I felt back then." He let out a frustrated sigh and shook his head. "But that's exactly what I've done. The people I love, they're feeling that same way right now."

There was a brief silence between the three of them. Frank looked at Gwen and nodded before placing his hand on Rivo's shoulder. "Son," he said calmly. "What if this isn't the end for you?" he asked. "Remember, Rivo, we told you that we weren't here to guide you to the afterlife."

Rivo drew his head back in surprise as he tried to understand his father's words. "What do you mean?" he asked in disbelief. "I died in that battle. I got crushed when the temple collapsed. I just saw it again. There's no way anyone could have survived that," he said adamantly.

"Rivo," his mother said firmly. "Listen to your father."

"Son," his father interjected. "There's something we need to tell you." He took a deep breath. "It's been about two weeks since you fell in that battle. But something happened during that time."

Rivo's eyes widened. "What do you mean?" he asked.

Frank put both his hands on his son's shoulders and looked him directly in the eyes. "Shortly after the battle, right around the time of the memorial service, some Forest Folk were rummaging through the debris at the temple. There, they found a young man, unconscious but alive, barely clinging to life."

"They found you, Rivo," his mother added. "They didn't recognize you at first, but you know how superstitious they are about leaving men to die. They carefully brought you back to their hideout and have been taking care of you. They've been applying oil to your wounds, feeding you soup and porridge...they've been keeping you alive, Rivo."

Rivo immediately thought of Bon. "Is he there? Does Bon know?" he panted.

"Yes, Rivo," answered Frank. "He's been watching over you nonstop. He's hardly left your side."

Rivo stood in shock. "Bon," he whispered.

"Rivo," said Gwen. "It's time now. It's time for you to go back. It was good seeing you again, but your time here is over. We'll meet again, a long time from now," she said as she and Frank both held Rivo's hands.

"We love you, Rivo. We'll always love you," said Frank, as the two began to vanish from sight.

"Mother...Father," whispered Rivo. "What's happening?" he asked frantically, looking at his translucent arms as they slowly disintegrated. "What...what's going on?" He felt a gust, as he had before, but this time, all he could feel was an eerie darkness. His spirit body was gone—it was just nothingness.

Then he heard what sounded like the shuffling of feet walking through dead leaves and the faint muttering of voices in the distance. Rivo gasped for air and slowly opened his eyes. He looked around to find himself lying down in a makeshift shelter made of large twigs tied together. It was only a few feet tall and wide, walled in on three sides, with rags and garments used as a curtain covering the open side on his right. He moaned as he strained to move his arms; his body was no longer translucent, but solid and heavy.

"Rivo?...Rivo!" a familiar voice gasped excitedly.

The curtain was pulled back as Bon entered and knelt beside him. "Rivo!" he shouted.

"Bon? Is that really you? Can you really see me?" Rivo groaned, his eyelids heavy with fatigue.

Bon put his hand on Rivo's shoulder. "Aye," he said softly, with a warm smile.

Rivo slowly scanned his surroundings, his neck stiff and sore. The weight of his arms and legs as he began to move them felt surreal. His heart raced as the realization finally settled in. For the first time in what seemed like ages, Rivo was back in his real body.

Chapter 38

A Familiar Face

"Bon," Rivo said faintly. "This is real! I'm really back!"

Bon smiled big and nodded. "Aye!" he replied.

Rivo rubbed his eyes, trying to collect his thoughts. "Oh, Bon...I'm so sorry about everything—everything you went through, about your papa, about Zon," he moaned as he clasped the boy's hand.

The boy began to sob, "Papa...Bub-Bub..."

Rivo grabbed the back of Bon's neck. "Bon...you don't need to worry anymore. The monster's gone. I saw to it myself. He can't hurt you or anyone you love ever again."

Bon wiped the tears from his eyes and nodded. "Aye. Monster gone. Rivo...thank you."

Rivo slowly sat up, *My body's stiff, weak, and really sore*, he thought. *But, other than that, I feel alright. Bon, you've really been taking care of me, thank you.*

"Bon," Rivo said, grimacing as he felt a sharp pain shoot through his side. "I can't thank you enough. You saved my life." He stopped to favor his aching ribs. "But I need to get back to—"

"Home," Bon interrupted as he nodded knowingly.

Rivo let out a remorseful sigh. He wished that there was some way he could repay the boy and the other Forest Folk for rescuing and taking care of him, but he had to go back. He had to let Pearce and Naomi know that he was still alive. He had to see Renee.

"Yes, Bon," Rivo replied faintly. "But first," he added, realizing how weak he felt. "I think I need some solid food." He lay back down, so drained that he felt he might fall back asleep, but he forced himself to stay awake, frightened over what might happen if he slept.

"Aye, food," Bon replied as he went to get Rivo some bread and meat.

Rivo wasted no time in scarfing the food down. It had been two weeks since he'd had a proper meal after all. "Bon, I hate to ask you for another favor. But I have to go, and I can't wait until I'm strong enough to walk on my own. Is there any way—"

"Bon help!" The boy volunteered eagerly.

Rivo let out a weak chuckle. "I would be grateful. Where are we exactly? How far are we from the nearest town?"

"Close. Close to friends," the boy said as he pointed off to the distance.

The Forest Folk had set up a camp high up on a hill in the woods. From there, Rivo could look out over most of the northern forest region. He squinted and saw a familiar sight in the distance. There it was, the temple where he had battled Tuval, or what was left of it anyway.

A bittersweet smile crossed Rivo's face. "So back to the old outpost then," he remarked as he lay his head back down. "I wonder who all is still out there."

Bon whistled, and one of his comrades came over. He motioned toward Rivo, and the man seemed to know what he was wanting. Bon and the man got on either side of Rivo and helped him up, then slowly got under his arms and helped him to an open carriage that was on the outside of their camp. Rivo heard the chatter among the other Forest Folk watching on; the only word he could make out was *"Beastkiller."*

As they helped him get into the back of the carriage, they placed some garments and sacks underneath him so he would have some sort of cushion for the bumpy ride. Bon jumped up next to him as the other man got on the perch to drive the horses, and off they went.

Rivo grimaced in pain after every dip and bump, each one a reminder of his battle with Tuval. And a reminder to be thankful for having a body that could feel pain again. He kept reassuring himself, *my family, my friends, they're worth it... She's worth it.*

A few hours later, they arrived at the outpost. Bon helped Rivo get out of the carriage. Soldiers were standing guard next to the demolished tower from Rivo and Tuval's first battle. They approached the wagon to see what the Forest Folk had brought, only to find Rivo being helped along by his friend, Bon.

"Who in the stars' light is this?" asked one of the soldiers as they approached the newcomers.

The other soldier chimed in, "No way... That's him! The guy that fought with Cade."

The first soldier turned to him, shocked. "What? No way! I thought he died."

The other soldier shook his head and grinned. "There's no doubt about it. That's Rivo, the Beastkiller."

Rivo could barely lift his head up. He looked at the officer with a faint smile. "It's me. In the flesh...this time."

"Somebody get the captain!" the soldier hollered.

The soldiers took Rivo from Bon, but not before Rivo could put his hand on the boy's shoulder, "Bon," he said, "thank you. I'll never forget you."

Bon then clasped both his hands together as he did back when they first met, a sign of their friendship. "Rivo, Bon."

Rivo clasped his hands together in return. "Bon, Rivo," he replied, his voice quivering. And with that, Bon of the Forest Folk got back on the wagon and rode off. Rivo never saw the boy again, but would think of his dear friend often.

One of the soldiers helping Rivo patted his back to get his attention, "C'mon, kid, let's get you to the infirmary."

Chapter 39

A True Warrior

The outpost had a skeleton crew. Most of the soldiers had either gone back home or moved on to other assignments. There were still some wounded being treated, along with some medical personnel and a handful of guards. Rivo was brought in and taken to the same room he was in before. As he lay in the bed, he recalled how the last time he was in that room, Vickie was there, warning him not to die. Rivo couldn't help but laugh at the memory. "Man, I can't wait to see the look on her face."

Just then, he heard a familiar voice. "I have to see this for myself! Where is he?" Captain Tremlee shouted from outside his door. He marched into the room and stopped dead in his tracks as he looked at their new patient. "Stars be damned, Rivo of Greencourt," he gasped as his eyes widened. "How in the stars' light..."

"It was the Forest Folk, Captain," Rivo interjected. "They found me, nursed me back to health, and brought me back," he replied with a wry smile.

"Rivo..." the Captain gasped as his eyes welled up in a rare display of emotion. "Rivo, I'm so sorry we left you." He approached Rivo and placed his hand on his shoulder. "If I thought there was any chance... Please forgive me, son," he pleaded, shaking his head in disbelief. "The building was collapsing. I just couldn't risk anyone else—"

"It's okay, Captain," Rivo assured him as he patted his hand. "You did the right thing."

Tremlee began pacing back and forth frantically. "I have to make it up to you," he pleaded. "I'm going to send for a transport to pick up Pearce and Naomi immediately."

Rivo shook his head and waved the Captain off. "You don't need to do that right now. I think I'd like to surprise them. The only thing I would ask for is a ride out there."

The Captain spun around to face Rivo and stood upright, as if being called to attention by a superior officer. "Rivo, that's the least I can do for you," he said in a commanding tone. "We'll have a steam car ready for you whenever you would like." The Captain paused for a moment. He walked up close to Rivo, putting his hand back on his shoulder. "You saved the kingdom, Rivo. You—are a true hero."

Captain Tremlee turned to look out the window, his arms behind his back. "The Blade of the Shooting Star," he said with gravitas as he looked over the grounds of the complex. "That's what they've been calling you, Rivo. Cade told us that's the last thing you said before taking down Tuval. The name just kind of stuck."

Rivo sat up, looking at the Captain, bemused. "What?" he chuckled. "Who's calling me that?"

"Everybody, Rivo," the Captain replied. "Your name and your story, it's spread across the kingdom like wildfire. You've brought hope back to this land, son."

Rivo sat there, both humbled and perplexed. "Thank you, sir. I'm honored." He sat silently for a moment, taking it all in. *Life's never gonna be the same for me again, is it?*

As he thought over everything the Captain had told him, he remembered his old brother-in-arms. "By the way, where's Cade?" he asked. "Did he leave already?"

"Oh, and let you come back from the dead and hog all the glory? I don't think so," said a booming voice from the hallway just outside. Cade walked into the room with the aid of a crutch, a broad smile across his face, replacing his trademark scowl. *And I thought the Captain's show of emotion was rare,* Rivo thought.

Rivo's face lit up as he laid eyes on his old comrade. "Well, look at you! Still a true warrior, even without a war," he teased.

Cade threw his head back in mock surprise. "Me a warrior?" he replied, placing his hand on his chest. "Look at you, Rivo. Saving the kingdom and my hide along with it," he said as he hobbled closer and pointed at Rivo. "You, Rivo, are a *true* warrior."

In yet another rare showcase of emotion, Captain Tremlee laughed at the sight of his two Beastkillers finally getting along. "Well, I'll leave you two alone to argue over which one is the truer warrior and go make sure a steam car is set aside for Rivo," the Captain said as he patted Cade on the shoulder and headed toward the door. On his way out, he turned back toward Rivo. "Oh, and Rivo. Expect to get a personal invitation from the king soon. He'll be scrambling to meet you once he hears about this," the Captain added as he gave a salute and walked out the door.

With the Captain now gone, Cade closed the door and locked it, then hobbled back toward Rivo.

Rivo looked at Cade with a puzzled expression. "Cade? What's going on?" he asked.

Cade dropped to his knees at the side of Rivo's bed, sobbing. "Rivo," he said through his tears. "I'm so sorry. For everything. For underestimating you, for talking down to you like I did. For abandoning you at the temple after you saved my life. I owe you, Rivo," he cried. "Everything I have and everything I am, my life, everything. I'm in your debt. I will work the rest of my life to repay you."

Rivo gently patted Cade's shoulder. "It's okay, Cade. Really. It all worked out," he told him.

Cade shook his head, unable to look Rivo in the eye. "I can't accept that, Rivo. I need to repay you," he begged.

Rivo put his hands up defensively. "Cade, I don't need anything. You don't need to make it up to me," he said adamantly. "I know you would have done the same if the situation were reversed."

Cade lifted his head up and tightened his jaw with determination; he wasn't going to take no for an answer. Just then, a thought occurred to Rivo. "Well, there is one thing you can help me with," he said, leaning toward the other Beastkiller.

Cade shot up straight. "What is it? I'll do it!"

"Are you in good enough condition to drive one of those steam cars? I could use a ride."

Cade nodded. "I will do my best!"

Rivo leaned back and ran his fingers through his hair. "Great! The doctor should be coming by soon. Once he gives me a clean bill of health, we'll get a good night's rest and then leave in the morning after breakfast. Sound good?"

"Yes! Tomorrow morning," Cade said as he nodded again. "Until then, I will stand guard at your door. Don't hesitate to let me know if you need anything."

Rivo wearily rubbed his forehead. "Cade, you don't need to stand guard; we're not at war anymore."

"Nevertheless, I will be posted just outside your door. Just in case!" Cade barked as he marched, still limping, yet still looking like a brigadier general to stand guard outside of Rivo's room.

"Oh brother," Rivo said to himself. "This guy's something else." He took a deep breath as he gathered his thoughts. "So, I'm really going back... Hold tight, Renee...I'm coming."

***

Rivo slept soundly through the night, despite Cade periodically marching into his room to check on him. As the morning sun rose, Cade delivered Rivo his breakfast: sausage, eggs, a biscuit, and a glass of fresh goat's milk; all food Rivo had been craving for so long. He made quick work of his meal and drank the last of the milk.

"Are you still hungry, Rivo?" Cade asked urgently.

"No, I'm good. Did you eat anything?"

"I ate a pancake with blueberries and whipped cream before you awoke."

Rivo froze and looked at him in bewilderment. *Pancakes with blueberries and whipped cream? What is he, a six-year-old?*

"Are you thirsty? Would you like more milk?" Cade asked earnestly.

"Well—"

"I will get you more milk!"

"Cade, hold on. Your leg, you need to take it easy."

"I will get you more milk!" Cade insisted as he marched off to fetch Rivo another glass.

"I'm not sure I can get used to this. It's hard to watch," Rivo remarked, shaking his head.

Having received an okay from the doctor and feeling well rested and well fed, Rivo decided it was time to head back. He and Cade bade farewell to Captain Tremlee and the rest at the outpost, then loaded up in the steam car.

"Alright, Cade," Rivo said as he slowly took a seat, still sore all over. "Let's head to Greencourt. There's a couple of people who I think might want to see me." He looked thoughtfully out in the distance. "Then," he said to himself, "it's time to see Renee."

Chapter 40

A Steam Car Named Desire

The steam car took a commonly traveled merchant route back to Greencourt. It was a different route than the group had taken a few weeks earlier from Rhemilia, so Rivo didn't get to take in the familiar sights one more time. It didn't bother him too much, though. *I've seen it twice already,* he thought to himself.

It was quite a unique experience. Rivo had moved that fast a few times before on horseback, but it wasn't for a very long distance, and Cade wasn't the one in control. It took Cade a little while to get used to how to steer the machine. His injured leg didn't help. The Captain offered to have someone else drive, but he wouldn't hear of it.

The bumps along the way made Rivo wince in pain from time to time, but once Cade finally got a handle on how to maneuver the vehicle, the ride went a little smoother. Rivo took in the sights as best he could, enjoying all that the land of Wyverly had to offer— things he had overlooked before, things he had just taken for granted. But with his new lease on life, the rolling hills, the tall trees, even the birds in the air and flowers on the side of the roadway, made Rivo see how much of life's beauty and splendor one often becomes too accustomed with to truly appreciate.

The two rode on, taking very few stops, and approached Greencourt, just as the sun was setting. Rivo couldn't believe how far they had come in such little time. What would have likely taken weeks on foot took less than one day in the steam car.

The car slowed down as they neared the entrance to Rivo's old stomping grounds. "Can we stop right here, Cade? I don't want to draw too much attention right now," said Rivo as he covered himself up with his cloak. He didn't want to risk having anyone recognize him before he met with Naomi and Pearce.

Cade pulled the car over about a hundred paces before the town entrance. There was a gray brick partition, about three feet tall, that ran along the edge of town and ended at the entrance. Rivo recalled how he, Naomi, and Pearce used to walk along that partition on boring afternoons when they were little, trying to balance themselves the whole way.

There were no guards or police posted at the entrance—there was never any need. Rivo noticed that a new welcome sign was in place. The previous wooden sign simply said "Welcome to Greencourt." He remembered when that sign had been put up; it was one of the earliest memories of his life, actually. He must have been three or four years old at the time. He and Naomi sat on the brick partition and watched the men as they proudly hung it up. The new, freshly painted sign still said "Welcome to Greencourt," but it had a new message underneath, "Birthplace of Rivo the Beastkiller, hero of Wyverly."

Rivo's heart raced at the sight. "Wow, I'm at a real loss for words. I never thought I'd see anything like this," he said sheepishly.

"Hogging the glory as always, I see," Cade said as he playfully slapped Rivo on the shoulder.

Rivo served as a tour guide of sorts as they passed through town. Pointing first at the lively pub near the entrance, with the town hall just across from it. Then on to the local bed and breakfast, run by old man Chambers and his wife of over fifty years.

"My parents told me the Chambers have been running that since before they were born; the town's not big enough to have an inn, so travelers always stay there," Rivo told Cade, who was essentially a captive audience for this unsolicited tour.

Rivo went on, pointing out the woodworker's shop, the blacksmith, the general store, the town doctor, everything. He stopped when he noticed that they were starting to draw some attention. Since it was sundown, most of the children were home, but there were a few nosy old folks hanging out on their front porches, wondering who these two cloaked men who were walking through town might be. The next thing they knew, people started poking their heads out their windows, peering at their new visitors. "Maybe we should just head to the cabin," Rivo said quietly as they picked up the pace as best as the two sore, worn-out soldiers could.

They made their way through town and wandered down a forest path on the outskirts, which led to a tiny cabin. "This is it, the only home I've ever known," said Rivo. He looked through the window and saw that his room was still exactly as he had left it, a few changes of clothes folded up in the corner, and a small desk next to his bed with some notebooks sitting open on top. Apparently, Naomi hadn't been able to bring herself to go in there quite yet.

As they walked past his bedroom, Rivo peeked through the kitchen window and saw Naomi and Pearce sitting at the small round dining table, sipping hot tea. He couldn't tell if they were chatting with each other or not.

"Well, what are we waiting for?" Rivo asked rhetorically as his heart began to pound. "Let's do this."

"Rivo, are you sure I should be here for this?" Cade asked hesitantly. It was clear he was feeling out of his element. "I can go get a room for myself at the bed and breakfast if you want. This seems like a family thing."

"Don't worry, Cade," Rivo whispered. "I want them to know you brought me here. I'm sure they'll be thrilled."

Pearce and Naomi's teatime was interrupted by a sudden knock at the door. "Who's there?" hollered Pearce, his voice agitated.

"Well, I've come all this way to visit, and this is how you talk to me?" Rivo replied sarcastically. "Maybe I'll just go back if you're gonna be like that!"

Rivo and Cade heard tea cups crashing to the ground, followed by the sound of loud footsteps speeding towards the door. Pearce swung the door open with Naomi at his side. They stood paralyzed at the sight, wide-eyed with their jaws practically hitting the floor.

"Rivo!" Naomi shrieked as she lunged at him and hugged him as tightly as she could, tears streaming down her face. Rivo's side was still hurting, but he didn't want to say anything.

Pearce wrapped his arms around both his wife and Rivo. "Rivo! I can't believe it. I can't believe it's you! How!? How did you make it?"

"It was Cade over there," he said as he pointed his thumb toward the mighty warrior, who was standing awkwardly behind him. "Plus, I had some help from our forest friends. Let's go inside and I'll tell you all about it."

They all went inside the cabin and listened to Rivo tell them the whole story of his rescue and return. Leaving out the details about his spirit watching their journey. *That's a little tidbit I'll save for Vickie,* he thought.

Naomi was in such a state of shock that her hands were shaking. Pearce was tearing up uncontrollably.

Cade sat quietly, trying not to show any emotion at the touching reunion. "Guys, I think I should retire to the bed and breakfast for the evening. You three need some alone time," he said as he stood up from his chair.

"Oh, c'mon, Cade. You're welcome to stay the night here," Rivo replied.

"Cade, we'd be honored to have you as our guest," Pearce reassured him, with a teary-eyed Naomi nodding in approval.

"I thank you for your hospitality, but I really think this is best. I'll make sure to come over and say goodbye before I leave in the morning," Cade replied as he headed towards the door.

"Not so fast there, Beastkiller," Rivo interjected, leaning back in his chair. "Can you do one more favor for me?"

Cade spun around abruptly and stood at attention. "Of course, name it," he replied adamantly.

Rivo grinned as he scratched his chin. "I need one more ride. There's someone I need to talk to in Rhemilia."

Cade chuckled with a crooked smile. "I see, this is about that girl, isn't it?" he asked as Pearce and Naomi exchanged a knowing glance.

"Yeah, Cade," Rivo replied, smiling as he rubbed the bridge of his nose in embarrassment. "It's about that girl."

Cade sighed playfully and nodded. "Sure, Rivo. I'd be happy to," he said before closing the door behind him.

Naomi threw her hands in the air in disbelief. "Rivo, you can't leave, you just got here!" she pleaded.

Rivo let out an exhausted sigh. "I'm sorry, Naomi, but I have to see Renee before they leave. I can't miss my chance."

"Well, then let us come with you," Pearce said with a shrug.

"I like that plan," Rivo said, tapping his fingers on the table. "It'll be our own little reunion."

"That works for me," Naomi said, sipping some tea from a new cup. "I'd love to see them again."

"Wait a second," Pearce said, thoughtfully tapping his chin as he glanced at Naomi, then back at Rivo. "What's making you think of Renee now all of a sudden?" The question went unanswered as a thud was heard from under the table from Naomi kicking him in the shin.

Rivo shook his head and laughed at the sight of Pearce grimacing in pain. "So that's the plan then, let's get some rest and head out in the morning," he replied.

"Rivo, I don't think any of us are gonna get a wink of sleep tonight," Naomi said, placing her elbows on the table as she rubbed her face.

"Speak for yourself," Rivo chuckled, "I'm exhausted."

Pearce shook his head as he looked toward Rivo's room. "Rivo, you are something else, buddy."

Naomi lightly slapped her hands on the table. "Well, I'm still trying to make sense of all this. I'm putting a sleep sack in Rivo's room tonight. Otherwise, I'm gonna have to keep running in to check on him and make sure this isn't all just a dream."

Rivo waved his hands in indifference. "Suit yourself, just keep the snoring down, please," he said with a wry smile.

Naomi inhaled sharply as she pursed her lips. "I'm gonna let that one go this time," she replied.

With that, the newly reunited family went to their rooms. Naomi sat up, leaned against the wall, by Rivo's side, the whole night. She couldn't bring herself to close her eyes. "Get some rest, Rivo," she whispered, looking at him as he slept, "I know I won't."

***

It wasn't even sunrise yet when Naomi found herself in the kitchen preparing breakfast. She was still beside herself that she was once again setting up a table for three. The commotion awoke Pearce, who was accustomed to getting up before dawn anyway. He walked up to his wife and gave her a warm embrace.

"He's really back, isn't he?" Naomi said as she pressed the side of her face against her husband's shoulder.

"Hard to believe still, but yes. If there's one person who could have pulled it off, it's Rivo."

There was a knock at the door; this time, they knew who it was. "Come in, Cade," Pearce hollered.

Rivo was slowly rolling out of bed as Cade walked in. "Morning all," he said as he yawned, his hair going in every direction.

Cade got right to the point, "Morning. You ready, Rivo?"

"We're just sitting down for breakfast. Would you like a plate?" Naomi asked as she began to reach for another plate and cup.

"No, thank you, I already ate."

"Pancakes with blueberries and whipped cream?" Naomi said with a smirk.

"Yes, how did you know?"

Rivo and Naomi exchanged a light chuckle. The three sat down to eat. Cade joined them at the table but didn't eat, instead opting for a glass of goat's milk.

Rivo devoured his meal in no time. "Alright, let's head out," he said, slapping the table as he stood up.

"Rivo!" Naomi said with a giggle. "We barely just started."

There was another knock on the door. "Who now?" Pearce mumbled as he put down his biscuit in frustration.

"I'll get it," Rivo said, walking to the door. As he opened it, there stood old man Chambers along with his wife, Mrs. Chambers, and half the town of Greencourt.

"I knew it!" hollered old man Chambers. "Rivo! I can't believe my eyes!" the old man said with a broad smile.

"I told you I thought that was him walking alongside that fellow last night, Pa!" Mrs. Chambers chimed in, wagging her finger at Rivo excitedly.

The amount of clamoring and chatter made it impossible to have any sort of conversation. "Yes, that's right, I'm back," Rivo announced with his hands up, trying to calm the crowd. "I'd love to tell you all about it some time, but right now I just need some peace and quiet."

The disappointed crowd reluctantly respected Rivo's wishes, but not before they all exchanged handshakes and hugs with Greencourt's most famous resident. These were people Rivo had known his whole life. They'd been watching out for him for as long as he could remember. He wished that he could have done more for them at that time, but there was a young lady in Rhemilia who required immediate attention.

After the townspeople left, Rivo turned toward Cade and the rest, rubbing the back of his neck. "I kinda figured things were gonna be different from now on," he remarked sheepishly.

Cade rolled his eyes and shook his head. "All right, hero," he said obnoxiously. "Let's go get your woman," Cade added as he walked out of the door with Pearce and Naomi behind him, bags packed and ready to head off toward Rhemilia.

Chapter 41

My North Star

Whispers of the Haundo had been circulating for a while. Mr. Sundry and his crew, however, weren't overly concerned. They hadn't encountered these creatures yet, perhaps due to the fact that they traveled in such a large group. The beasts had decided it wasn't worth the effort when easier targets were available. Either way, every town welcomed the troupe's pleasant distraction with open arms, and Rhemilia was no exception. "So why stop now when demand is so high?" Mr. Sundry would ask—rhetorically, of course.

"You three unload the wagons while the rest finish setting up," he ordered. "I've got to pick up some supplies and hobnob with the locals."

"Of course you do," Vickie mumbled under her breath as he walked away. Mr. Sundry always managed to find something else to occupy himself with when it was time to do the dirty work.

"Okay, well, I'll start unloading the barrels. Might as well get the grueling part over with first," Judd groaned as he hefted a barrel onto each shoulder.

"Okay, so there should be fourteen large crates, sixteen small crates, and three barrels, including the two that Judd just took," Renee muttered quietly to herself, counting everything and pointing her finger at the wagon to keep track.

Vickie noticed Renee had gone completely silent. She looked over and saw her sister's finger had trailed off, her gaze fixed on three young visitors who had just arrived in town: a young man and woman who, judging by the rings on their fingers, appeared to be husband and wife, accompanied by a handsome boy around Renee's age. He wore a blue headband and leaned casually against a wagon.

Vickie eyed her sister and smirked. "You're not one to usually check out the local cuisine, Renee," she teased.

Renee was caught off guard, "Huh? Oh no, it wasn't like that!" she stuttered, embarrassed that she was caught.

"Oh, it's fine, sis. You're only human after all," Vickie chuckled. "Ya know, if you want, I can go fetch him for you."

Renee returned to taking inventory, or at least tried to. "Cut it out, Vick. Please don't embarrass me."

"Looks like I may not have to. He's heading over right now."

"Oh no! Vick, please tell me you're joking!" Renee moaned.

"Nevermind, it's the other one," Vickie remarked casually as she studied her nails.

Renee let out a sigh of relief as Judd came back for another barrel.

Pearce approached the three. "Good morning. My name's Pearce, and that's my wife Naomi and her cousin Rivo. We're from Greencourt, and we're soldiers for the kingdom. We're looking for some good recruits and thought you three might be—"

"We're not interested," Vickie interrupted.

"Very well. Have a good day," Pearce replied as he turned to walk away.

"Send the other one, the boy in the headband," Vickie muttered with another smirk.

"Vick!" growled Renee sharply through her clenched teeth.

Pearce either didn't hear Vickie or just didn't care to acknowledge her. He walked past his comrades and started unloading their wagon.

Renee shook her head in frustration at her sister's antics. "Why do you always do stuff like this, Vick?"

"He's coming," Vickie said flatly.

"Vick, I said, cut it out."

Judd couldn't help but chuckle. "He really is!"

"Oh no! Vick, please help me, I can't do this right now!" Renee pleaded.

"Don't worry, sis. I'll chase him away."

"Just don't be too mean." Renee took a deep breath. *Play it cool, play it cool, play it cool*, she told herself as she went back to counting crates.

"Hey, I'm Rivo of Greencourt," the young man said with a smile.

As Renee feared, Vickie came down way too hard on the boy, who, to his credit, seemed to take it quite well. This did, however, present an opportunity for Renee to introduce herself properly and smooth things over by inviting him to see their show. *At least I'm able to be the good cop*, she thought.

"He seemed like a nice boy, Vick. Did you have to be so rude?" Renee asked.

After Vickie left, Judd and Renee continued unloading. Renee kept an eye on Rivo, who had run over to join a group of kids playing rushball in a nearby field. *Just a big kid*, she thought to herself, smiling as she watched on.

Judd saw her looking over that way and couldn't help but laugh a little. "Go ahead, Renee. I'll finish this up."

She grinned at the strongman. "Thanks, Judd. I'll be right back," she said as she ran off to join Rivo and the others.

Vickie was by the wagons when Renee returned. "Welcome back, Renee," she said to her out-of-breath sister. "What was all that about? I'm not used to seeing this side of you, especially around boys."

Renee still had a grin on her face. "We need to start getting ready for the show," she said, trying to change the subject.

"Oh no, you don't," Vickie said with a giggle. "You never talk to me about boys. I wanna know—what do you see in that one?"

Renee kept walking past her, then turned around, smirking. "I just want that headband, I think it looks cute on him, that's all."

"Yeah, right. The headband," Vickie chuckled, shaking her head. "Why do I have the feeling that boy's gonna get us into all kinds of trouble?"

***

Renee's dreams had tormented her ever since the battle at the temple. They were usually either nightmares about the Haundo coming back, or dreams where she and Rivo were still traveling together. One dream caused her to wake up in terror, the other, in despair; both unpleasant in their own way.

This dream, however, was different. She found herself by the streams near her childhood home. The same streams she and her father would often spend their afternoons at when he was home. She was by herself, though she didn't feel scared or alone, aside from wishing her father were there with her. She could see and hear the running water—it was so vivid. She decided to step into the stream, the smooth rocks pressing against the soles of her feet, the cool water rushing over them, "It feels so real," she said as the water kissed her ankles.

"Renee?" a familiar voice called from the banks nearby.

She turned around to see a brawny, dark-haired man with a full beard and an even fuller smile.

"Daddy!" she exclaimed as she ran to meet him.

The two embraced each other. Renee felt his muscular arms wrapping around her, and his flannel shirt brushing against her cheek as she pressed the side of her face against his broad chest. She swore that she could even smell the scent of pipe tobacco, ingrained in his clothing.

"This just feels so real, Daddy," she said through her sobs. "It's like we're really together again."

"In a way, it is, Renee," he replied softly as he stroked the back of her hair and kissed the top of her head.

"What do you mean?" she asked, looking up at him.

"Well, Renee, didn't you make a wish on a shooting star when you were little, after I died?"

"Yes, I wished that you would come back, but it didn't come true. That stuff's just a fairytale for kids."

"Is it, Renee?" he asked, still stroking the back of her head. "I'm here, it's in your dream, but I'm really here. I can't come back to life, but I can come see you this one time."

"What? No, this can't be," she said in disbelief, "It's just a dream, nothing more."

"Renee, I know this is hard to believe, but I can only come visit you once. Let's make the most of it, shall we?"

"But why now?" she asked. "I made that wish when I was little."

"Time works a little differently where I'm at, Renee. To me, it was as if it were just a moment ago when you and I were playing along these streams. You were just a tiny thing back then, but look at you now," he said as he brushed the back of his fingers across her cheek, "you've blossomed into a beautiful young woman."

"Beautiful?" Renee chuckled cynically. "Now I *know* I'm dreaming."

"Oh, Renee," he said, holding her face gently in his hands, "don't let the world beat you up. You, Renee...will always be my North Star."

Renee gasped, her eyes wide. "That was it! That's what you used to call me—your *North Star*!" she said as tears streamed down her face. "It's like it was blocked from my memory, I couldn't remember for the life of me!"

"Oh, Daddy, it's really you!" she said as she wrapped her arms tightly around him again.

"I'm glad you understand now, Renee," he said as he patted her back. "I'm sorry I couldn't be around to watch you and Vickie grow up. I intend on paying her a visit sometime as well, but don't tell her, I want it to be a surprise."

"Okay," she chuckled.

The two held hands as they walked along the banks of the streams, like they had so many times when she was small. "So Daddy," she said as she wrapped her arm around his, "did you just come by to say hello, or was there something else you needed to tell me?"

"As a matter of fact, there is, Renee," he replied as he stopped and turned toward her. "I know you've been having a lot of troubling dreams as of late. And that these have come from some turmoil you've been going through."

Renee's eyes began to well up, and she cast them to the ground.

"Renee," he said as he gently lifted her chin, "you're sad right now, but when you wake, you're going to sit up with a smile on your face. Today, Renee, is going to be the first day of the rest of your life."

"I don't understand, Daddy," she said, confused.

"You will, Renee," he said as he held his hand against the side of her face. "I can't stay much longer, you're going to wake soon, but I just wanted to make sure to tell you that."

"Okay," she said with a tearful smile. "But, Daddy?" she asked.

"What is it, baby?"

"Can you hold me until I wake up?"

He gave her a warm smile. "I would want nothing more," he answered softly as they embraced one last time. "Goodbye, my North Star. It was good to see you again."

Renee woke to the sight of the sunrise out her window, a pink light illuminating the Rhemilian sky. She sat up on the side of her bed, a smile on her face, just as her father had told her. "Thank you, Daddy," she whispered.

She heard the door to their room open. Vickie walked in with a muffin and a glass of milk.

"Renee? Glad you're awake. I got you a little breakfast. Please eat something today," Vickie said as she set the food down on the table nearby.

"I will," Renee said, still staring out the window. "Actually, do you think we can go to the café and get some real breakfast?"

"Of course," Vickie replied cheerfully. She looked over at her sister, curious about the change in tone from what she'd seen lately. "Renee...is that a smile I see?" she asked in amazement.

"Yeah," Renee replied softly.

"Oh, I'm so glad to see that!" Vickie ran over, put her arm around Renee, and kissed her on the side of her head. "I don't remember the last time I saw you smile."

Renee patted Vickie's arm and noticed the children were already heading out to the field to play. "I think after we eat, I might go and play with the kids for a bit before we leave."

"I think that's a great idea, Renee. We'll get some breakfast, then you go ahead and join the kids. Judd and I will take care of loading the wagon."

Chapter 42

Just Paying Back a Favor

It wasn't even noon when the group arrived in Rhemilia. Cade did as he had at Greencourt and pulled the car over just before the entrance to town, so as to avoid too much attention. The three pulled their cloaks over their heads and walked into town. Cade opted to leave his hood down. "Stars be damned, Rivo," he said with a short laugh. "How many towns are you famous in? Do we need to see if they put up a new sign for you here, too?" had added, shaking his head.

They retraced their steps from what seemed like ages ago, though Pearce, Naomi, and Rivo all felt like different people since the first time they came to Rhemilia looking for recruits; the town seemed good as new. Any damage done by the Haundo had since been repaired. It was almost as if the attack hadn't even happened.

They walked past the inn where they had stayed, where Rivo came up with his battle plan against Drokner and his hounds. Then down the same street where the battle had taken place. Off in the distance, Rivo saw the fairgrounds, where he had first met them.

Where he first met *her*.

Where the circus tent once stood was now littered with merchant tents, selling their goods. Off to the right was a caravan. Rivo saw Mr. Sundry. He was talking to some of his workers, who were loading up the caravans. The circus was finally leaving town. It turned out that Mr. Sundry and most of his performers and workers had stayed there the whole time. Being in the middle of a war of that nature, traveling performers weren't exactly itching to get on the road if there were other, safer options available. Rivo later learned that they stayed and helped guard and rebuild the town while he and the others went off to war.

Then he saw them, Vickie and Judd. They were helping load the wagons. "Man, I was cutting it closer than I thought," Rivo muttered under his breath as he debated how to approach them. "Glad we left when we did." He rubbed his jaw thoughtfully as he contemplated how best to reintroduce himself to his old comrades. "Well, what do you think? Should we—"

"Vickie! Judd!" Naomi yelled as she put her hood down and ran to her old friends.

Rivo chuckled, shaking his head. *Well, there goes any hopes for a crafty surprise.*

The two looked pleasantly surprised to see Naomi. "My stars, Naomi! Good to see you!" Vickie said as she and Judd took turns hugging their old friend. "What brings you here? Did you come all the way to Rhemilia just to say goodbye?"

"Not exactly," she replied as she looked towards Rivo, Pearce, and Cade. "You three, what are you just standing there for? Get over here!"

Vickie looked to see Pearce, Cade, and a mysterious hooded figure standing between them. Pearce, she was happy to see, but she couldn't help but wonder why in the world Cade was with them. She then eyed the other visitor with suspicion.

Pearce walked up first, followed by the other two. He gave Vickie a hug, and the two exchanged a kiss on the cheek, while he offered Judd a handshake, which was swatted away by the strongman in favor of a brotherly bear hug.

"This is great! I didn't think we'd ever see you again!" Judd said excitedly, a big grin spreading across his face.

Vickie looked cautiously at Cade, who was still standing with the stranger several steps away. "Cade? I didn't expect to see you with them. What brings you to town?" she asked flatly, her lack of enthusiasm at his presence showing.

"I'm just paying back a favor," Cade answered plainly with a nod.

Vickie had a puzzled expression on her face. "Really? A favor for who exactly?"

Cade sighed and turned towards Rivo, his face still mostly covered by his hood. "Well, kid, when are you gonna show her?"

"Show me what—" Vickie's question was interrupted as she saw Rivo remove his hood. She gave a loud gasp and covered her mouth; her eyes teared up.

"Boy, do you and I have a few things to talk about," Rivo said with his eyebrows raised and a smirk across his face.

"Rivo!" she screamed as she ran to her old friend and gave him a tight hug. "How?"

"We'll have to sit down and have a long talk, Vickie. There are definitely a few things I need to tell you," Rivo said as he patted her back.

"It's really him!" Judd said as he ran up to Rivo, sobbing like a baby. He gave the young man a big bear hug like he had given Pearce. It was then that Rivo was reminded that his sides were still hurt from the battle.

"Easy there, big guy," Rivo groaned as he rubbed Judd's head, "I missed you too."

Vickie held her face in her hands as she started gasping for air, overcome with emotion. Naomi put her arm around her side to keep her from losing her balance. "Rivo...I don't know what to say. I really...you know, for some reason, I just had a feeling you were still alive. But then here you are, and I can't believe it."

"Like I said, we have a lot to talk about," Rivo said as he grabbed her by the hand. "But first... Where's Renee?"

"Renee? I think she said something about going over to the field to play rushball with the kids one last time."

"If the rest of you don't mind, I think Vickie and I need to take a quick walk over to the field. We'll be right back." Rivo told the group, and he wrapped his arm around Vickie's, "Let's go, Vickie. I need to see Renee," he whispered.

As they began walking arm-in-arm together, Vickie rubbed a tear from her eye. "Renee," she gasped, shaking her head in disbelief. "Talk about someone who'll be glad to see you."

Rivo let out a quick laugh. "Not as glad as I'll be to see her. I promise you that."

Vickie stopped to look Rivo in the eye. "Rivo...what do you mean by that?" she asked firmly.

"You'll see."

"No, Rivo," Vickie snapped, "I want to know. That's my sister. You may not realize it, but she's been through the abyss and back since that battle. I'm not gonna let you—"

"Just come back and sweep her off her feet," Rivo interrupted, finishing her thought. "I need to suffer first, right?" he said, looking her directly in her eyes, his eyebrows raised.

Vickie's eyes went wide as she stumbled back, almost falling, "Rivo?" she gasped.

"Isn't that what you meant? I need to suffer first, I need to come back as a spirit and watch it all over again, starting from the first time I put on that stupid headband that she thought looked so cute on me. I need to see everything I put her through." Rivo talked like he was reading from a script. "Tell me more about what it's like to go through the abyss and back, Vickie," he said with a tinge of anger, narrowing his eyes.

Vickie put both her hands to her mouth, crying as she listened to Rivo repeat her wish back to her, her stomach twisting. "Rivo, how do you...how do you know I—"

He took a step toward her and leaned in closely. "I heard it all, Vickie. Every word. And it happened just as you wished."

"Oh, Rivo...some of the things I said." Her voice quivered as her hands began to shake. "I'm sorry, I didn't really mean it. I was just in a bad place, I–'"

Rivo interrupted her to give her a hug, "Vickie...thank you," he whispered in her ear.

Vickie sighed in relief, tears streaming down her face as she hugged him back and pressed her head against his chest. "Oh, Rivo, you have such a kind nature. Don't ever change."

"I'd like to see Renee now," Rivo said, calmly patting Vickie on the back of her head.

"Of course," Vickie said softly as she wiped her eyes. "Let's go."

As they approached the field, there was Renee, running back and forth, kicking the ball around with the kids. He turned to Vickie, "You stay here. I'll handle this," he said as he made his way to the field.

Renee was engrossed in the game with Gordon and some of the other children and didn't notice someone walking toward them. She heard a familiar voice calling out. "Oh no, you don't!" the voice shouted.

Renee looked up and gasped at the sight. There stood Rivo with Vickie behind him, wearing a tearful smile on her face.

"What, are you trying to recruit these young kids now? I don't think so," he said as he slowly approached the field, wearing a wry smile.

Renee's knees quaked as she almost collapsed, "Rivo?" she gasped faintly. "What..." Her voice faltered as she covered her mouth with her hands.

"Or were you just having a little fun because they said you could join them?" he asked playfully. "That's just as bad, ya know, a young woman like yourself running circles around these kids? That doesn't sound fair to me."

Renee felt sick to her stomach, "This can't be real... Rivo, what...what's happening? How?" she said, choking on her words. Gordon and the rest of the children all stood silent, equally in shock at what they were seeing.

"I was watching you this whole time. Ya know, you should be ashamed of yourself," Rivo said as he stopped at the end of the field, leaving a good fifty paces between him and Renee.

"Rivo...stop... What are you doing? You're alive... How?"

"That's a long story, Renee," he said gently. "And we have the rest of our lives to talk about it."

"What? Rivo, what are you..." Her voice trailed off as she hunched over and braced herself on her knees.

Rivo reached his arm out towards her with his hand open, as if waiting for her to join him in a dance. "You're coming with me, Renee."

Renee looked back at him, hesitantly. "What? Coming with you where? What are you..."

"How about we go for a swim first," he said, nodding toward Lake Rhemilia. "And this time, Naomi won't stop us—nobody will stop us."

"Rivo?... Is this..." Renee stood herself up straight, closed her eyes, and took a deep breath to gain some composure. "Is this something for me, or is this...just another lake party with your recruits?" Renee asked, covering her quivering lip with her hand as she stiffened up slightly and wiped her tears.

"Just you, Renee," he said adamantly. "You're coming with me, and we're leaving. I'm going to build a house for us. It'll be in a forest somewhere...by a stream."

Renee's eyes were fixed on his. "Rivo? Do you really..." She paused to look at Vickie, who was standing a ways behind Rivo. She tearfully nodded with approval at Renee, as if to assure her that this was really happening. By that time, Pearce, Naomi, and the others both stood by Vickie.

"Come on, Renee. It's time to go," Rivo told her, with his arm still extended, waiting for her to come grab it. "Sorry, kids, we're going to have to finish this game another time," he hollered.

Renee felt her knees still shaking. She stood in hesitant disbelief at first, but then took a couple of wobbly steps toward Rivo. The steps then became firmer and faster. Before she knew it, she was in a full sprint, her feet pounding the ground. She ran to Rivo and leaped into his embrace, wrapping her arms around his neck as he hugged her waist.

"Let's go, Renee," he said softly, placing his forehead against hers. "I owe you a swim, don't I?"

"Right now?" she asked with an awkward laugh.

"When better? Let's take our shoes off first, I know you hate the feeling of wet shoes," he said as he playfully looked her in the eyes.

The two took off their shoes, grabbed each other's hands, and sped off towards Lake Rhemilia. They made it to the bank and jumped in—just the two of them.

As they emerged, Rivo wrapped his arms her around the waist as Renee held the back of his neck.

"Renee," Rivo said softly. "It was you, all along, it was you. Watching out for me. Risking your life. You loved me and I was too dumb to see it...Thank you, Renee."

Renee looked in his eyes and laughed.

"What's so funny?" Rivo asked, smiling back at her.

"After all that? Everything you put me through?" she asked playfully. "You owe me a lot more than just a *thank you*."

Rivo gave out a quick laugh in return. "You're right... I love you, Renee. I want to spend the rest of my life with you," he said softly as he leaned in to give her a kiss.

"That's...more like it," Renee replied as their mouths met and the two shared a passionate kiss in the middle of the lake under the summer sun of Rhemilia.

As they separated, Renee ran her fingers across Rivo's face as she looked at his wet brown hair, going in every direction.

"My hair again?" he teased. "*His wet hair lay plopped upon his head like a dead octopus—*"

"*But in a good way*," she added as she moved a stray strand out of his face and kissed him again.

The intimate moment was interrupted by the giggles of Gordon and the other children Renee had just been playing rushball with.

"Hey, you! What do you think you're doin'?" Rivo shouted playfully as he started toward them. "C'mon, Renee, let's teach these kids a little respect!"

Renee grabbed Rivo's wrist as he tried to swim away. "Not...yet," she said softly as she snuck in another kiss. "Now...let's go show them!"

The two rushed out of the lake and ran back to the field, hand in hand. They ran past Pearce, Naomi, and the others. Naomi smiled broadly and grabbed Pearce's hand, her motherly instincts kicking in. "Ya know, Rivo, at some point we need to plan what we're gonna do the rest of the day," she hollered at them as they ran past.

Renee slowed down to turn around, her face glowing. "He's not just yours anymore, Naomi. You all can go ahead. We'll be fine," she hollered as she was backing up.

Cade couldn't help but crack a smile at the sight. "Way to go, kid. You finally realized it."

Vickie looked at Cade, her eyebrows furrowed. "What do you know about that?"

Cade returned the look. "I know more about women than you might think."

"Really, is that so? I wouldn't have guessed."

"I was quite the ladies' man when I was his age," Cade said as he proudly reminisced.

"Ya don't say? I'll need you to explain that one to me sometime."

"Perhaps," Cade said as he raised his eyebrows.

"Well," Naomi spoke up. "I guess we just need to just take a little stroll through town for a bit. Let's give the new couple a little space."

"Good idea," said Pearce. "I wouldn't mind catching up with Mr. Sundry and some of the townsfolk who were so helpful during the battle last time."

Judd leaned in toward Vickie. "I have the feeling we'll need to let Mr. Sundry know that Renee won't be part of the troupe anymore," he whispered.

"I have the feeling you're right," Vickie said with a sigh. As happy as she was for Renee, she was going to miss having her sister around.

"I think I'll go ahead and get a room for myself at the inn," said Cade. "I'm thinking Rivo doesn't need me around anymore. I'll just get in his way."

"Sounds about right," Vickie responded.

Cade gave a low growl at Vickie's jab, then turned to Pearce. "As I was about to say, Pearce, Naomi. Let me know when you're ready, and I can drive you home." He then gave a sideways glance to Vickie. "And you, maybe I'll see you before I leave?"

"Perhaps," Vickie replied dryly.

Chapter 43

Special Day

"Ouch! What did you do that for?" hollered Rivo as he rubbed his side from being pinched.

"You!" Vickie barked back, "I can't believe you sometimes, Rivo!"

"What?"

"Having your wedding on the same weekend as your Knighting ceremony? Who does that?" Vickie scolded.

"Well, it just seemed to make sense. We were all invited by King Roland himself," Rivo said, trying to make a case for his defense. "Then he offered to have the wedding on the castle grounds. It just seemed perfect. We were all here anyway."

"This is supposed to be *Renee's* special day, you dope. Now the attention is gonna be on *you* instead!"

"But she agreed to it!" Rivo shot back.

"Of course she did!" Vickie snapped. "She just wanted to make you happy!"

"Ya know, Vickie. We haven't seen each other in four months. I was hoping you'd be glad to see me."

"And that's another thing! A four-month courtship? Why did you make her wait that long?"

"That's not long these days, Vickie," Rivo replied. "Oh, and how long have you and Cade been seeing each other exactly?" he pressed, his voice dripping with snark. "I haven't heard anything about a wedding."

"That...is none...of your...business," she replied firmly.

"I see you two are getting along well, as usual," Naomi chimed in as she and Pearce entered the guest chamber, her baby bump showing.

"Naomi! Look at you!" Vickie ran to her old friend, gave her a hug, and then felt her belly. "I am so excited for you two!"

"Looking sharp, Rivo," Pearce said as he gave his old comrade a hug. "What is this getup, anyway?"

"It's the official military dress uniform of Wyverly. What do you think?" Rivo asked as he spread out his arms to show off his deep blue suit with black trim and belt.

"Looks handsome!" Naomi said as she scurried over to give her cousin a hug and a peck on the cheek.

"Well, Judd and Cade should be here any minute. You guys can have fun doing gross guy stuff while Naomi and I get Renee and find her some dresses," Vickie said as she grabbed Naomi and headed out.

"So, Rivo, the knighting ceremony is tomorrow, followed by the wedding the next day, right? How did you want to spend your last days of freedom?" Pearce asked with a smirk.

"I'll tell you how," said a booming voice from the hallway. "We're gonna get him outta that ridiculous costume and show him how real warriors have fun!" Cade shouted as he walked in with Judd right behind him. By the looks of it, those two had already hit the local pub.

To Rivo, it felt like it had been a lifetime ago since he had last seen them. "Hey guys! Good to see you two!"

"Don't, hey guys, me, we are warriors! We must feast and celebrate as men of war do!" Cade hollered, pounding his chest, the smell of mead on his breath.

"Okay, just give me a minute to get out of this uniform," Rivo said as he carefully began to unbutton his jacket. "So what exactly did you all have in mind?" he asked.

"Duke Kincaid insisted that we join him for a royal bachelor party at the dining hall," Cade replied with an expansive gesture.

"And who are we to refuse the Duke?" Judd added.

"A bachelor party with Duke Kincaid?" Rivo muttered. "Ugh...I don't know if I'll be able to keep up with you guys. Sounds like it might get a little wild."

"It better!" bellowed Cade. "You don't have to keep up, but you have to come along. Let's go! Judd, my boy, give me a hand!"

The two large men grabbed Rivo by each arm and took him out of the room, Pearce following closely behind.

***

For as much as Rivo felt out of his element, Renee felt even more so. The three ladies all went to a luxury boutique where they met with the royal ladies' tailor, Lady Amelia. She was to pick up her custom-made dress for the ceremony tonight, along with her wedding dress.

All Renee could think about when they entered was how she used to look through the windows at shops such as these when she was a girl, never allowing herself to believe that she would ever be able to even enter such a place, let alone put on a dress. She felt out of place, but was thankful that Vickie and Naomi were there with her.

She tried on both dresses; her outfit for the ceremony had a color pattern that matched Rivo's, deep blue with black trim. Her wedding dress had a train that was so long, two of the royal maidens were assigned to help carry it down the aisle. Renee couldn't help but feel awkward about having others serve her that way.

"You're marrying the hero of Wyverly, my dear," said Lady Amelia, a tall, thin woman. "Her Royal Highness insists on the best for you. This time tomorrow, you'll be referred to as *Lady Renee*."

"I don't think I'll be able to get used to that," Renee chuckled nervously. She couldn't come to terms with the fact that not only did Queen Helena know who she was, but also made sure that Renee received such special treatment. She was both beside herself and uncomfortable at the same time. She had the dual desires of both wanting to bask in the experience, while also just wanting it to be over with.

"Stunning, my dear, absolutely stunning," Lady Amelia said as Renee walked out in her wedding gown. "You look like you were born to wear that dress, my dear."

"Wow, sis. I'm speechless!" Vickie gasped.

"Renee, you really do look fabulous," Naomi added.

"Thank you." Renee didn't know what to say; she had never received that kind of attention before. "And Naomi, thank you for being so good to me the last four months," she added.

The two had grown close since Rivo returned. While he and Pearce would often spend the daytime building the cabin in the forest between Greencourt and Rhemilia, just as Rivo had promised, Naomi and Renee would be with each other in Greencourt all day. Rivo insisted that the cabin be a surprise, so she wasn't allowed to see what it looked like until after the wedding.

"And, my dear, your honeymoon is going to be fabulous, just fabulous," said Lady Amelia.

"Oh yeah, the honeymoon. What is this place exactly?" Vickie asked.

"The King's vacation estate in the Northern Isles. It's paradise, my dear. And they'll be there for two weeks." Lady Amelia answered as she tugged and adjusted Renee's dress.

"Wow! All that just for Rivo killing a wolfman and somehow escaping with his life," Vickie remarked facetiously. "He really puts the dumb in *dumb luck*."

Lady Amelia gasped and put her hand to her chest. She wasn't used to hearing such crass talk. "My lady, we don't speak about a gentleman in that manner."

"Okay, sure. Show me a gentleman and I won't talk about him like that." Vickie laughed, looking off to her side. "And I hope nobody expects me to call him by that ridiculous nickname, *The Blade of the Shooting Star*. What idiot came up with that title?"

"I'll have you know, my husband served with Lord Rivo and nothing but the most admirable of words to speak of him," Lady Amelia said proudly.

"Really?" Naomi remarked. "Who's your husband?"

"That would be the honorable Captain Tremlee, my dear," Lady Amelia replied as she worked on Renee's hair.

"Tremlee?" Vickie said, rolling her eyes. "You're married to that uptight bast—" Her words were cut off by an elbow to her side from Naomi. "I mean, good for you!" Vickie added with a fake smile.

"Stop, Vick," Renee tried, but couldn't hold back a giggle.

"I almost forgot how much fun you were to hang out with, Vickie," Naomi laughed.

***

The knighting ceremony went off without a hitch, save for some hoots and hollers from Cade, Judd, and Duke Kincaid. After watching them at last night's bachelor party, Rivo was surprised that those three could even make it to the ceremony.

The wedding day was a blur to Rivo, so much happening in such a short period of time, between making last-minute adjustments to his outfit, tracking down the wedding party, and making sure everyone was in the right place at the right time, he was overwhelmed by the whole experience.

Things finally began to slow down as he stood at the altar and watched Renee walk down the aisle. She stole the show, as expected. All eyes were on the beautiful bride. Her gorgeous white gown glowed like a bright candle in a dark room. The vows were exchanged, and it was official. They were now husband and wife. The couple was introduced to the crowd as *Sir Rivo* and *Lady Renee*, titles they would never fully get used to.

***

As the weeks turned into months, Rivo and Renee sat on the swinging bench on the front porch of their forest cabin, watching the sunset with the sounds of the roaring streams in the background. The night slowly overtook the day as Renee lay with her head on her husband's lap. The stars began to shine, and the porch was now lit by the blue light of the moon. Just then, a shooting star dashed across the sky. They both looked, then gazed back at each other and smiled.

"Well, Renee, did you make a wish?" Rivo teased as he ran his fingers through her hair.

She let out a thoughtful sigh. "If I had to make one wish," she said as she grabbed his hand and placed it over her belly. "Maybe it would be that I could finally work up the nerve to let you know that there'll be another member of the family joining us pretty soon..."

The End

A Note From The Author

Read through it? Review it!

I thank you from the bottom of my heart for taking time out of your life to read my work. I poured my heart and soul into Rivo's story and I hope you enjoyed reading it as much as I enjoyed writing it.

Self-published authors don't have the reach or the resources of a traditional publishing house. As such, we rely heavily on word-of-mouth referrals and reviews. If you read through this work, I humbly ask that you consider leaving an honest review on the storefront you purchased this from and/or your platforms of choice.

To discover more work from independent authors, you can check out some of the many writing groups on social media. One of my favorites is the Fellowship of the Indie Author (www.thefotia.com).

Thank you for supporting self-published authors!

-Matt

Acknowledgments

I'd like to thank my wife, Sheila, and our two kids for being so patient with me during the late nights I spent putting this story together. I'd also like to give a huge thank you to my editors, Daniel Riley with whimsyland.org, who came through for me when things fell through with my original editor as well as Pauline Lovett, who was immensely helpful with some last minute editing and developmental feedback (x handle is @LovettLovesBooks). I cannot go without also thanking my endlessly patient cover artists, Daren Hatfield and Jeff Dehut, my beta readers: Patrick Skelton, J.Z. Pitts, Dennis Klatt, and my wife, Sheila Linton. I would also like to thank all the members of the online writing community who have given me invaluable feedback, guidance, and support throughout this process. And last, but not least, I thank God, from whom all good things come.

I certainly can't forget to mention the authors whose work inspired me: The works of C.S. Lewis, J.R.R. Tolkien, and David Eddings are certainly at the top of that list for me.

I'd like to also take a moment to acknowledge the stories, people, and events that inspired this story. I see the story of Rivo and his friends as a tribute of sorts to all of them and the special memories they made for me in my life. Memories of a more innocent and carefree time that I hold dear. Memories of the magic of childhood, a magic which can never be recaptured, but can still live on in stories.

I'll never forget the sense of wonder I felt as a child the first time I watched *The Princess Bride* and *The Neverending Story* and how they set my heart on fire for heroic and epic fantasy tales.

I remember the feeling of awe that filled me as a young boy the first time I laid eyes on the original *Legend of Zelda* on the NES with the gold cartridge, the cool music, and the adventure that followed while playing the game.

I remember my childhood friends, Nate and Bobby among others. Life got in the way and we lost touch over the years, but I'll never forget the time we spent as young boys venturing out to the woods behind my house to find the right sticks that would serve as our swords as we would go on to slay invisible monsters.

We were young. We were fearless. We were brave.

We were Rivo.

About the Author

Matthew Linton was born in Syracuse, NY and spent the bulk of his childhood in a small town called Chittenango (hometown of *The Wizard of Oz* creator, L. Frank Baum).

Matt has lived in four different states and has been calling South Carolina his home since 2000. He lives with his wife, Sheila, their two kids, Owen and Erin, and their pet turtle, Sheldon.

When he's not writing, Matt enjoys reading, going for long walks, and spending time with his family and friends.

Matt's love of stories, and the fantasy genre in particular, was piqued at a young age. He grew up watching movies like *The Princess Bride* and *The Neverending Story* and playing video games like Zelda, Suikoden, Chrono Cross, and many more.

For more information on Matt and his upcoming work, you can find links to his social media accounts and website at

linktr.ee/matthewlintonauthor

Keep your eyes peeled for my next novel, Franko: Blade of the Shattered Star. The story of Rivo's father, Frank. To be released in 2026!